T0247832

Advance Praise for
The Accidental Joe

"Tom Straw's Sebastian Pike is a wonderful addition to the annals of amateur sleuths of the crime/spy genre. Wisecracking and wounded, his clear, innocent voice carries a deep understanding of the world we know and, more importantly, the world that we suspect. *The Accidental joe* is a Hitchcockian spy story: surrounded by more spies than he knows, Pike is the ultimate amateur, a chef-provocateur for a cable TV reality show balancing a tower of croquembouche in the South of France amidst a dizzyingly fast-paced mission filled with assassins and betrayals."

—**Walter Mosley**, author of *Every Man a King* and the forthcoming Easy Rawlins, *Farewell, Amethystine*

"Tom Straw has set the bar for culinary, espionage travel thrillers. Actually, I think he invented the bar. And it's a bar I'd meet him at anytime."

—**Alton Brown**, culinary personality but also totally a spy

"A masterful beginning to a series I hope runs forever. The writing is superb, the action thrilling, the story both exciting and gut-wrenching. Bourdain, le Carré, Herron, and Greene, make room for Straw."

—**Reed Farrel Coleman**, *New York Times* bestselling author of *Sleepless City*

"I couldn't put it down—and I sure didn't want to! Great action, clever tradecraft, behind-the-scenes TV production, and food porn, all offered up by one of the most appealing narrators I've come across in years. I hope Tom Straw is intending this to be a series because I'm already on line for the next one."

—**SJ Rozan**, bestselling author of *The Mayors of New York*

THE Accidental joe

THE Accidental joe

THE **TOP-SECRET LIFE** OF A **CELEBRITY CHEF**

TOM STRAW

A REGALO PRESS BOOK

ISBN: 979-8-88845-295-0
ISBN (eBook): 979-8-88845-296-7

Cover design by Conroy Accord
Interior design and composition by Greg Johnson, Textbook Perfect

Publishing Team:
Founder and Publisher – Gretchen Young
Editorial Assistant – Caitlyn Limbaugh
Managing Editor – Madeline Sturgeon
Production Manager – Alana Mills
Production Editor – Rachel Hoge
Associate Production Manager – Kate Harris

As part of the mission of Regalo Press, a donation is being made to World Central Kitchen, as chosen by the author. Go to http://wck.org to find out more about this organization.

Regalo Press
New York • Nashville
permutedpress.com

Published in the United States of America
1 2 3 4 5 6 7 8 9 10

To Jennifer.

It's still a lovely ride.

Let's keep the meter running.

Trust everybody, but cut the cards.

—FINLEY PETER DUNNE

one

I might be dying, but nobody will tell me. Not that I blame the docs. They're a little busy with my gunshot wound to engage in my razor-sharp conversational French banter, so I'll do my job, which is lie here and try not to become the next headliner at that Great Gig in the Sky.

Giving up control isn't my strong suit. But when they hustle you in on a gurney and cut your pants off with a nasty pair of scissors, you've pretty much already handed the whole deal over to them. I'm not even embarrassed that I went commando today.

If I don't seem full-blown panicked, thank the drugs. Whatever they gave me on the medevac chopper took care of that. And thank goodness. One of the doctors is poking around my nether regions like she's searching for a lost earring between the couch cushions. She's either probing for the slug or trying to stop the bleeding. Or she lost an earring.

Just so you know, I'm lucky to have your company. Not only to keep me from being alone, which I dearly appreciate, but somebody should know how I, a globe-trotting TV chef, ended up in a foreign trauma center riding the seesaw of life's tipping point.

So, reader, draw near. I'm about to take you someplace you've never imagined. I know I never did. I promise you one hell of a ride. I'll try to get all this out while I still can. Are you with me?

two

believe there are no accidents in life. Even if we can't see it, there's a whole Rube Goldberg mechanism of cause and effect making shit happen. Case in point: what led to me taking a 9mm slug was an email.

It came while I was in Paris last week. Like a good little host, I'd parked my butt at the desk in my suite at Le Pavillon de la Reine to write my opening voice-over, the verbal salvo of pretentiousness and snark that starts every episode, when my inbox pinged. Incoming from my brand-new producer with the rundown of the next day's shoot.

Her email looked pro forma: crew call times, load and roll schedule for the vans, nuts and bolts, skim, skim, skim. Until I saw her rundown of my interview segments. French film director, check. Paris cuisine author, check. Victor Fabron…? Who the hell is Victor Fabron? I fired back that exact question to Cammie Nova: "Who the hell is Victor Fabron???" I could have gone with one question mark. Cammie Nova was brand new, and I wanted to make a point. You never, ever book a guest without clearing it with the host. Especially not at the literal eleventh hour.

Back came Nova's automated reply. Not checking email now. If it's an emergency, call, etc. I let it go. I'd take it up with my newbie producer in the morning. Make it a teachable moment. God, I was sounding civilized.

I uncapped my blue Lamy, smoothed the blank page of my composition book, and got to work.

HANGRY GLOBE
Season 4, Ep 4 / Paris
V.O. for Cold Opening
by Sebastian Pike

Surprise me.
That's what travel is all about. And, since this series is a culinary adventure, that's what cooking is all about, too. Face it, life is not a cabaret but a flatline bore, and if this particular chef is hangry for anything, it's not the thrill of seeing Paul confer two Hollywood handshakes in the same Brit Bake Off episode. Sorry, Alton Brown, even one of your humongous pizzas, cooked onstage on your giantized Easy-Bake Oven superheated by thousand-watt klieg lights, won't do it for me. I'm that hangry. I want a jolt. Get me excited. Make me sweat.
Gimme swelter.
If my relentless globe-trotting has taught me anything, it's that life, like the perfect meal, is of an instant.
I want it fresh.
So, I'm in a foot race to get there quick and grab it while it's hot. You may call me a chef, but I see myself as an explorer, although without the pillaging and heedless spreading of smallpox to the locals. You've seen enough of me to know I duped a TV network into paying my way to scout food as a gateway drug to culture. Shame on me if I don't get out there and immerse myself in the naughty bits on a sacred quest for cheap thrills and the elusive surprise.

It's no vacay. Even in Paris. Truth be told, I have a love-hate thing with the place. The hate part isn't what you'd think. It might surprise you that I have zero problem with the tourists. Generation Selfie, pretending to balance the Eiffel Tower in the palms of its hands? Fine. Same with the hormone-dizzy, corn-fed sweethearts fastening padlocks to foot bridges before littering the Seine with the keys—I say go for it. You bought your tickets to the world.

Consider me discerning, not elitist. Albeit refreshingly judgmental.

The hate part? Well, that's too personal to mention. So don't even.

I said, "Don't even."

Let us instead focus on my love affair with the City of Light, which gets played out in fevered assignations off the beaten path. It's in neighborhood cafés at sunup, jammed elbow to elbow at the zinc bar with Pauls and Paulettes rushing in for an espresso fix before work. It's at a certain hole-in-the-wall crêperie, whose Marais location you'll have to waterboard me to divulge, that performs forbidden alchemy with batter, sugar, butter, and a just-so squeeze of lemon. It's also in the off-the-radar cultural shrines like L'Amour du Noir, a destination mystery bookstore on the Left Bank.

The other Paris you don't want to miss is a hipper-than-thou neighborhood far from the parade of lemmings at the Louvre. Top off your personal hydration vessel and stuff it into your ethically crafted messenger bag. We're headed for the bank of the Canal Saint-Martin in the Tenth Arrondissement.

three

When our convoy reached the Tenth the next morning, I slid out of the last van, even though, as usual, I'd been first to arrive in the hotel lobby. Whatever anybody needed me for would come after the tech setup, therefore I always let the crew and gear load and roll first. That also allowed Rayna, a.k.a. the culinary coordinator, a.k.a. the Food Sarge, who took the lead vehicle, to have the espresso machine spitting and hissing in the craft services tent by the time my Merrells met pavement.

Weird, but I hadn't set eyes on my new producer yet. I planned to get Cammie Nova aside for a private word about her guest-booking transgression, but she no showed the lobby call. Tardy on her second day. One more demerit to address.

"Did you know Balzac drank fifty cups of coffee a day?" I offered my empty for a refill. While Rayna pulled another ristretto of dark, syrupy perfection, I went on. "That's why the man was insanely prolific. He said getting jacked on java made his ideas march, get this, 'like the armies of a great battalion onto the battlefield.' Of course, he died of a heart attack at fifty-one." I raised my fresh cup. "To your health."

I downed it at the curb and rubbernecked the film set down the street. My first segment was to interview the director of a TV police procedural for *Canal Plus* that was shooting on location. We planned to video an action sequence to cut into in his piece, and I wanted to see the setup, but later for that. My crew was waiting for me inside Le Verre Volé, a happening wine bar we borrowed for the day as *Hangry Globe*'s home base. I found the kitchen already lit, cameras mounted, and my marks set for rehearsal. "Look at you toadies, all locked and loaded."

Latrell, the director of photography and A-camera operator, greeted me with, "Decided not to wait for the producer." He put no stink on it, but the DP and I had spent years joined at the lens perfecting The Great Unspoken. On camera we communicated through knowing glances and silent signals. So, his benign statement about not waiting for Cammie Nova hit me like a Klaxon. It warned me the crew was miffed.

Starting from the cutting board, I pantomimed the choreography for the cooking demo we'd execute for real later that day while Latrell and Marisol, who operated the handheld B-cam, blocked their shots. My audio tech, Declan, made sure his mic boom stayed out of frame. Rayna, the Food Sarge, studied my moves to count how many backup dishes she'd need in six hours when the sautéed salmon with grapes was not imaginary. Hoss the Roadie lurked unobtrusively in the background, or as unobtrusively as a man creeping up on 285 could.

During the reset for a second pass, Declan lobbed the first volley. "Kind of a new record, isn't it, Chef? AWOL, first day?"

Rayna joined in. "Help me out—is it Cammie Nova or Cammie No-show?" I held my mark at the *mise en place* and waded in. If this spread, or if they sensed I had my own issue with Nova, she'd never dig out.

I signaled a referee's T. "A friendly word? Cammie Nova is our producer. She does not need to justify producerly business that delays her, all right? Besides, we're ahead of schedule. Why? Because you guys are self-starters. We could do this in our sleep."

"Like you in Singapore?" Latrell landed it. Everyone else laughed at my expense, which is what a happy family does.

I counted off on three fingers: "Red-eye, Ambien, minibar. Always read the label, kids." Through a window above the sink, I saw a taxi pull up. When Nova got out, I called a wrap on rehearsal.

I JOINED HER IN VIDEO VILLAGE. That's the nickname for our HQ, the nomadic observation post, a pop-up canopy stocked with headsets, two-way radios, monitors, and Twizzlers. I didn't coin it, although I wish I had. It's called Video Village on every set I know of in TV and film. "Good afternoon," I said. Nova was too smart to miss my sarcasm, but instead of apologizing or going defensive, she returned the serve.

"Problem?"

The crew emerged from the wine bar, toting gear our way. I told her we should head down to the cop show. She started to walk, but I gestured to the nearest transpo van. "Step into my office." I got behind the wheel. Nova seemed puzzled but slid in the passenger side.

In the privacy of the Renault Kangoo, I gently but firmly schooled Cammie Nova on her unforced errors. Worthy of note: when I asked her why she was AWOL, she hesitated. When she recovered her reply was vague. "Granular essentials." Then she switched topics by admitting that she knew she should have checked with me before booking that guest.

"Then why didn't you?"

"Because I needed to snag Victor Fabron or lose him. I decided, better to seek forgiveness than permission."

"Curse you, initiative, you two-edged sword." Our laugh cleared the air, and I was glad I addressed it openly. Two things I don't want on my show: tension and secrets.

THE MAGNITUDE OF THE POLICE procedural's infrastructure dwarfed ours. I stopped counting crew heads at forty. Then there was the equipment. A main camera plus one atop a serious Louma crane. Plus, a Steadicam. Plus, a drone cam. And enough HMI lights to brighten the overcast day for the first shot: a hit man's getaway chase scene along Canal Saint-Martin. The director of *Coups Criminels* trotted over, gushed about being *"un grand* fan," and invited me to sit in his director's chair to watch the sequence. "Chef, I will gladly have time to devote to our interview while the company resets from the rehearsal." My own crew was recording all this so we could edit it in later. I already knew my expression would be all kid-at-Disneyland, because some things you can't hide.

On the director's action cue, the doors of a townhouse across the street flew open, and a stuntman in a black sweater and watch cap burst out, hopped on a motorcycle, and zoomed off. A detective, the lead actor, sprinted out of a nearby tea salon and chased on foot. The camera on the overhead crane followed the motorcyclist, who stopped at the canal, fired two shots at the cop, and sped away, leaping the gap of water onto the open swing bridge. Then, trouble. The motorcyclist made an unscripted skid and fall. The director called "*Couper,*" or cut, then, how can I put this delicately, he lost his shit.

"*Merde, merde, merde!*" He threw his headset at the monitor and stalked over to his assistant director and the stunt coordinator issuing a tirade of *merdes, dégages,* and *s'en foutres.* When the director had made his point, he chased them away, tails between their legs, and approached me. "*Désolé,* Chef. No interview. No." Nova slid in beside us and suggested maybe later. The filmmaker glared at her. "No interview." He showed her his back, then stalked off to his trailer, slamming the door.

Cammie rested a consoling hand on my arm. "I am so sorry about this."

"Hold that thought." I twisted to find my crew standing on the fringes, two cams and a fish-pole mic. "You guys get all that?" Three thumbs up.

I turned back to Nova. "This will make my kind of TV. This behind-the-scenes hissy fit beats any interview the auteur could have done." I sprung out of the director's chair. "To steal from Édith Piaf, *je ne regrette rien.*"

BACK UP AT OUR HOME BASE, the first of my other guests had arrived. Eva Jacoby-Jobert was a dear old friend, a smart, cranky contrarian—just the way I liked 'em. She sang out, "Welcome to Bobo Land."

"All right, Eva, enlighten me. Bobo?"

"Slang for bourgeois bohemians. This neighborhood's crawling with them. Tell me you didn't notice the skateboard boutique, the co-working spaces, and all the vegan bistros on your way here. C'mon, Pike, stop and smell the tofu."

"Now that you mention it, I did get a twinge of hipster nostalgia."

"Yes, it's Brooklyn without the murders." Immediately, her expression gloomed over, and the big woman threw a hug on me, whispering, "That was insensitive. I still ache about Astrid." That happens a lot. Most of the time it irritated the piss out of me because it either picked at the scab or strangers saw it as their mission to change my life by spouting platitudes about grief. Save it for the Hallmark aisle. Or better yet, leave me alone.

Nobody knew about the Gordian tangle of complexity I was coping with over my fiancée's sudden death. Nobody but me and Astrid. And trust me, like every tragedy, it comes with excruciating layers. But Eva, she gets a pass. Eva knew both of us, and her feelings were not only genuine, but she also knew the emotional line, and never crossed it. That's why I pitched her to Nova for the booking and was cheered to see her.

A Chicago ex-pat who studied cinema at the Sorbonne, Eva's first publication, a study of French noir, became a textbook at her own university. Her follow-up, *An American Eats Paris*, remains short-listed among the best food writing of this century.

While Declan wired her with an RF mic, I went inside Le Verre Volé and found Cammie alone, behind the bar, reading a sheet of paper. When she heard me, she quickly folded the page like I'd caught her with porn. "Day one, and you're already prepping your résumé to bolt?" She dismissed that with a wave and grinned. It looked forced. "My first guest is here," I said. "So at least I'll have one interview today."

"Victor will show. Apparently, he was up all night editing his documentary."

"Maybe I can steal a clip from it to fill the gaping hole in this episode."

Nova stuffed the paper into her bag. "Help me out. Do you always get pissy like this on shoots, or just today for my benefit?"

"You're witnessing your bad-boy chef in the panic throes of wondering what to ask this Vincent guy. Call me crazy, but going into an interview I like to feel curious about something."

"It's Victor, not Vincent. I emailed you background prep. Didn't you read it?"

I opened my phone. "So, you did. Ten minutes ago."

"If you're looking for a hook, go to the *Le Monde* article that called him the Michael Moore of France."

I took that in, bobbing my head side to side. "Actually, not bad. I've done more with less. Thanks."

Out front I grabbed some alone time to read her packet. I caught a light whiff of smoke and looked back inside. Cammie Nova was burning a piece of paper in the bar sink.

EVA WAS A HIT. Learned and a born storyteller, she drew connections between French cinema and the Parisian food scene starting with the

10

1956 noir classic *Voici le Temps des Assassins* to Truffaut's *Shoot the Piano Player* to the gangster film *Bob le Flambeur*, which was shot in actual restaurants around the Pigalle.

She gave me an idea. "OK, smarty. Let's play a little game I call Stump the Geek. I name the movie; you name the Paris restaurant featured in it."

Eva pursed her lips. "Now? Don't I get any warning?"

"Spontaneity, my friend." I hoped my new producer was learning how I rolled, taking liberties without a net. But over in Video Village, Nova had her headset off and her nose to her phone. More than distracted, she looked uptight.

Eva showed her game face. "Hit me."

"*Something's Gotta Give.*"

"Le Grand Colbert. Too easy."

"*Midnight in Paris.*"

"Le Grand Véfour. Next."

"Crap. *Rush Hour 3.*"

Her eyes searched the sky. "There was a *Rush Hour 3*?"

"No stalling. Big Jackie Chan fight scene…? Famous restaurant…?"

While Eva pondered, a man in a crooked toupee wandered right in front of us. He stopped and wavered, unsteady on his feet. "Pardon," he said in a heavy French accent, "but you are Chef Pike?" His Beaujolais breath knocked me back a half step. From the audio trolley, Declan signaled to Hoss. The roadie duckwalked closer to shoo the man away. But the guy ignored him and said to me, "I am Victor Fabron. I have arrived for my interview."

Perfect. Fabron. Jammed down my gullet, late, and now composting the day's only viable segment. I craned toward Video Village again. Nova was gone. Bloody hell? Gone during a take? Video kept rolling. It fell to me to deal. I chose the low road. To play my inebriated guest for cheap laughs. I might even salvage this as a blooper. Blotto guest crashes party.

I lowered my hand out of frame and signaled Latrell and Marisol to keep rolling. "Monsieur Fabron, you're a longtime filmmaker, *n'est-ce pas?*"

"*Bien sûr.*"

"See those things behind you, Victor? Those are cameras."

Victor rotated to them and squinted. "Ah, *bon*. Then everything is in order for my interview."

A police whistle blew two bursts a hundred yards down the street. Multiple voices, unseen assistant directors, hollered the same warning in French, "*Silence, nous roulons....* (Quiet, we're rolling)." I searched again in vain for Nova. We were supposed to get a heads-up before the cop show shot its chase scene. What could I do but shake my head and smile. The way this day was going, I could turn the entire Paris episode into a blooper reel.

The director called action over his bullhorn. I heard the echo of a front door slamming, followed by the revving of a motorcycle. All were familiar sounds from the rehearsal I'd witnessed an hour before. Tires squealed. The motorcycle raced up the street. Marisol, the B-cam operator I had poached from a news crew when we were shooting in Puerto Rico after Hurricane Maria, had the savvy to ad-lib. She panned her C300, tracking the action as the bike passed mere feet from us, then stopped at the swing bridge. The rider turned, fired his pistol twice, and roared off. But instead of making his stunt leap across the canal, he turned left on Quai de Valmy, speeding the wrong way up the one-way street. I couldn't see the director, but everyone heard the meltdown over his bullhorn. "*Couper, couper. Merde, merde, merde!*"

It's considered good form to button a lighthearted scene with a wisecrack. I turned to Fabron, who was still swaying in place before me. "Looks like you and I both got a lesson in humility, *mon ami*. There's always somebody with a bigger budget to blow your shot."

I wasn't sure Fabron heard. His wobble grew more unsteady, and he sagged against me, clutching my arm to stay upright. I steadied the poor lush and turned to Latrell's camera. "Here's a first. I think my guest is peeing on me."

Latrell didn't crack a smile. Instead, I saw alarm—on him and the rest of the crew. Behind me Eva choked out a scream. Then I saw why. Victor Fabron had blood spreading from two bullet holes in his back. More spilled out an exit wound through his chest.

four

Both sets became crime scenes. Police from the nearby Commissariat Centrale cordoned off the area to preserve evidence and facilitate the tandem questioning of the cop show's company and my *Hangry Globe* crew. The investigation brought a real detective to my location, not the life-worn lead actor from *Coups Criminels*, but a stocky lieutenant in a nylon bomber jacket whose face looked like he came from going ten rounds at the gym. Right off I got a flutter of quakes when he shouldered past to crouch beside the body, then trace an arc upward from the corpse to me. The detective stood, then jabbed a finger at the open door of the wine bar.

In the empty dining room, he patted a corner table and kept me stewing at it while two other plainclothes *flics* came in for a whispered huddle over at the entrance. The Food Sarge had loaded me with a cold Evian on my way in, but my fingers were trembling, and I couldn't muster a grip on the cap. The detective tossed his notebook on my table. "I am Detective Tirard of the *police judiciaire*." He pulled up a seat. Then studied me.

Man, I craved a cigarette. I hadn't lit one in about ten years but, you know. Nerves. I grew up in Queens, New Yawk, where ball-buster cops braced me for miscreant behavior more than I could count. Over time I took it in stride and became quite the savant at disarming them with wisecracks or ass kisses, whatever worked. Not then. I was too tweaked by the killing. The French Steve McQueen's stare made me certain I was going down for it. The cop took my water bottle and opened it, one-handed. I took a sloppy gulp. "Thanks. Still a little shaky from the murder."

"You call this murder. You know this for a fact?"

A touch of small talk, and already I'd dug a hole. "No, I just assumed. The bullets." He said nothing. And waited. As a host I had used his interview technique countless times, getting guests to open up by making them feel the need to fill the silence I imposed. Knowing what he was up to didn't help me. I blathered. "Although, I dunno, I guess it's possible it could have been an accident. Live ammo on a set. It's happened." I told myself to shut up. "So I hear."

Detective Tirard ran a finger across his pad. "Sebastian Pike, correct?" I oversold with my nod and sloshed a few drops. "My colleagues just reported that the actual motorcycle stunt driver has been discovered behind the locked cellar door of the townhouse where the scene began. He had been stripped of his wardrobe, gagged, and bound by zip ties at his wrists and ankles. His prop pistol, the one that fired only blanks, turned up in a bucket of cleaning supplies across the room. The motorcycle is at this moment getting fished out of the canal where the shooter dumped it two blocks from the Gare de l'Est train station."

"So. Not an accident." Still shaken, I barked a single nervous chuckle at my understatement.

"You seem amused?"

"No, no, not at all." I felt the cool study of the cop and sobered. "It's tragic. This is a sad day."

"Sad, you say. Then you knew the deceased well?"

"That's the funny—I mean, not funny, unusual—the unusual thing is, I met him for the first time this morning. On camera. Before that, I had no idea who he was."

"This is true?"

"Wouldn't know him from Adam. I knew he made documentaries. Investigative stuff, I hear. To be honest, I couldn't name one of them."

"Would you be able to tell me if Monsieur Fabron had any enemies?" I wagged no. "Help me understand, Monsieur, er, Chef Pike. On your television program, I am told you interview and…commune, shall I say…with numerous guests?"

"That's what I do, exactly. Yes."

"And do you make it a habit of talking with guests you know so little about?" The detective gave me the Inspector Javert stare.

This was going uncomfortable places. I irrigated with another hit of Evian. "You know, Detective, once in a while, I like to be spontaneous. Mix it up."

"…Mix it up."

"Exactly. Nothing beats a surprise. Except for, well, you know. What happened to poor Vincent."

The Javert appraisal again. "You mean Victor."

"You see? Didn't know the poor man." Through the window behind the detective, the coroner vehicle eased away carrying the body of Victor Fabron. As I watched it go, it passed Cammie Nova, pacing across rue de Lancry, talking on her cell phone. It was one intense conversation. She had her free hand covering her eyes while her thumb massaged a temple. From her reaction I wondered how well she knew him. Were she and Fabron friends? Is that why she pushed him on me so hard?

"*Allo?*" I turned back from the window. Detective Tirard was appraising me like a stink bug dragging a hairball across the parquet. I flicked him a stupid smile, probably affirming his conclusion. He flipped his spiral pad to a fresh page. "And what about you, Monsieur Pike?"

"What about me?"

"Your enemies?"

I nearly told him he would need more paper for that list until I realized what he was getting at. "Hang on. Are you suggesting someone might have been trying to kill me?"

"It is my job to explore all possibilities."

"Well, I can't think of anyone who would want to kill me, if that's what you're asking."

"You have no enemies?"

"I didn't say that." Not only was my mouth dry, I had sweaty hands. My body was sprouting microclimates. "What about a random act? Or terrorism? Or some nut with a grudge against *Canal Plus* for, I dunno, moving the *Peppa Pig* time slot? If you're exploring all possibilities, what about that?"

He sniffed. "Thank you for the professional guidance—Chef." The verbal jab didn't get lost in translation. Frankly, it pissed me off enough to make me want to clench this gym rat in an illegal choke hold and flop his oxygen-starved, rag-doll arrogance all over the floor, belting out "La Marseillaise" until he bewailed his insolence unto me.

But I let that go. Need I remind you he opened my twist top one-handed?

Tirard stood. I dared to hope. "Are we done?"

"For now. Except I will need one more thing. Forensic evidence. I must take your bloody shirt."

I dispatched Hoss the Roadie to hit the wardrobe trunk for my backup white Faherty Laguna plus a pair of unsullied jeans. Tirard stepped out to confer with his partners, saying he'd be back. When I met Hoss in the doorway for my clean doubles, I caught another glimpse of Nova. Still on her phone. Still intense. But now farther away from everyone.

Nova. When I slid the little dead bolt inside the men's loo, I wondered, Was there a chance she would quit? Nobody would blame her after what happened, but damn, I sure would hate to be stuck mid-episode in Paris without a producer. By the time I hung my shirt on the door hook I dismissed that idea. Cammie Nova showed too much steel to cave. Which was one of the things I liked about her. Independent. Strong. Dauntless. Same as I present myself to the world.

Which is how I knew she must be shredded inside, too.

Changed and washed, I rolled my jeans and took my bloody shirt off the hook, wondering, Fold, roll, or finger dangle? I set my pants on the commode and folded the shirt in half. Soon as I did, something fell out of the pocket and clattered on the tile. I snapped on the overhead and scanned the floor. There, under the john. A...flash drive? I picked it up and turned it over and over, looking for a label. It didn't have one. But, man, was it sticky with blood.

five

Detective Tirard wasn't back when I came out of the pissoir. As if my head wasn't already in a salad spinner, now came the added stress of finding him, wherever the hell he went. He was French; maybe he went on strike.

I stepped outside carrying my grim load. Nova was off her phone and seated in Video Village. She saw me coming and met me halfway. We both said the same thing at the same time. "Are you OK?" We chuckled mirthlessly, then let the shocked stupor fill the vacuum between us.

It was I who finally broke our lull. "Tell me, are you all right?"

"I called off the rest of the day's production, of course."

"Effing-A. And you? How are you holding up?"

Cammie gestured behind her, oblivious to my attempt to connect. Or ignoring it. "We are struck and loaded out, except for Rayna." The Food Sarge was across the street packing the last snacks and beverages from craft services into her van. As if she knew we were talking about her, the Sarge looked our way, then resumed loading. "The rest of the crew's en route to the hotel. I paid transpo drivers from the cop show to take them and Rayna in our vehicles. I didn't want any of our people behind the wheel. They were pretty nuked."

People react to trauma in different ways. Newbie or not, Cammie was crew now, and that made her family like all the others. I wanted her to know that. "What about you? Are you nuked?"

I wouldn't call the smile she gave me brave. More like impermeable. So was her reply. "What about you, Pike? You look…well, look at you." I'd caught a glimpse of my traumatized self in the bathroom mirror and knew what she meant. I was the Nick Nolte mug shot, minus the Hawaiian shirt. But I could deflect, too.

"Have you seen the cop, Tirard?"

"Not since he left you. Is something wrong?"

"Let's start with weird. I was folding my shirt to turn over to the detective when something fell out of the pocket. Something not mine." I held up a ball of toilet paper in my hand. "Go ahead, open it up." Her slender fingers spread the tissue folds, revealing the memory stick nested within. "A flash drive," I said.

"I know what it is. But if it's not yours, how did you get it?"

"No idea. Well, one. It's got blood all over it. I think it came from Vincent."

"Victor."

"The deceased."

She addressed me but never took her eyes off the plastic lozenge glazed in red. "How could it have come from him?"

"I don't know. I mean when he got hit, he ended up draped all over me. It might have come off him."

"…From his pocket."

"Into mine. I know, I know, beer ponging from his pocket into mine defies Newtonian physics."

Nova sucked her teeth. "Was Victor holding it?"

"I don't know. I was too focused on keeping him from screwing up the scene with Eva."

"Could it be hers?"

"Doubtful. Why would Eva bring a flash drive to a TV interview?" I closed my fingers around the USB stick. "I'll turn this over to Detective Tirard. Let it be his headache."

"Right, right… But I don't see him." Nova weighed the situation. "Here's what we do. You go back to the hotel. I'll give it to him."

Slipping away seemed both appealing and problematic. "No, I'd better hang here."

"I disagree." She put an edge on that. And transitioned to a stiffer mode. "You absolutely need to leave. I won't take no."

"No."

"Stubborn much? Come on, let's not make a scene."

"I am standing ten feet from where my guest—your booking—got killed, holding the clothes that made me look like Jackie flying home from Dallas, and you're worried about making a goddamn scene?"

"I think we're already there, Chef. Come on, let me handle this."

"Why not me?"

She gained two inches in height to answer. "Because I'm going to do my producer job here. As your producer I think it's a bad strategy for my host to engage with the police unless it's absolutely necessary."

"I don't have anything to hide."

"We know that. But you never know how these things can turn. I'll see that he gets the drive and your shirt and insulate you from getting your hands dirty. If Detective Tirard needs to follow up, he'll know how to find you." She held out her hands to take the load off me. "I am your producer. Let me produce."

This. This was the hit-the-ground-running Cameron Nova who wowed me at her job interview.

WHAT DOES A PRODUCER DO on a show like *Hangry Globe*? Simply put, work miracles. Every logistical detail of mounting a global production is a feat. From travel arrangements to interview bookings to making sure there is electricity to charge camera batteries in the middle of a jungle, that and more falls to the producer to make it all happen. On schedule and without screwups.

Three weeks ago, my longtime producer Sheila imploded and checked herself into rehab. Good move for Sheila. For me? A mad scramble to find a replacement who could parachute in and keep us up and running. Sheila had already set up our coming episode in Laos, but I needed a kick-ass successor like yesterday. The network kept pushing someone I'd never heard of, Cameron Nova. As a man who famously does not give a rat's ass about the network, I was not about to have one of their lackeys rammed down my gorge like some foie-gras duck. I told them no, that I would red-eye in, and they were to set me up with a day's worth of candidates to interview. Only then would I make my choice.

Cameron Nova's résumé did look solid. No wonder the network kept pushing her. A degree in communication, culture, and media studies from Howard, and as if excelling at one of the most respected Historically Black Colleges and Universities weren't enough, Nova then got a degree from the New England Culinary Institute. From there, a steady rise of media credits from associate producer gigs on PBS cooking shows to three seasons on an Australian Bourdain knockoff, a food-centric travel show. She was the first finalist I saw when I dropped in, bleary-eyed, to the network's Chelsea Market conference room for my binge day of producer interviews. Cameron Nova opened big.

"I won't be shy. This is my dream job. I've seen every episode of *Hangry Globe*…twice. I've not only studied your show, I've studied you. I'm probably as big a fan as a person can be without getting hit with a restraining order."

I laughed. Ms. Nova had led off with a selling point wrapped in self-effacement and comedy. A sense of humor topped my list of qualifications, and she delivered from the starting blocks. "Funny," I said. "And with bite."

She hitched a thumb toward the glass wall at the other candidates sitting in the waiting area. "I'd send them home now."

"And confident. Not the kind to cave under pressure?"

She locked eyes on me, an unwavering gaze. Yep, she would find a way to plug in a camera in the Congo. Then she regarded the open duffel on the table. My clothes, a tangle of clean, dirty, and passable, spilled out like roadkill innards topped by the electric shaver I hadn't had a chance to use in three days. "A producer would get you a hotel."

"I'm only in New York a few hours. Tonight, it's on to Vientiane, then—"

"Paris."

This woman definitely had my attention. "That cannot be a lucky guess."

"One of my old production assistants books travel for your network. I like to be informed."

"What have you heard about me?"

Nova spread her arms. "I'm here."

I rocked back in the ergonomic chair and sipped tepid French roast. "I can be prickly. Headstrong? Depends how you define it. Or if I slept. I don't suffer fools or bullies, and I hate to be lied to. But I never fire inside my own perimeter. If you're family, I'll take a bullet for you." I paused to appraise her reaction.

"I'm still here."

Time I moved to the next level. "What I need from a producer is an eye for substance. That's the sweet spot of this show. I cook and I goof, but I always look to balance it with a big dose of gettin' real."

"Like in Portugal. You surprised Emeril Lagasse by taking him to his grandfather's ancestral home and made him cry."

Pulling that one out, definite points. So far. "Exactly. Food is my gateway. Last season at Wembley—"

"Backstage with Adele. You cooked her a vegan meal…red quinoa pilaf…and got her going about privacy hounds. Then you coached her to say 'Fuck off' to the tabloids. That got bleeped, but hello. Like we don't know the word?"

Intrigued, I decided to test her, rapid-fire. "Afghanistan. Season One."

"Nangarhar Province. You surprised a unit from Texas with home cooking."

"Specifically?"

"Burnt ends and beans."

"Rio, Season Two."

"Ipanema gigolos."

"South of France."

"Season One finale. You made brunch for Bono and the Edge at a villa at Èze-sur-Mer. When you told Bono 'Pride (In the Name of Love)' was the most powerful musical tribute ever to Dr. King, he sang it, and you teared up. I think it was more than just a song that moved you."

"You know more about me than I do."

"Count on it."

She tempered her certainty with a smile. Natural and welcoming. Was she too good to be true? I'd find out after the other interviews. But Nova was the one to beat. "Very impressive, Cameron. I'll be making a decision soon."

"Excellent. And Cammie's good."

We both rose to shake. But when I sat down again, so did Cammie Nova. Kind of threw me. "What do you call this, déjà interview?"

The face she gave me this time came without a smile. "You're slipping."

"Excuse me?"

"It's subtle but I see it. Even if nobody else does. Or will tell you."

"Am I hallucinating from jet lag, or are you critiquing me in a job pitch?"

Her unwavering look again. Nova stayed on point. "You're having a rough time. I will watch your back." I didn't say anything. What do you say to that? So, I listened with a small knot cinching under my ribs. "Do you know what you always were? The guy who came on TV, and my breath caught. You had that 'look-at-me-something-exciting-is-about-to-happen' mojo. Until something happened."

This shit was landing. An obligatory meet and greet had taken the most personal turn possible. It reached inside me and squeezed. She continued, taking pains to proceed gently, compassionately. "We all know what that was." Hell, the world knew. The sensational death of my fiancée. The shock I still bear. "But what I'm talking about is how it affected you. And how it feels now. On your show. Like you're 'doing Pike' instead of being Pike." I'm rarely speechless, but this candidate, this stranger, left me holding my breath and leaning into what she would say next. "I can produce your show. But I can also help you find that charismatic contrarian again." Cameron Nova folded her hands on the conference table. "That's all I got."

Strange. Invoking what happened to Astrid didn't trigger the usual emotional crash. No mourning. No toxic taste of loss. Instead, I felt something new. That for the first time in a year, someone understood. Oddly I didn't feel discomfort at being seen. Or that this outsider had boundary issues. I swiveled to look at the other candidates through the glass, then back to her. "Is your passport current?"

ON THE FIRST SEASON OF *Hangry Globe*, I began a tradition of wrapping each day's work by treating my peeps to Crew Cocktails. It's a holdover from my days slogging restaurant kitchens when you'd blitz the dinner rush with maniacal intensity, then kick back after closing with your scullery mates, some good wine, and serial trips to the alley for some herbal restoration. Crew Cocktails is a chance to reward my show-saving artists for all their hustle. More than that, I truly like these folks. The chance to get human, if not goofy, together after the skull-whacking toil of cranking out a road show three hundred days a year is something I cherish. My group text said the hotel lobby lounge was still on, but I wouldn't fault any no-shows after the bat-shit day on Canal Saint-Martin. Everybody showed. Everybody except Cammie Nova.

As far as I knew, she was still dealing with the La PP, local nickname for the *prefecture du police*. When they asked, that was my answer. Nobody pressed. All were understandably subdued. They ordered serious cocktails unblunted by mixers. This crowd sought sedation.

They didn't seem traumatized, though. I wouldn't say they'd seen worse, but they'd seen plenty. Over the years we'd taken warning shots from rhino poachers, ducked incoming mortar fire in Afghanistan, and gotten stuck in a UN food distribution that turned into a riot. Little by little they did what I had hoped, relaxed and talked it through. The best sign was when they were able to giggle recounting the look on my face when Victor Fabron reeled into my interview. Declan and Hoss even reenacted the scene to purifying laughter. Of the bunch, only Rayna, usually rowdy, sat in solemn contemplation of her melting ice cubes.

Latrell got up off the sofa and took out his iPhone. The library-lounge captivated his cinematographer's eye. The room was a literal study in red. Bookshelves lined with matching leather-bound volumes in garnet and rust hues sat beside enameled vases in cherry and merlot. Dramatic accent lighting illuminated crimson walls. Leave it to my DP to call it. "I feel like we crashed a Stanley Kubrick set." He snapped off a few pics of the decor. Then he arranged us all in a group pose and gave his phone to our server for a class photo. I wished Nova had been there. To join the family. To let her hair down. To achieve normalcy.

After I signed the bill, I asked Latrell to upload the video from the Fabron sequence to me. It wasn't ghoulish fixation. I didn't tell him, but I wanted to see how that flash drive found its way into my pocket. The lines in his forehead smoothed the way they do when he feels on the spot. "I can maybe do it later," he said. "I don't have the video now. Nova has it."

"...Nova?"

"Yes, Chef. She came over and asked both me and Marisol for our media." That was too weird. A definite first. I struggled not to lose my cool in front of him. But like I said, Latrell reads me. "I asked her why, not to be insubordinate, but because that's our master vid."

"Did she say why?"

"In case the police needed it." My turn to read him. His look was dubious. "This was before they got there. La PP, is that what you called them?"

My suite was on the second floor. I took the stairs so I could call her on the way up without risking lost reception in the elevator. "Hey, Pike, I'm in traffic but heading back to the hotel. Everything good?"

"Well...that depends." Our hotel kept its room keys on oversized fobs that you leave and pick up at the front desk. I paused to work mine out of my jeans as I approached my door.

"Uh-oh. I'm picking up tension. How can I help?"

"Hang on a sec." I finally freed the key and used my phone hand to push the heavy door. I heard rustling noises when I stepped in. When I cleared the corner of the little foyer, I saw a man crouched under the stairs to the loft. The room was dark, but the mini-Maglite in his mouth shined inside my shoulder bag while he rummaged through it.

SIX

Quietly as I could, I started to back out. But Nova asked if I was still there. Her amplified voice carried. The man whirled. The mini-Mag blinded me, but when he let it drop, I got a flash of him charging. I've been in enough fights to know how to take a hit, but nothing prepared me for his. It felt like getting rugby-tackled by an Orc.

The force threw me backwards into the wall. I landed on the padded bench arranged against it, which kept me from going down. Instead of waiting for another slam, I got a fix on him in the shadows and sprung, going low, shoulder down. I caught him in the gut. He oofed out a hard groan and landed on his back on the coffee table, sending stemware crashing and an ice bucket clanging. He rolled sideways away from me toward the sofa, upended the coffee table, and used it to snowplow me across the living room onto the desk. The back of my head bounced off the flatscreen on the wall. Dazed, I brought up my forearms to defend against a blow. But it never came.

He fled. As the door closed, the hall light swept across busted glass on the floor. It twinkled like discarded stars. I rushed to the corridor, but his footfalls were already fading down the stairwell. Back inside I parted the window sheers. All I saw was his back as he sprinted through the courtyard and out into the night.

"Pike?" Nova, coming from the phone. "Pike, what's happening?" I flipped on the chandelier and hunted for my cell. "Talk to me." I found it underneath the steps leading to the loft.

"I'm here." My voice didn't sound like me. I struggled for air. "I surprised some guy when I came in my door. He's gone now."

"Oh my God, are you OK?"

"Going to be damn sore tomorrow." I regained my breath. "Place looks like Mötley Crüe's hotel room."

"How bad are you hurt?"

"I'm fine. Although this is my second trashed shirt of the day." I inspected a rip in the shoulder seam. "At least no blood this time. He was pawing through my bag. Been through the desk, too."

"Did he take anything?"

"Too soon to know. I don't have anything valuable out. Passport's in the safe. Also, some emergency euros. Hang on, we're going upstairs." I trudged up and found the in-room safe wide open. "Wow, safe's been cracked. Weird. Passport's here. So's the money." I sat on the bed. "My suitcase is open, but it was already empty. But I see the dresser drawers have been clawed. And yes, I do unpack if it's more than one night."

"Very strange. Has this ever happened before?"

"Once in Somalia I grabbed a dude swinging one leg out my window trying to make off with my laptop. But this is a first-world first. On a day of firsts. I don't think it's a coincidence."

"Meaning?"

"The flash drive."

"But you don't have it."

"I'm assuming my visitor didn't know that."

"Pike, nobody knows about that except us."

"We don't know that for sure." Even though she was pushing back, talking with Cammie settled me down. "Look, I'm only spitballing here, but what if he saw Fabron slip it to me? Or knew he intended to. Your bio said Fabron was an investigative documentary filmmaker. Maybe he unearthed something sensitive, something worth killing to keep quiet?"

"Well, he told me he was uncovering nepotism in governmental appointments…."

"Not sounding so unhinged now, am I?"

Cammie laughed. "I never called you that. You're just grappling to make sense of this."

"You never said it. But you thought it, didn't you? If not unhinged, quaintly delusional?"

She cleared her throat. "You? Quaint?"

"You said you knew me. Be advised, I'm more than ruffian charm."

"I'm calling the police."

"Nice dodge. And don't bother, I'll call them. Or have the front desk do it."

"I already pulled up Detective Tirard's number for redial. You lock your door and wait for the police, if I don't get there first. In the meantime, you might want to do a more thorough inventory to see if you are missing anything. And Pike."

"Yeah?"

"I'm glad you are all right."

A HALF HOUR LATER, I roared by Place de la Bastille in the back seat of an unmarked SUV, destination: Police Prefecture. A pair of plainclothes detectives sat up front. A third, who arrived with them, stayed back in my suite to do forensics and deal with the hotel manager. My sergeants had the same look as the detective who interrogated me at the crime scene, urban toughwear and demeanors to match. The driver spoke exactly once, and that was a *merde* when traffic slammed shut. He lit up his flashers. When nobody moved, he hit the siren, that loop of two plaintive notes that always reminds me of French black-and-white films and lovers on the run. He got the clearing he wanted and jerked a hard left onto a cobblestone ramp that led down to the Seine. That didn't feel right. "*Pardon*," I said. "Isn't *la prefecture là bas?*" I extended my arm toward Ile de la Cité across the river, but these gents were deaf to me. At the bottom of the ramp, a police patrol boat waited. A uniformed officer stood on the quay. She was holding the bowline. A small console light illuminated another cop standing at the helm of the black Zodiac. He fired up the twin Yamahas on the stern when I slid out of the SUV. My detectives gestured me to get in the boat. I hesitated. Not out of fear, but the jab of a piercing memory: Astrid, taking her death ride in a rigid inflatable pretty much like this one. I can't tell you how many dawns seeped into my bed while I lay awake seeking sense and absolution. Absolution has never come. The only sense I made was to recognize how much of life is about the peril of motion. I decided, nothing to do but live it, and stepped aboard.

The skipper illuminated his light bar and gunned it, throwing up a rooster tail aft and jamming me against the aluminum backrest. "Where are we going?" I hollered to the woman in black fatigues. She didn't acknowledge. I tried again, louder and in French. The officer never turned; she kept her eyes on the water ahead.

Wherever our destination was, we were heading away from central Paris. The blinking lights on Notre Dame's scaffolding disappeared over my shoulder, and instead of the Louvre and Eiffel Tower, the night scenes to port and starboard were industrial. Container cargo vessels were docked on one side, grain and cement barges on the other. I knew my geography well enough to know we were nearing the spot where the Seine intersects the Marne.

A white light flashed twice on a boat two hundred meters ahead. The policewoman returned the signal with a handheld. Our skipper turned off the light bar and reduced speed. I strained to make out the oncoming vessel in the darkness. Clearly a large yacht. As we drew closer, I could see it was one of the dinner excursion boats you normally saw working the other end of the river. But not one of the tourist tubs. As the helmsman passed it, then carved an easy circle around its stern, I figured the *Don Juan 2* ran about fifty meters in length. It appeared 1930s vintage, a classic wooden motor yacht that had been meticulously refurbished.

Drifting along the starboard side, I saw boarding stairs that had been folded out of the bulwark. A man in a dark suit and bow tie waited on the teak grid of the lower platform. When the policewoman secured us to its side, he smiled and extended a hand. "*Bon soir*, Chef Pike. Allow me to assist you aboard."

seven

Topside the maître d', Monsieur Laurent, swept an arm to the carpeted stairs. The boat surged slightly as it got underway. I kept a loose hand on the curved banister on the way down and arrived at a ghost room. The elegant salon of rich wood, brass accents, and windows on both sides offered views of the passing riverbanks, but the six dinner tables shrouded in white linen sat empty. They weren't even set. "Your party is in the aft salon." I made my way to the portal leading to the next dining room. Only a single round table sat in its center. Surrounded by acres of open carpet, it was set but also vacant.

Behind me Laurent was already padding up the stairway. A middle-aged man who could have stepped out of the smart-casual page of an Orvis catalog came around the bar to my left beaming a wide grin. "Gregg Espy. Welcome aboard."

When he went to shake, I hesitated. "Pleased to meet who-the-hell-are-you?"

Far from put off, the man tipped his head a few degrees to appraise me. "Interesting. Are you really this chill, or is smart-ass your defense default? I'm not criticizing, I'm truly curious."

"Me first. You still haven't answered my question, and I've got a few more."

"Fair enough." Espy gestured to one of the leather chairs at the table. When I sat, he took the one opposite. "Ask away."

"Where do I start? How's this? What the fuck?"

Gregg Espy laughed. "Reasonable and succinct." He took off his tortoiseshell glasses and steepled his forefingers against his lips. I could picture Espy in a lit prof's office at Yale. "First, apologies for the dramatics. We had a sudden need to isolate you for a friendly briefing."

"I love that you say friendly. I say kidnapp-y. And exactly who is this 'we' you're referring to?" I heard feet mushing carpet behind me, but it wasn't Monsieur Laurent with a steamed towel. Imagine my surprise when I twisted around and saw Cammie Nova slipping in.

"Cameron," said Espy.

"Gregg," said Nova.

I tried to make sense of this. And of their relationship. "I reiterate. 'What the fuck?'"

"I expected some disorientation. Let's clear that up and we can move forward." Nova closed the pocket doors behind her, then Espy leaned toward me in a candor pose. "I work for the US government in a certain capacity."

"You're a spook."

"Central Intelligence, to be forthright. I'm director of special activities."

I shifted toward Cammie. "One down, one to go."

"Ms. Nova works with me as a specialized skills officer, or SSO."

"Whatever that means. It damn sure wasn't on your résumé."

"It means she is trained to perform duties consistent with intelligence gathering."

"Like this morning's fiasco."

Espy and Nova traded quick looks, and she said, "When did you figure that out?"

"Am figuring. It's hardly a Mensa challenge. I drew a Venn diagram with intelligence gathering in one circle and gunplay in the other. How'm I doing so far?"

The CIA man grinned. "You're too smart for us."

"I dunno. You're the dude with the fifty-meter bateau and the Paris police doing your bidding. No aspersions, Gregg. Frankly I'm relieved my Zodiac trip didn't end up like Fredo's last ride in *Godfather 2*."

"We don't operate that way."

"Tell that to Victor Fabron."

Nova snapped, "That was not us." But her edge wasn't angry. Defensive, like she needed me to know that she would never put a hit on one of my guests.

"But he was there because of you. More to the point, because you jammed him down my throat."

She came back more sharply. "Victor Fabron would have made a fine interview." Espy held a palm out to her. Nova bristled at being put in her place, even wordlessly. She flopped into the free chair and crossed her arms.

Espy sounded a conciliatory tone. "When we lose an asset, it gets emotional."

My eyes found Cammie's. During my interrogation when I'd spotted her out the window, I wondered if Fabron's death landed personally. Now I saw that it had. "I get it. No harm done." I answered him but said it to her.

"Good, good," said Espy, "because we didn't bring you here to lock horns. On the contrary, Nova and I want this to be the birth of an amicable relationship. By the way, manners. Can I get you anything? Name it."

Oh, would I have loved me some wine. Or something potent from that bar. But this felt like an occasion for a clear head. I saw some bottles in an ice bucket. "Sparkling water, maybe?" I reached, but Espy jumped up, eager to serve. After he poured, I said, "The flash drive. That was your deal, your intelligence gathering, right?"

Nova got a short head dip from her superior. "That's right." She uncrossed her arms and sounded more like the Cammie I knew. "It had sensitive information on it that Victor was supposed to brush pass to me on location. That's why the in-person booking. When he got shot, he slipped it to you."

"Haven't you people heard of email?"

The director of special activities plucked something invisible from his tablecloth. "Too insecure. The intel in question is far too volatile to risk on digital platforms. Even encrypted."

"And yet now the police have it." As soon as the words came out, I scoffed. "Of course they don't—you never handed it over. That's why you insisted I leave it all to you." She smiled sheepishly. "And why my hotel room got tossed."

"Somebody obviously saw him pass the flash drive to you. The transfer wasn't on our video. I checked." Which was why she confiscated the media from Latrell and Marisol. The more I learned, the more I felt used.

"Who killed him?" I clocked another Espy-to-Nova permission signal.

"That's one answer I did get. Thanks to Marisol's video, we were able to ID the shooter. His name is Thorvald Grepp." Regret descended on her. "Grepp's an agent I ran back in the day. We don't know who he's working for now, but he was once in Norway's E14 intelligence unit."

Espy jumped in. "You aren't cleared to know that."

"Yeah, well you aren't cleared to use my TV show for your bullshit spy games." I stormed over to the sliding door.

For the first time, Espy looked alarmed. "Pike. Please stay. Please? We need your help."

"Doing what?"

"Exactly what you are doing. One more time, for us." Espy pulled my chair out and waited. I felt like a dick standing there so I sat again. He patted my shoulder and retook his seat. "I've been in this service a long time. Rarely does the abstract model intersect the actuality. This time it exceeds it."

I frowned toward Nova. "Your man might as well be speaking Mando'a."

"I'm saying there's a reason we embedded SSO Nova with you." Her tiny smile made me look away. "We drew up a model for this enterprise. It's perfect cover. A globe-trotting celebrity chef with outspoken views and insurgent credentials who all the world wants to meet. And not just culinary types. You know what I'm talking about. Your show—your star power—gives you all-access to the world's movers and shakers. Popes to poets, despots to dissidents, news writers to news makers."

"Thanks for all that. I may even steal it for a promo. But I refuse to whore out my series as some government façade."

"Nobody would know."

"I would. And that doesn't sit well with my, what did you call them, insurgent credentials? No sale. Not worth it to be one of your joes."

Espy smiled. "You even know the lingo. Somebody's been reading his le Carré."

"Enough to know that the le Carré joes are field grunts who do all the scut work and get banged up, tortured, or shot." I almost cited Victor Fabron but didn't want to tweak Nova. "I'll miss you, Cammie. I really will." Bittersweet's how I felt watching her. I not only respected her professional chops, she felt like someone I'd enjoy slogging through a season of drudgery with. Unflappable, sense of humor, a rare match. "Too bad. I had this gut feel you and I would make a damn good team. But I'm out."

A silence ate the room. Only the low purr of the bateau's engines filled the void. The Hôtel de Ville eased by the window I was facing. Espy set both hands on the tablecloth and locked them together with laced fingers. "Here it is. I'm letting you in." He threw a switch from congeniality to soberness. "We need to perform a rescue mission. A man's life is at stake."

"Oh, no, please don't. Not the humanity card."

"That was the message on Fabron's flash drive."

Nova affirmed. "A good man who has performed invaluable service to our country is in danger. You'd be saving the life of a hero."

"And now the patriot card."

"It's the entire deck," said Espy. "Because you haven't committed yet, I can't give you a full briefing. But I'll bend the rules to see if I can tip you over to a yes. Will you hear me out?" I flicked my brows, a noncommittal go-ahead. "We have an asset placed at the highest echelons of the Kremlin. A mole who has been operating as a double on our behalf for years. The message on that flash drive was urgent. His cover is about to get blown, and we need to get him out. We need to perform an exfiltration, and soon. Every day that passes, he's closer to getting burned, and once he is, it would mean torture, then death for him, as well as for the hundreds, literally hundreds, of our human intelligence sources in his orbit."

"I get the urgency, OK?"

"Good."

"And I'm down with striking a blow against the thug empire."

"Excellent."

"But I'm no spy. I'm more James Beard than James Bond. You say Kremlin and exfiltration in the same breath, and all I hear is danger."

Espy adopted a lighter tone. "You won't ever be put in harm's way."

"I won't?" I tried to sound skeptical, not wavering, but Espy smelled a close.

"Because you won't be involved operationally. Try this on." The grin returned. "You'd be our MVB. Most Valuable Bystander. You be you. Do your show, and leave the spy stuff to us pros."

"What about my crew? These people are family. I refuse to put them in jeopardy."

"Same guardrails for them," said Espy. "In fact, your crew will not only have elite protection, they'll never have any idea what's going on."

"Exactly what would be going on? We'd go to Russia? If so, when? And what is my role?"

"We just got the alert today. If you give us a yes, we will be able to draw up a plan by tomorrow. Like I said, we need to move fast." Cammie dragged her chair close on my other side. Her scent reminded me of summers at the shore and assurance.

"There's one thing we need to make this mission work, Pike, and it's you."

"No pressure, right?" I was trying to laugh it off. Their stares were fixed on me. Espy's was full of hope. Cammie's felt like she was peering straight down the dark shaft to my guarded soul. I tried to turn away from her but couldn't. "You're saying it would be only this one mission?"

She counted off three fingers. "A, B, C, and out. And we're already at B."

I lacked enough fingers to tally all the justifications I had to say no and walk. But her presence—her bearing—tempted me to again embrace the peril of motion. Like I used to.

In a Joseph Campbell I read during my year of emotional repair, he quoted an elder's advice to a young Native American. It went, "As you go the way of life, you will come to a great chasm. Jump. It's not as wide as you think." For reasons illogical but powerful, I took the leap.

eight

Gregg Espy took yes for an answer and quickly ended the meeting. The contented DSA, having bagged this reluctant chef, sailed on solo to wherever spook bosses go. Nova and I split off in the police Zodiac. The bateau had reached the Eiffel Tower, and as we motored away from it, we watched the ten o'clock light show of glittery strobes. "Where did this cruise take me, Vegas or Paris?"

"Oh, that reminds me," she said. "The Jules Verne." I frowned, not following her. "The answer to your question this morning about *Rush Hour 3*. Eva never answered. The restaurant fight scene was up there. In the Jules Verne."

"I am floored. Not even flying lead could knock you off the trivia game?"

"What was the opening line of your voice-over?"

I had to think. "'Surprise me?'"

Cammie opened her palms. "Here I am."

When we lost our view of *la tour Eiffel* passing under a bridge, I said, "Questions. I still have questions."

"Happy to answer. The ones I can."

"Really? It's that easy to get you to talk? Unless you're blowing smoke. This is the problem, see? Now that I know what you do, I'm not sure I can take you at face value."

"Welcome to my world." She pointed a V at the police officers standing at the pilot console with their backs to us. "Let's talk in the car."

We disembarked at Port de la Concorde, where Nova's Peugeot waited in the service lane. She made a daredevil lurch from the turnout onto Quai des Tuileries, heading toward our hotel. "OK, questions. Hit me."

"What about my crew? I meant what I said back there. I have this primal thing about protecting them."

"They'll be safe. As will you."

"Can I at least let them know what's going on? Not disclosing makes me feel, I dunno, shady."

"Hear this clearly. You cannot tell your crew. Not some. Not one. Nobody. I don't care how tight you are. Promise?"

I put one hand on my heart and raised the other. "They won't have a clue. Look at me. I found out I was your joe by accident."

"I've fooled lesser people."

"To be fair, you had the shadowy hand of the full intel community behind you. Which, on reflection, means somebody at the network's in on this." She was a stone wall behind the wheel. "Is it HR? Programming? Goldman? Wiley? Salzberg. It's Salzberg, I know it."

"Even if you guess right, you'd still be wrong."

"Spy talk! How cool is this?"

"God, you are wired. You're pinging like Donkey from *Shrek*. Never took you to get nervous."

"I am kind of amped. Not in a bad way. Call it happy-scared. I haven't…haven't felt that in a while." I turned away, pretending to be interested in the illumination of the Pei pyramid as we cut through the Louvre.

Nova brought her hand across to rest on my wrist. "It's hard to lose someone you love."

"I'm working through it. Yeah."

"I know." She let her fingers stay a moment and let go. I appreciated her for not pressing. People who poke at your sore spots are usually out to hear themselves talk. The space Nova gave opened me up. "I was so gut punched I started doubting myself. And doubt is not my best look. Shakespeare had a great line about that."

Without a pause Cammie said, "'Our doubts are traitors, and make us lose the good we oft might win, by fearing to attempt.'"

I was stunned. "Consider my gob fully smacked. My quote. I cannot believe you know my Willy Shakes quote." Staring at her, I wondered, Who is this woman who not only can quote a lesser-known Bard comedy, but one of my darlings? "Who are you, and how did you get in my head?"

"Don't be too impressed. Career side effect. I know all the traitor quotations." A slice of a different Cammie broke through the pro-spy façade. A vulnerable glimpse I liked. She said, "Do you think I'm weird?"

"No, I think I'm weird. Because I don't think you're weird." We laughed together. When it subsided, I took a fresh look at this enigmatic woman. Who was in there?

The GPS kept telling her where to make turns. Nova ignored it and improvised, cutting six minutes off the ride to the Marais. "Impressive. With skills like that, you could work on *Hangry Globe*."

Cammie chuckled. "For now." That delivered me a reality check. I bided my time, counting off two blocks before I probed the topic.

"So where are we in the alphabet? You said we're already at B. Did you mean we already did B, or is B next? Because if we're coming up on C, I want to know how soon you might…maybe…move on. Not that I'm in a hurry. Because I'm not."

At a red light she turned to me, and the specialized skills officer iteration of Nova spoke. "Pike. Let's not get too invested."

"You mean personally?"

"Personally? Oh, hell no. Absolutely not."

"Good. Because I meant not personally."

"Right. Good. Of course."

"I ask only because of show logistics. I'll need to replace you. Professionally."

The SSO kept it all business. "Maybe Sheila will be out of rehab."

"Ha. I officially no longer buy the rehab story. Come on. Too convenient an exit. Totally bogus, designed to make room for you. I call BS."

"For someone new at this you're good."

"Lifetime skeptic, borderline cynic."

"You're more spy material than you think." Nova eased to a stop outside our hotel. "Your ex-producer is enjoying a government-paid getaway at a resort spa in Sedona. As for me, day at a time."

"Sure, sure. I just like to know what's the next step."

"For you? A good night's sleep. I got notified your room's been restored to baseline. Leave a fat tip for housekeeping. You've had a helluva day, Chef. Rest up."

"I'm still kind of cranked. Feel like a nightcap?"

"Nightcap? What century is this?"

"That was me being ironic. But if you want the chambermaid to deliver some grog or a hot beef tea, Cameron, that could be arranged."

She put the transmission back in drive. "Thanks anyway. I have things to do. Espy and I promised a plan tomorrow, remember?" When I came around to the sidewalk, she powered her window down. "Hey? Now it's my turn."

"To what?"

"I get to welcome you aboard." I could still hear her laughing while I stood under the stone archway watching her taillights disappear into the night.

Naturally I figured I'd be tested on keeping the secret from my crew. But I never imagined how soon it would come. Before I reached the elevator, my phone pinged with a text from the Food Sarge. "I need to speak with you about something important. Tonight, alone—away from the other Globers."

AFTER THREE-PLUS SEASONS, Rayna Stanhope not only knew how to wrangle all things culinary for the show, from ingredients to appliances to food styling, she also knew my personal tastes. Such as where I liked to go when I wanted a no-nonsense cocktail in a city of aperitifs.

Rue Daunou was hopping at that hour. Hipster bars were at capacity, and the overflow spilled out into the street. Young urban comers milled around, fisting craft cocktails and beers the way London does happy hour. I strode past them all.

Near the end of the block, I pushed through a pair of swinging saloon doors and stepped into Harry's New York Bar. How old-school is Harry's? It's the same watering hole where George Gershwin wrote *An American in Paris*. The Bloody Mary, the Sidecar, and the French 75 were all invented under its brown tin-stamped ceiling. The Sarge flagged me from a deuce she had claimed in the alcove at the top of the stairs above the piano lounge. I went for a Redbreast old-fashioned. Rayna had a head start and ordered a reload of her stinger. *Saluts* and first sips out of the way, she thanked me for calling off the next day's production. "We all appreciate it. Compassionate of you." She hoisted her rocks glass to me, then took another pull. A healthy one, I noticed.

"Enlightened self-interest," I said. "Nobody, including your cordial host, would be doing their best work after what went down. Safe to say we are all pretty bugged."

"Except maybe one of us." She gave me a stagey nod, and I wondered if that was her second stinger or third.

"And so, we jump to your topic. Or do I not sense a ball getting teed up?"

"I'm not fooling around. This is a big deal. It's about our Fearless Producer."

"Hey, be nice." Same as at the morning rehearsal, I couldn't sanction her undercutting my producer.

"Nice?" She tipped back another swig. "I mean, did you see her today? After the guy got shot?" I almost answered no, but Rayna had something to spew. I let her run. "That beyotch was cold. Half of us are crying. Declan's ralphing his croissant in the gutter. And what's our Fearless—what's Nova doing? Hovering around the body. Getting on her cell. Acting like it's another day, lah-dee-dah."

"First of all, no, I didn't notice any of that. And second, people have all sorts of reactions to stressful situations." I was having my own response to this particular one. Not only because I felt a visceral need to protect Cammie in absentia, but also the ribbing about her tardiness on the set had hit a new level. Then came a newer one.

"Uh-huh. See, I was afraid of this. The way you're defending her." She leaned back, displaying a hard smugness I'd never seen. "I was right."

"About?"

"Can I say it?"

"I think you're going to."

"You're into her. Our Fearless Producer."

"What? That is a stretch. No, more than that. It's petty."

"Bullshit. I saw the two of you after the crew left the set today. I caught your little looks."

Talk about absurd. So, I answered in kind. "Busted. Nothing stokes the libido like handing over your blood-soaked wardrobe."

"Whatev. At least I know you won't sleep with her."

"Rayna—"

"With your moral compass, and all." She shook the ice in her glass. "Unless this is different."

I should probably explain. About two months after Astrid's death, Rayna and I were friendly colleagues closing a Caracas bar, talking out our mutual lives' shit shows when, later, she knocked on the door to my room wearing nothing but a smile and hotel bathrobe. Not only was I not ready for that (way too soon), the big firewall was the impropriety. Even before MeToo, going back to when I worked Manhattan restaurants, which were the sexual Wild West of workplace misconduct, I'd never hook up with an employee. Sure, I got tempted. Rayna's approach might have been captivating some other time. But I'd never act on it. We talked it out that night. I took pains to make sure she didn't feel humiliated for the invite, and we moved on. At least until Cammie Nova entered the picture. I decided the best course was to move off that topic, get the freaking check, and vamoose.

As benignly but clearly as I could put it, I said, "My moral compass remains true north. So let that ease your mind." The Sarge looked anything but convinced. I needed to douse this with a fire extinguisher before she touched off a rumor that raced out of control. "Besides," I said, "this goes no farther than this table, right?" I waited until she agreed. "Nova? No way."

"Uh-huh…"

"Not a chance. Zip. Zero." She seemed amused. I drove it home. "No magic. No chemistry. No there there."

"None?"

"Too wonky." Rayna seemed puzzled, so I helped her process. "As in earnest."

Her torso rocked with a big, tipsy nod. "You mean cold, tight-ass beyotch?"

"I'm happy with wonky." A hand from behind clamped down on my shoulder. I bolted to my feet and spun with my fists up.

"Ho, ho, easy." A pear-shaped tourist took a step back, knocking into his wife. "Sorry to startle you, Chef Pike. Kelly and I are huge fans. We heard on the news what happened today. God-awful. Here I thought we were the only ones with random shootings. Can we buy you another of what you're having?"

Their kindly midwestern faces made something crumble inside me. I managed to slap on my official smile. "Sorry for going into attack mode. A little jet-lagged, I guess." I asked their names, autographed the coaster they held out, and said thanks for the offer, but I was just leaving. I caught the waiter's attention and drew an invisible pen in the air.

Even though her glass was empty Rayna said, "I'm not done." I sat while she continued. "Nova did more than walk around the body, checking him out. I saw her squat down and run her hands over him."

"Like maybe doing first aid? Checking for a pulse?"

"Your producer friend shoved her hands in his pants pockets." Rayna said it loud enough that I checked the other tables. Nobody seemed to have heard. "Ran through all of them like she was searching. Or trying to steal something."

"I heard his wallet was still on him."

"I don't know what it was about, but it stuck with me all day, trying to make sense of it." She planted her forearms on the table and leaned in to me. "Know what I think? She's some kind of cop."

"Come on—Nova?"

"Or a spy."

"Oh, please." I pooh-poohed it, then craned for that garçon with the check.

"Did you know she has a gun? That's right. The other day when all our connecting flights met up in Brussels, she didn't know it, but I was at the back of her security line. Three guards took her aside. When I moved up, I saw them behind a partition. Nova showed them some kind of document, and they handed a pistol case back to her. Pike, I think Cammie Nova is a cop. Or spy."

Holy zamoli. Was this happening? Really? I made another check of our surroundings, mainly to buy time to think. I was warned not to share with the crew. So, I had to deny. And do it in a way that quelled the blaze. "We both have seen lots of people get pulled aside for a private search, right? And how do you know it was a pistol case and not...I dunno, jewelry or...some electronic production gadget." God, I sucked at being a spy. Can I say that? All those Graham Greenes and John le Carrés I devoured, and there I sat grappling maniacally for purchase on a steep cliff of loose gravel.

"Then why the document?"

"That's it. Probably some medical device with a doctor's permit." I needed to shut this down. "Sarge, know what I think? I think the trauma of this day has hit us all big-time. I'm not saying you didn't see what you saw, but I'm going all in on a deep, cleansing breath. Let's sleep on this. Maybe tomorrow, the feelings you have about Cammie might not be as raw. And won't color what might have been checking her friend for a pulse or name of next of kin or something."

"He was her friend? Well, I didn't know that. I admit I do have a bias against the beyotch."

"Like I said, sleep on it." The waiter appeared with the bill. When I finished with the transaction on his portable, I stood. Rayna said she was going to hang there for one more. "Use the show's credit card," I said. "And Sarge, let's not speculate about Nova with the others, OK? If you need to talk, talk to me."

She rose unsteadily and gave me a hug. "You're the best."

"Shut up, you are." And then I got the hell out of there.

PAIN IS A TRAVELER. It's been my companion so long I should sign it up for reward miles. I wish that were funny. There's a term in substance recovery: taking a geographic. An itinerant cook I worked with who had a nose for blow told me that one. He learned it when his sponsor held up a mirror to tell him that no matter how many times he changed restaurants, cities, and coasts, his problems were portable. My friend pretended he got it. Later he used the mirror to do lines.

There is no geographic for me. This salaried traveler with royalty points in *Hangry Globe* has been outdistancing Carmen Sandiego for years, but the pain tags along. I needed to be alone when I returned from Harry's to my restored hotel room, but pain waited up for me, coloring everything.

It even made Paris feel foreign. That may sound like an unintended joke, but I once declared myself an adopted son of that beloved city. And not based on visits. You've heard me mention Astrid. Well, when the two of us started getting serious, I rented a Left Bank apartment. The idea was that we share it during my series hiatus, a long break that coincided with her yacht being put up in dry dock for maintenance. By her yacht, I don't mean she owned it. I mean the one she worked on. I can see I'm going to have to give you the highlights of how we met. It's thrilling if you are into love at first sight. If you're not, you can't know my story if you miss this one.

I met Astrid on the pilot episode of *Hangry Globe*. This bad-boy chef was hell-bent on planting the black flag, creating a show where food and culture smacked heads, and what better opener than a leap into the profligate maw of rock-and-roll decadence? And where better than aboard the private luxury yacht owned by Europe's wealthiest rocker? My crew and I boarded in Positano for a cruise along Italy's Amalfi Coast hosted by Kogg, the macho superstar singer whose working-class upbringing infused his lyrics with harsh, street-level poetry. With obvious comparisons to the Boss, Kogg's hardscrabble brand of rock excited a disenfranchised male blue-collar fan base with huge crossover appeal to women. And it made him a goddamned fortune.

Kogg put on a show for our cameras, leading me on our video tour of the *Thumos*, his 140-foot mega-yacht. Oligarchs would chuckle into their iced vodkas, but that skiff was tricked out. Strutting his decks in a packed Speedo, the rocker motioned to his toys with a bottle of Louis Roederer gripped by the neck: a pair of Kawasaki Jet Skis, a Zodiac MilPro, a Boston Whaler, three kayaks, stand-up paddleboards, and scuba gear for six. The appointments weren't shabby, either. A whirlpool, a sundeck, an alfresco cinema, five staterooms for ten guests, Kogg's master suite, and quarters for his crew of nine. He started counting them off for me: captain, engineer, first mate, bosun, deckhand… but it all went to a blur when we entered his galley and I laid eyes on the yacht's executive chef.

My brain went to polenta. I remember fixating on the name stitched on her white tunic and uttering my first word to her. "Astrid."

Your iconoclastic TV host fell hard for her right there on camera. The segment called for us to team-cook a lunch on the super-yacht, and by the time our *scialatielli ai frutti di mare* got served alongside a simple caprese with olive oil and fresh basil, I was too smitten to eat. She was too moony to do anything but.

Our romance lasted over that season in spite of travel obstacles. I was globe-trotting with my new series, and Astrid set sail for weeks at the whim of the most whimsical of rock egos. We managed to meet up for stolen weekends in her ports of call over the summer and autumn. But that winter, when my lengthy hiatus from shooting coincided with the yacht's refitting, we took that apartment on Rue Jacob and became a couple.

Over seven weeks, when Astrid and I managed to leave the bedroom, we surrendered to the Paris trope and starred in our own rom-com montage. *Mon Dieu*, we ate good. I turned her on to Frenchie; she introduced me to Allard. We shopped fresh everything at the Rue Poncelet market for home-cooking date nights, picnics in Luxembourg Gardens, and day trips to Giverny. We did the zinc bars, the sidewalk cafés, the museums. We stayed in and read Dickens to one another. We even quarreled—all natural, especially for two alpha loners learning how to become a pair. But mostly, we walked, practicing the most Parisian of habits, *flâneurie*. Strolling was all about slowing down the motion and taking the time simply to be together in love. When the *Thumos* came out of dry dock and we were both about to go back to our jobs, I proposed. Astrid said yes. Actually, what she said was, "Please, sir, I want some more." We held each other and laughed, then danced all night to our Anita Baker mix.

We parted as an engaged couple with our coming lifetime together peeking over the horizon. But things change. Sometimes they do more than change. They knock you sideways.

One morning I woke up in London, hustling to make the lobby crew call, when a Breaking News bulletin came on BBC: "Rock star and one other dead as dinghy explodes at Athens luxury mooring."

How it went down:

Kogg had finished a sold-out concert at Peace and Friendship Stadium, and Astrid hitched a ride with him from the Athens Marina out to his mega-yacht to weigh anchor for his next gig in Istanbul. They never reached the *Thumos*. Forensic investigators determined Kogg had brought aboard a duffel bag packed with ingredients for making crystal meth using the "shake and bake" method, volatile chemicals combined inside two-liter soda bottles. Something screwed up. One of the bottles ignited. The flash fire set off four others, which detonated the Zodiac's fuel bladder.

Devastating? Shattering? The word for what I felt hasn't been coined in the English language, and believe me, I've hunted for it. But please spare me the condolences.

Please?

51

You see, there's a secret reason I get pissed off about the sympathy blankets people bind me in. And now it's you, dear reader, who's going to get pissed because I won't tell you why. I've never told anyone. I'll offer only this much, but you can take it to the bank. In every tragedy there is an element of guilt. I live with it, I choke on it, I have formed my life around it. Whatever pain I am enduring reminds me that I have it coming.

I'm leaving it there for now.

At dawn I woke up still sore from the brawl with my intruder the night before. Sitting up in bed, I did some stretches to test myself out. Not too bad. I flipped my phone over to assess the incoming. Before I went to sleep, I'd turned it face down so the screen wouldn't pester me every time it lamped up with the endless calls, texts, and emails from reporters seeking comment on the Victor Fabron killing. The morning haul was more of the same. On my way downstairs from the loft, I stopped at the landing to peek out the drape. Light rain was falling, and I felt glad I didn't have to shoot a segment in that. I turned from the window, put one foot on the short flight to the living room, and startled.

A large man was sitting in the easy chair. He was relaxed, owning it like an athlete on the sideline bench. The picture of casual, except for the pistol resting on his lap.

nine

"Morning," said the man with the gun. My eyes darted around for an escape. Upstairs was a dead end. The window. I'd be a sight climbing out of that in my skivvies. But forget that. I'd never breach the curtains before the man, or his bullet, got me. I held up my hands.

"Ah, that's not necessary. I can see you're cool. And I'm not here to hurt you. DSA Espy would frown on that."

I gave him a long look. "I've seen you before. You skippered the police Zodiac last night."

"Good eye. Really, you can lower your hands. Come on down." He indicated the gun without picking it up. "This isn't for you." I took a seat on the bottom step. "Name's Kurt Harrison. I'm not with the Paris police. I'm American. A security agent attached to DSA Espy's cadre."

"Are you my bodyguard?"

"Was last night."

"You were here all night?"

Harrison smiled. "You walked right past me on your oh-three-eleven pee."

"How did you get in?" Before he could answer, I did. "I'm an idiot. Kind of what you do."

Harrison had warmth in spite of his military commando bearing. But you can be warm and still be all business. "Soon as you shower and dress, we'll go."

"Go? Where?"

"Twenty minutes enough time?"

"To be clear, are you my bodyguard or my babysitter?"

"Today, I'm your daddy." The security agent stood. Six-two of corded muscle in cargo pants and a hoodie. Dwayne Johnson when he had hair. "Wear something comfortable. Nothing you mind getting dirty or ripped. Just in case."

"Of what?"

He holstered his gun inside his sweatshirt. "We'll roll in twenty, Chef."

HE DROVE US OUT THE A13 through suburbs and countryside to a French military base that apparently granted privileges to Americans of a certain stripe who wore plain clothes and loved their acronyms. SAC was Harrison's. He told me that was CIA-speak for Special Activities Center, in which he was a PPO, paramilitary protection officer. Once we cleared the gate, my daddy knew his way around, pulling his Renault Captur up to a hangar on the far side of the air station. He grabbed a gear duffel from the hatch and led me inside. The hangar was empty except for a line of human silhouette targets in front of some sandbags and a collection of gym mats. "Welcome to training day, Chef Pike."

"Appreciate the private tour but if you had mentioned this, I could have saved you the drive."

"Firing range is this way." Harrison strode toward the wall of sandbags. I hesitated, then caved and followed.

"This is all going to be basic. Seriously, how much can I teach you in one day?"

"Agreed, so why bother? I'm not making a career of this."

"Take that up with the boss. After yesterday's close calls, I've been tasked with teaching you some rudimentary self-defense." He unzipped the duffel and fished out a pistol. "This is a Beretta M9. Semiautomatic. Nine millimeter, fifteen-round magazine. Standard US military issue. Personally, I prefer my Glock 19. But we'll start you off with this."

Resistance was futile. Not because of intimidation from Harrison. Me and my testosterone kind of liked the idea of playing Dirty Harry with live ammo. But before I got to hold the M9, he walked me through its operation. Then grip and stance basics. "Firm, two-handed like this. Arms extended, shoulders relaxed, that's the way. You're a righty. So scoot your right foot back about twelve inches from your left. How's that feel?"

I answered by yanking the trigger, completely missing my target but killing a sandbag. "Feels good."

The PPO gave me a hard stare. "Have you ever fired a gun?"

"I went duck hunting in Italy on one of my episodes with a Michelin-star chef."

"He still alive?"

"Not to worry. I'm kind of a jock." I fired again, another complete miss.

"See, you're jerking that trigger. What you want is an easy, steady pull with the pad of your forefinger. Try going softer."

I may not be a small-arms expert, but I am a natural athlete, and things improved over the course of the hour. By then all my shots hit the silhouettes, including half a dozen kills. Next, we moved to the mats for hand-to-hand combat.

"Is this part necessary?"

"It is if someone comes at you with a knife." Harrison made a lightning lunge out of nowhere into my belly. "Now, this one is a rubber demo. If someone tries this with a real one, you'll thank me. Unless you'd rather have your intestines on the sidewalk."

"Teach me, Obi-Wan."

Although commando skills weren't in my CV, I did have some martial arts training and competitive fencing in my past, not to mention a glut of street rumbles growing up in Astoria. None of which applied. My trainer introduced me to eye gouges, throat punches, groin kicks, and something called the nutcracker choke, which was not one bit as whimsical as its name. "The main thing when someone comes at you with a weapon, be it blade or gun, you deflect, disable, disarm. Deflect, as in get your ass out of the kill zone. Sounds crazy, but that means pulling yourself up close to your attacker with the weapon pointed away from both of you. Disable, as in rendering the attacker inoperative, then disarming. Sometimes those can be combined by breaking an elbow, wrist, or thumb in the process of stripping the weapon."

Harrison choreographed those defense moves in slow motion with me in the role of assailant. More for pride than anything, I kept at it through the afternoon. My early moves, rote and by-the-numbers, eventually showed occasional fluidity. Enough to get cocky when we wrapped up. "Better watch yourself, Harrison. You may have created a monster."

The PPO chuckled, then unleashed a disarm with such blinding speed that somehow, I found myself looking up from the mat at Harrison, who was holding the rubber blade to my throat. "One slice of the carotid, and you're gone in seconds."

"Lethal efficiency for today's millennial in a hurry. I'll file that one away."

"Last item." Harrison took a small canvas case out of the duffel and handed it to me. "Open up." Inside rested a revolver, a small, stubby, nasty thing in black matte with olive-green grips. "That is a K6s TLE. Don't let the size fool you. Holds six rounds of .357 stopping power. Two-inch barrel fits in a pocket, and it's hammerless. Won't snag on the draw."

"Cool." I tried to hand it back.

"No, that's yours. Snubbie's what you need. Compact, uncomplicated, and good at close range, kind of in line with your skills. No offense."

"All yours. I'm strictly short term. It'll go to waste as soon as we're done." When Harrison hesitated, I put it in his duffel myself.

"OK, fine. But at least take this." All deadpan, he handed me the rubber knife.

"Now you're talking. I'm more about knife skills, anyway. If the bad guy would just hold still, I could chiffonade him like nobody's business."

WHEN MY TRAINER AND I stepped out of the hangar, the rain had let up and a Mercedes GLE beaded with water was idling at the door. Gregg Espy sat behind the wheel with his face down in his smartphone screen. "Looks like you rate a ride with the director of special activities."

Not only did I like the big man's understated macho manner, two violent incidents made me take his lessons seriously despite my smart-assing. This was the guy you'd want in your foxhole. And he was in mine. "Appreciate the help, PPO Harrison. Truly. Hope I never need to put any of this to use, but if I do…" I left it there. He got it. I felt a rise of tension parting with him. My next skirmish might not be a rehearsal. "Guess I'll be seeing you."

"Only if I want you to." The security agent shook my hand. I was gripping a cinder block.

Espy gave me a cursory hello, then began our drive in silence. He wristed a wave to acknowledge the sentry's salute as we left the base, then casually lobbed his opener. "Question. Were you planning to tell us what last night's sudden meeting with Rayna Stanhope was about?" The CIA man had interrogation skills. In control, offhanded approach, a loaded question, all to throw me off kilter. All of which worked.

I did what I always do to regain balance—push back hard. "Is this how it is going to be? I'm supposed to account for my movements and report to you?"

"You're new, Pike, you get slack. But this isn't some game. Lives and national security hang on everything we do. Therefore, when a civilian crew member shares gossip that could burn SSO Nova, endanger her life, and blow up the operation, yes, it is incumbent on you to share it, and share it ASAP." He checked my reaction, then returned his attention to the road.

Implications tumbled. Not only did he know where I was and with whom, he knew what we were talking about. "You had somebody listening?"

"And recording." He gave me a so-there face. "In a public place like that we can only hope one of the bad guys wasn't doing the same thing."

"I didn't introduce the topic there."

"Understood. I got that from the playback. On the upside, you handled it deftly and didn't validate Ms. Stanhope's speculations. It shows me you can keep a secret. Let's move on and get to why I'm your chauffeur today. We've come up with a viable mission plan." He merged onto the A13 and settled into his travel lane before he continued.

"First priority, exfiltrate our mole. Hard enough. Harder yet from Russian soil. So, we figured out a way to have him come to us. With me so far?" I raised a thumb. No interruptions. "The plan we came up with underscores why we need you. There's an oligarch named Ignaz Tábori. He's Hungary's minister of agriculture. We want to get him on your show for an interview. Agriculture, food, whatever. You'll work out the angle." I raised my hand. "Go ahead."

"I'll overlook the fact you're screwing with my show's content so I can ask the bigger question. What does booking some buzz-killing Hungarian bureaucrat have to do with your exfiltration?"

"Everything. Tábori is high and tight in Putin's kleptocracy circle. So close that every time he does a media interview, Vlady sends a handler to babysit him. Guess who the handler is. I'll answer that. Our mole."

"Got it. I think I can take it from here. The oligarch comes for my interview, bringing your mole out of Russia to us. Soon as he shows, you work your exfiltration."

The director of special activities grinned and gave me the Paul Hollywood handshake. "You're a quick study. Sure you're not a spy?"

"No, I'm...what did you call me...your MVB?"

"Ha ha, that's right. Most Valuable Bystander."

"Hate to be the turd in the punch bowl, but your plan sounds like me doing zero bystanding and plenty of standing in the middle of danger."

"Not the way we do things. You be you, remember? Go about your interview, and everyone—you, your crew, even the Hungarian—will never know it happened."

So he kept saying. I wondered if maybe I should have pocketed that revolver from Harrison. "Help me out here. Why would this oligarch I never heard of want to be on my show?"

"He's already agreed to. We had intel his wife is a major fan of yours, and that set the hook."

"How soon is this supposed to happen?"

"Unclear. We've hit a little snag. In her capacity as your nominal producer, Nova circled back to the Hungarian's office to set a date. His chief of staff said Tábori left on his annual family vacation and won't tell us where."

"Funny that you call this a little snag."

"I know, I know. But we already have a lead. Tábori has a mistress in Budapest. Soap opera star. Her landlord is on retainer for us, and he says she left in a limo full of suitcases yesterday for the South of France. SSO Nova has already initiated a search for the oligarch there. I need you and your crew to pack up and head down to Provence and be in position when we locate him."

"Can I point out that your tail is now totally throttling my dog?"

"This is top priority. And not only for the Agency. I have some skin in the game. This mole isn't just high value. He's my joe. I cultivated him. I turned him. I've been running him for years. He is a good man. I owe him, Pike."

His display of emotion sold me. "I suppose we might find something to shoot in the South of France." Espy chuckled. "Sorry I didn't notify you about the Food Sarge last night."

"Lesson learned, moving on."

Then I tested the waters sideways. "Do you want me to give a heads-up to Nova?"

"Don't need to. She listened to the playback with me." My worst fear. That meant Cammie had heard Rayna's projections about me "being into" her. But that's not the gut twister. She also must have caught my volley of cringeworthy denials to sell why I was not into her: No magic. No chemistry. No there there. And let's not forget wonky. Because I'm sure Cammie won't. I remembered prefacing all that by telling Rayna none of this leaves this table. Shit, I felt stupid.

"Listen, Pike? A word to the wise." My feeler wasn't as adroit as I'd hoped. The spymaster saw right through it. "Keep your head on straight. And watch your back with Nova."

"Not sure I understand what you mean."

"That's why I'm offering. She's top Agency talent, but there's an inner political game to all this, and Nova plays it like nobody I've seen. She is one artful manipulator."

"Is that bad?"

"You don't want to find out." Taillights lit his face in the back-up near Versailles. Espy checked the Rolex Daytona on his wrist, which looked anything but government issue, unless your government was Qatar. "How long would you guess I've been doing this?"

"I dunno. Twenty years?"

"Try thirty-one. Man, I have seen it all. I'm starting to think I've seen enough." The thing that's earned me a rep as an interviewer is that, for whatever reason, I'm the sort of guy people open up to. That evening it was a spook on the A13. "There's a price to being on the road so much. You know that as well as anyone. My wife left me, my kids are estranged.... You're out here long enough, you mark time with losses."

Telling Espy he was preaching to the choir might trigger him to ask me to share, which no way was going to happen. So, I let it go with, "I'm sorry." Luckily, he kept to his own download.

"And professionally, with all the changes in the world like Ukraine, strained alliances, Brexit, nationalist splinters, stateless actors, toxic politics back home—sometimes I feel like my era has passed." He turned to me like it was Saturday night and I was his priest. "I never wanted to be a man who outlived his Age."

"Then what's the alternative? What's act two for someone like you? Live out your time and go raise pigeons?"

"Espy's Rule Number One about surviving as a spy: always have an exit strategy."

"I get that. What's yours?"

"Espy's Rule Number Two: tell no one your exit strategy."

ten

The Espy briefing, the personal combat training day, and the offer of the snub-nosed .357 combined to make me paranoid enough to stay in and not tempt fate on the enticing boulevards of Paris. A decidedly different stance for me, a baller out to meet the world as the great Bourdain once put it, without fear or prejudice. My fledgling clandestine experience was threatening to erode that.

TV didn't help. Everywhere I flipped, CNN International, France 24, and the Beeb, featured "startling new developments" in the Victor Fabron killing. An anonymous tipster in silhouette with an auto-tuned voice said Fabron received death threats sparked by his new documentary investigating nepotism in government jobs. Ghosty security cam video, time-stamped a week before, showed a motorcyclist resembling the shooter leaving a suspicious package on Fabron's doorstep. When the biker left, it detonated.

Skeptic that I am, it reeked of spooks stage-managing the epitaph of a dead man. Look, I'm anything but naïve about the spin machine, whose gears are lubed by blood and cognac, but getting this close to the contraption made me want nose plugs. Apparently, if you're the CIA, a man and a story can both be killed.

I realized they had managed me, too. Isolating me on a military base for a training day, away from the press, while they executed their PR game plan. I'd agreed to put on the CIA uniform, but I confess I was straining at the fit.

Halfway through steak tartare and an ice-cold Leffe the concierge had delivered from Ma Bourgogne on the corner, I got a group email from Rayna. Subject: Family Emergency.

"Guys, I am sorry to blow out of Dodge like this, but my mother suffered a stroke. While you read this, I am on a flight home to Boston. It sucks not to say goodbye, and I would never do anything to hurt the show, but I need to hurry to her side. Cammie is working on a replacement, so hopefully this won't mean a hiccup in production. Hugs and prayers, OK?"

My first response was compassion. My second was that the Sarge never mentioned her mother in three years. And what's this crap telling me in a group email after our history? See what was happening to me? My new twisted worldview had me wondering if Rayna was so pissed at me or jealous of Nova that the real message was a big flip-off as she took a hike.

Then came my third response.

I speed-dialed Nova. "Hey, it's me. Where are you right now?"

WHEN NOVA LET ME IN her room, I had to walk around her luggage, a suitcase, and a carry-on bag stationed by the door. "You packed already?"

"Grab and go. I'm off to Arles tonight. I have legwork to do there and a network to rouse. You and the crew will catch up with me there tomorrow."

"We shall see."

"What does that mean?"

A tray on the coffee table held cold Badoits and a bottle of wine. I pulled it from the bucket to inspect the label. Sancerre. Either we had shared tastes, or she'd been expecting me. "How cordial. We can toast the end of our mission."

"What is with you?"

I wagged my cell phone, the incendiary email, live on the screen. "I assume you read Rayna's good-bye note. Or did you write it?" Nova didn't blink. I sat on the couch, boot heels on her coffee table. "Tell you what. I'll voice my theory; you tell me if it's foil-hat time or spot-on." She slid into the chair opposite. "Rayna's loose lips made her the Sarge who knew too much. You and Espy staged an intervention, and now she's conveniently off the continent. Where to? Boston, really? Or that spa in Sedona with Sheila?"

Nova took her time before she answered. "Close enough."

"And I'm not consulted? What the hell am I supposed to do for a Food Sarge? Even if I do stick with this mission—which, be warned, is doubtful—you can't produce a culinary travel show without a culinary coordinator. If you're even thinking about maintaining our cover, you should know that."

"All handled. We have someone on the way, a field agent with experience on a Food Network show. He's not only Agency personnel, but he also speaks Russian. See? We're making lemonade out of this."

"'We?'" All I could do was shake my head. "You know, for somebody in intelligence you're not too smart, SSO Nova. This contrarian persona the network promotes? That you said you were so charmed by? It ain't PR. I've been calling bullshit all my life. And the price I pay is that I have to be my own boss because I can't work for anyone else. So, I'm all indie all the time. Impetuous, mercurial, unfettered, and alive. A free man in Paris, that is until you people started fucking with me." Getting it off my chest wasn't cooling me off; I was getting more jacked. "Guess what. I don't like your A-B-C game. I'm O-U-T."

She held my gaze as steadily and dispassionately as an optical exam. "Then quit."

Last thing I expected. I took my feet off the furniture and remembered Espy's caution about how Nova plays the inner game. "Are you trying to mess with me? Is this some psyops technique? Well, it won't work."

"Pike, you need to be indie?" She gestured to the door. "Assert your independence."

"If I did, what about you? I assume you'd *adios*."

"Why does that matter?" She angled her head to one side and waited. A chess move. I knew that, but it still stung.

I shifted on my cushion. "For one, I'd have to break in another producer. And I'm, well, starting to enjoy working with you."

"Are you? Well, I am sure you could find someone else more compatible. Someone, say, less wonky?"

My face heated. "Ha ha, that. You picked that up, huh?" She stared blankly and let me sweat. "Pretty funny, don't you think? There I was trying to smother the Sarge's gossip, and I guess I did a little overselling in the denial department. All to protect you, of course. And how ironic that my one-on-one pushback ended up much less on the down low than I'd planned." Nova's silence squeezed me. Out came more blathering. "As far as wonky goes, I find wonkiness attractive. Not to sound inappropriate. Not wonky like sexy librarian wonky. That would objectify you. I say attractive in the sense of competency being attractive. And dignified. When it comes to wonky, sign me up."

"You can relax."

"I can?"

"Chemistry's subjective. You're wonk averse. I have a thing against fixer-uppers. Some things just are."

I nodded until the worm bored in. "Forgive me. Did you just call me a fixer-upper?"

"Mm, I don't think I mentioned you. Did you think I meant you?"

"Well, what did you mean?"

"I mean my history of trying to change guys carrying too much baggage always ends badly." She made a casual reach for the wine. "How'd it go with the DSA on the ride back from Fauville?"

What the hell happened? We're in the middle of my stay-or-go showdown, and she pivots the whole topic. I reconsidered Espy's caution about her being a manipulator. "The drive? All fine. He gave me the bullet points on the exfiltration plan. And decamping to the South of France to locate this oligarch."

"Anything else?"

"He mentioned you." She paused her reach for the corkscrew. "He said you were top Agency talent."

She raised the corners of her mouth. Not qualifying as a smile. "Gregg and I have a layered relationship. When…or if…you and I get to know each other better, I might tell you about it." I could guess, but I was gentleman enough not to ask.

Nova cut the foil on the bottle but studied me as she twisted the corkscrew. "When I debriefed her, Rayna said she was still mortified about showing up naked at your door that night."

"She told you about that?"

Nova popped the cork. "And said that you fended her off."

"What's right is right. Thankfully her moment of weakness didn't line up with mine. Not that I don't have them."

Cammie let down a smidge. Got more real. "Again, I'm sorry for your loss, truly." I heard myself mumble a thank you. She held out the bottle and filled my glass to the curve of the bell. I've spent my life attuned to service and noticed her hands weren't steady on the pour. "I had a similar blow. Although nothing like yours. *À santé.*"

I regarded her over the rim of my glass as I sipped. Since I first met Cammie, I'd admired her strength. I saw it as the core of her beauty. Now she was showing a different color. A hint of emotion. "I'm sorry. You lost someone, too?"

"Everybody's got a story, right?" Her brief show of vulnerability passed like an eclipse. "We all have shit to get over." She sat back in the easy chair, studying me at length with a pensive face until a tipping point came. She abandoned her glass on the table. "Can you keep a secret?"

I wanted to laugh. "I think you and the entire CIA are banking I can."

"I mean between you and me. This isn't for anyone else. This goes no farther than this room. I'm serious. You talk of this to no one."

"Not even Espy?"

"Not Espy, not anybody. If Espy knew about this conversation, he'd ship my butt out in handcuffs to some rendition bunker in Morocco. Clear?"

"Clear."

"Be sure. Because it involves you and will be extremely hard to hold close."

I fished an ice cube from the bucket and slipped it in my mouth. "I'm listening."

"I have reason to believe the explosion that killed Astrid was not an accident." I got hit by a micro-bout of vertigo and swallowed the ice cube whole. "I know this is big. Are you all right?" I felt the freeze trace down my esophagus. Weirdly, it helped shake off my disorientation.

When I could finally speak, I spewed a chain of questions. "Why would that be on purpose? ...How could you know that? *Why* would you know that?"

"All good questions. I understand them all, I do, but right now I can't go any deeper. What I can tell you is this. I came to that conclusion while I was prepping for this mission with you. No surprise, I'm very thorough. Some might say wonky." She didn't treat it like a joke; her demeanor couldn't be more serious. "Plus, I have the best intel resources in the world. Since whatever happened with Astrid would obviously be an important part of knowing you and, frankly, vetting you, I dug deep. There were too many things that didn't add up. Starting with the fact the Kogg was not a drug user."

"But the crystal meth."

"Exactly." She folded her hands in her lap.

And waited.

"This is…I want to say astonishing. But it's…I'm stunned." I struggled to compose myself. "Don't misunderstand, I trust you."

"You can."

"But is this true or a theory? Because you just threw my life into the spin cycle."

"I wouldn't have laid this on you if I didn't believe it were true."

"Do you know who did it? Or why? Because we should do something."

"Slow down. Remember I said this doesn't leave this room? We can't do anything. Not yet."

"Then when?"

"Once we get this mission done. Soon as we finish the exfiltration, I promise to bring this home for you. You have my word. But to get there you have to stay on board." I needed to cry. I needed to scream. I needed to start throwing shit around the room. Instead, I weighed my reason for quitting versus this mind-blowing possibility. "What do you say, Chef? In or out?"

eleven

HANGRY GLOBE
Season 4, Ep 4
V.O. for Provence Opening
by Sebastian Pike

*I confess I never burn out on the Riviera and Provence, this swath of
Frenchie heaven crowning the Mediterranean. From the drunk uncle that
is Marseille to the hot-mess coed of Saint-Tropez to the Python-and-Holy-
Grail ramparts of Carcassonne where the spirits of insolent knights in
shining armor who once farted in our general direction can still be felt.*

What's not to love?

*Wherever you walk around here, whether it's on rocks or cliffs, meadows
or beaches, you're treading on history. After crossing the Alps, Hannibal
came through here on his way to attack Rome with the latest in warfare
technology—elephants. Even now, I'd watch where you step.*

*Maybe they don't wear pants on the sunny side of France, but once they
did wear togas.*

*The Ancient Romans left their mark with coliseums, aqueducts, and
bridges that still stand. Back in the third century, Provence was invaded
by the barbarians. Those wild, uncivilized heathens were defeated and*

banished from the region. Except for Cannes, where every May they still gather for the film festival.

Massively appealing to a hedonist for hire like me, everything about the South of France is of, by, and for the senses. Fragrant pastures of lavender. Cuisine that connects the bounty of the sea to the game of the hills. Plus, breathtaking scenery served up under a sun so lavish that it attracted a pantheon of artists. Chagall, Matisse, Cézanne, and Picasso all came here. Plus, one notable who suffered for his sanity and took his life one starry, starry night with a self-inflicted gunshot to his heart.

Well, I'm chuffed. How 'bout you?

OUR COMPANY MOVE from Paris to the South of France happened fast. It needed to. Not only to make our deadlines (your humble chef still needed to crank out his pesky TV show), but we also had to be in position to shoot the smokescreen interview with the oligarch, if and when he turned up. We needed to haul the proverbial, and DSA Espy gave us the gift of speed. Instead of burning half a day driving or riding a train, he ponied up a Gulfstream IV.

A private jet was a first for my crew, so it required explanation. I couldn't go, "Cool, huh? Elite travel, courtesy of the US government." So, I lied. I said the tight-fisted network sprung for it to help make up for our days of lost production after the Fabron killing. It pained me to watch how easily they swallowed it.

And it wasn't even my first lie of the morning. Cammie Nova had already left for Arles the night before to activate her HUMINT network to find the vacationing Hungarian. I told my crew she was scouting locations and booking guests. Halfway through our forty-minute flight, I watched Lyon pass under my window and wondered, Is this how it's going to be? Serial fibs to my peeps? And how soon would my tiny white lies grow into whoppers? And when would I get caught? These folks had finely tuned antennae. One of them already smelled something hinky, and now Rayna was lounging in Sedona with cucumbers on her eyelids.

Rayna. Damn, I sure gave her an abrupt stiff-arm the other night at Harry's when she accused me of being into Nova. I overcompensated with denial-logue that bit me in the ass later when I found out Cammie heard it. Yet that didn't feel like embarrassment. But what, then? What do you call a twinge that feels like something taking wing? The Sarge called it when she speculated Nova was a cop or a spy. In hindsight she also may have nailed what she saw in my glances at Nova. Because, unlike me, Rayna wasn't wearing blinders.

IF I NEEDED CONFIRMATION, Nova met me in our hotel coffee shop in Arles, and when I spotted her, I got another little twinge. Cammie, however, was in a different place. She had finished an encrypted call with DSA Espy, and I'd never seen her that tightly wound. "You look like you could use a nourishing breakfast." I pulled out the other chair at my table.

"No time. Besides, after the ass chewing I just got, I may not be able to sit for a few days." She spotted the crew offloading gear through the window. "Let's walk."

We strolled a short distance to a park and stood on its verge watching old men roll pétanque balls on a sand pitch. "There's new pressure to hurry up this exfiltration. Espy says our mole has been discovered by someone who is blackmailing him. Not for money, but a prisoner release. Someone we captured in Crimea. They messaged our man that if we don't comply by the end of the week, they'll burn him to Putin."

"If your mole is so valuable, why not release the prisoner?"

"Because the prisoner they want died a month ago during interrogation, and nobody knows it." I reflected on the term "interrogation," which sounded like a disinfected euphemism for a purgatory of nasty deeds. "Espy's worked up, but it's not like I'm sitting back and eating bonbons. I'm flogging all my sources; I'm pushing every department and engaging every ally. We're doing all sorts of tracking, both electronic and through our network of watchers. No pings yet from Tábori's cell phone nor from his wife's or daughter's. They are security obsessed, so they may have encrypted units for travel."

"You think they may be onto us?"

"High security is SOP for an oligarch, especially on his level. Corruption brings threat. Not only contract hits but kidnapping. His G650 left from general aviation at Budaörs, but the flight plan is unavailable."

"I have to say, I'm a little disillusioned. Here I thought the vast resources of our intelligence agencies had all-knowing, all-seeing tentacles."

"Damn straight we've got resources, but we're not as omniscient as you amateurs think. No offense. CIA, NSA, DOD, we're all like any other workplace replete with all the flaws, all the personalities, all the competencies and incompetencies…. We're basically a legion of fallibles doing our best."

"I know I'll sleep better tonight."

"Do you have a better idea, Food Boy?"

What the…? "Did I hear right? 'Food Boy?'"

"Term of endearment. Don't get all bent."

But I kinda was. "Excuse me if I don't feel totally endeared. It sounds, I dunno, condescending? Like a shot."

"And smart-alecking about sleeping better tonight isn't?"

"No equation. One is my fresh-eyed epiphany about the limits of intel capability; yours is…"

"What."

"OK, here it is. I want a code name."

"Food Boy works."

"No, negative, nah. Listen. Don't answer yet. Just hear me. I want a cool code name."

She pondered barely a second. "I get it. You want me to validate you. After all your preadolescent, adolescent, and now latent-adolescent fantasies about being a spy, you want me to anoint you with a worthy handle. Are you that psychologically needy?"

"Something with some dash. When you say it, I want to rise up. … And not in a creepy way. I didn't mean it that way at all." I jumped off that subject. "I digress. Let's circle back. You asked if I had a better idea."

"I did."

"Pardon a lowly amateur, but if we can't find Tábori, can't your mole just vamoose? If he's that high up, he must have connections."

"You don't get it. He survived this long by operating in isolation. And his blackmailer has upped the ante by sowing seeds of suspicion, an inch short of burning him, but enough to have him watched. That's what prompted the DSA's call." The corners of her mouth tightened. "He says it's my career if I don't pull off this exfiltration, and soon."

A cheer floated across the park. One of the old men knocked an opponent's ball out of place. Money changed hands. Same in every game. Somebody had to lose for somebody else to win.

URGENT MEANT URGENT. Nova split off to liaise with her intelligence cohorts and French law enforcement. Liaise. Listen to me, I'm suddenly this spy sponge. Before she left, Cammie apologized that the crunch forced her to book a blogger as my guest for that afternoon's Vincent van Gogh segment without giving him a prep interview. Not too thrilled about that, but her divided focus was bound to impact things. Cammie didn't need additional pressure. I told her I'd do my bit and work with whatever we had. Besides, it was Van Gogh. How tough could it be?

The redheaded genius held a grip on me as far back as culinary school when I aspired to cook like the Dutchman painted. Rebelliously, vibrantly, unforgettably. Which explained my fist pump when I sat down to our first Arles location at a sidewalk table at 11 Place du Forum. That's a nondescript address unless you stood in the street and recognized the venue of Van Gogh's iconic oil, *Café Terrace at Night*.

My guest gave me pause, though. Jean-Bernard Lavoisier, an art historian specializing in all things Vincent, gave off the charm of a dorky academic with all the stunted social skills that came with it. Cameras up. Sound recording. Arms wide, I gestured to our setting. "Professeur Lavoisier, you cannot think of Van Gogh without envisioning this place, can you?"

"No."

That was it? One flipping word? Declan stood and tapped his headphones. A signal even that monosyllable was inaudible. Since we'd edit out that anyway, I freed the clip-on mic that had crept under the man's sweater and restarted. "Could you, um, tell me about this place?"

"Yes." He stopped there. I gave him my urging face, which meant dipping my head to meet his eyes. He acknowledged before looking away and said, "It is beautiful." Then stopped.

OK… Maybe I could lead a prof to water. "Seems like Café La Nuit has survived looking much the same as 1888, when Vincent lived here in Arles. They paved over the cobblestones, but otherwise the whole aura is the same, don't you think?" Nothing. I craned around the yellow canopy. "If it stays clear tonight maybe we'll get some of those gloppy stars he filled the sky with." Professeur Lavoisier stared at me, mute. "A tab of acid might help, too."

He tilted his head, a confused puppy. "Acid?"

Time to bail. Play a comedy one-liner to the camera, end on a laugh, and pull the rip cord. But that's when I saw Cammie Nova had shown up. She paced back and forth across the street fully engaged in a phone conversation. The tension she emitted rhymed with her body language after Victor Fabron's shooting. I read bad news on her and thought, if I tank this segment, it would not only hurt the show (I didn't come to France to feed my gag reel), but another production fail would demoralize her. What then?

What would yester-Pike do?

Level up. Show where my two Emmys and the Peabody came from. I took a beat to appraise my guest—geeky, misfit, marginalized.

Yester-Pike would give him a hotfoot.

I struck the match. "Here's my problem with Van Gogh. Good with the paint, yada yada. But let's face it, a freak."

Lavoisier's head whipped to me, eyes flashing. "You say a...freak? Vincent van Gogh?"

"Love to hear you deny it. Isn't the whole crazy artist thing kind of some narcissistic indulgence?"

"This is an affront, what you say." He squeezed his hands together hard enough to crack knuckles. "Indulgence? Freak? No, no, monsieur. Yes, they called him mad, but one must understand what it feels like to be...to be the eternal outsider." Bull's-eye. I'd hit him where he lived and now, he was mine. "Van Gogh's behavior was not indulgence but an artist's necessity. Yes, he cut his ear, yes, he tried to kill himself by eating oil paint..."

"Don't forget the gun. Shot himself in the heart."

"But before all that. The great expressions in color and dimension we revere all sprung out of that self-torture." He swept an arm at the café. "You talk of how much you love the setting, when the setting you love was presented to you as a result of his marginalized life. Think. Picture the double illumination of that painting—heavenly starlight backing the warm yellows of this very café. See, no feel, its reflection on every street cobble."

Jean-Bernard Lavoisier went on and on. I couldn't shut him up. Passion is like dynamite. Gotta be careful when you light that fuse. No complaints. What made the segment sing was that it stopped being about Van Gogh and became about cracking open an aesthete and witnessing the eruption of his uninhibited zeal. Yester-me would have been proud.

I thanked him for his contribution, sent him off with a box of tartes Tatin, compliments of *Hangry Globe*, then dashed across Place du Forum where Cammie Nova sat on a bench with her face in her hands.

As I drew near, she looked up. "He's pulling me. Espy. I've been canned."

twelve

Nova shook her phone at me as if the director of special activities was lodged inside it. "He's screwing up, but he's—" Cammie paused to collect herself. "I'm done. It's his call."

I knew better than to talk. She had just been handed her head, and the last thing she needed was to be crowded or quizzed. Instead, I called out across the street. "Latrell. That's a wrap." We walked to her crew van. I took the keys and drove this time. The streets in that neighborhood were a corn maze. So many one-ways or pedestrian-onlys that I ended up retracing my route and getting needled by her.

"Are you trying to lose a tail? Because if this isn't evasive action, you have the worst sense of direction I have ever seen."

"FYI, my internal GPS is impeccable."

"Yeah, if it was programmed by Super Mario."

"I didn't hear that. I'm too busy doing you a favor by driving."

"I'll return the favor by pointing out that, unless there are two fat guys getting unicorn tattoos on their bellies today, this is the second time you passed that ink parlor."

"These conflicting road signs and mad turns are evil. Like some fiend turned this city into an outdoor escape room." I only pretended to be wounded. Like me, her sarcasm was a way to cope.

Cammie grew silent, then opened up near the hotel, probably timing it to limit how long she had to endure the recap. "I called to press him to light a fire under NSA to get a track on whatever cell phones Tábori and his family and mistress are using. They're dragging their feet, so I asked for his intervention on a higher level. He accused me of making excuses. That's when he swung the ax."

"Five hours after issuing you a warning?"

"Espy's feeling pressure. Said we can't dick around anymore. It's done. I'm being replaced."

"I'm the rookie, but wouldn't somebody new start flat-footed?"

"Quote, unquote, from me to the DSA." I stopped at a light. A Gypsy woman started spraying cleanser on the windshield. Familiar with the transaction, I fished out some euros and handed them over when the light changed. Cammie said, "Going to miss our little road show, Chef."

"Same here, Spy Cam." Cammie whipped her head to me, and I detected a grin. "See? Now that is a cool code name."

"Not too shabby. Too bad it came to you as I was leaving." I studied her, already weighted by loss. Loss of a talented producer, loss of her companionship, and…forgive me for being human…loss of my prospects for finding out about Astrid. Cammie's gut-shot moment wasn't the time to bring it up. I didn't have to. She was reading me. "I know this is disappointing to you. You understand what I'm talking about. I want you to know that I'll still try to make good on it."

"That's generous." I let that sit there because I couldn't find words to match what was climbing around inside. "Generous."

"You're repeating yourself more than the streets back there."

"I know. I know." She laughed at that and looked away, sniffing once. It was the first unvarnished display of vulnerability I'd witnessed in this indomitable woman. It triggered an ache in me. "When's this happening?"

She looked at her watch. "I bet Espy's got my replacement on a plane right now."

FIFTEEN MINUTES LATER I stood on the balcony of my suite watching the disco glitter of the late sun dancing on the Rhône. I tapped the first speed dial icon on the screen and listened to a half-ring *brrr* on the other end. Then silence. This was my first time using the encrypted phone they issued me, and I thought the call failed. But then came a burst of white noise hash followed by the voice. "Pike?"

"Jeez, I have to get one of these to keep. You sound like you're in the next room. Tell me you're not in the next room."

Espy chuckled, but the immaculate signal helped me hear how hollow it came off. "I'm guessing this is about a conversation I had a while ago. I apologize for not giving you a header, but primary first, then you. Protocol, right? I was about to log in a call." The DSA's smoothness irritated me. Language creating distance from personal responsibility: a conversation; a header; primary; protocol; log a call. Struck me as a lot of slick for three sentences. They must love this guy at Langley. "I hope I didn't put a kink our relationship."

"That's going to depend."

Telling pause. "I'm listening."

"It's going to depend on whether you reinstate SSO Nova."

"Whoa."

"Whoa is right." I waited. Let silence do the work. Mister Slick could do some lifting.

"That's kind of a nonstarter, Chef. You're smart enough that I don't have to apprise you how under the effing gun we are. It's a big effing gun, and the game's gonna be called on us if we don't deliver, and pronto."

"And you think bringing in somebody new is going to give you ground speed when Nova has the momentum going already?"

"You're overstepping with this. Makes me want to ask what's behind it. With Nova. Something you want to share?" I knew what he was fishing for. But I wouldn't dignify it. I fed him more silence. The line was clear enough to hear the flywheels engaging in the CIA man's head. "I'm trying to get a handle on your position, Sebastian. Kind of an unexpected request."

"Let's not call it that. Let's call it a demand."

"Hey, now."

"You heard correctly, Gregg. This is me, swinging my dick. Because if you pull her, I pull out. Without me and my show as your beard, where's your effing gun and your effing game then?"

"Why are you doing this?"

"Because I can." I hung up. The showman in me knew an exit line when it landed. I watched the sun go down and the headlights crossing the river turn the Pont de Trinquetaille into a string of pearls. Clouds rolled in. Rain in the forecast. Forget any gloppy Van Gogh stars to paint the sky. But I thought, Who needed stars when you just set off fireworks?

DOWNSTAIRS I SLID INTO a spot in the hotel bar with the crew, back from wrapping the location. For the first time they had reserved an empty chair for Cammie. The gossip mill churned ever onward, and I couldn't fault them. The topic remained our suddenly departed Food Sarge, and they leaned on me for tidbits. Anything new? Had I heard from Rayna? Who would replace her? How soon? I fended them off, claiming ignorance and throwing out the measly crumb that the choice of her replacement was in process. After lying by omission, it was nice to be truthful on the latter point.

Nova appeared during second-round orders but didn't sit. She had on a blazer and a Nationals cap. "Maybe when we get back." She hitched a side nod for me to come along.

I SIGNED THE TAB and followed her out of the lobby, falling in step as we walked narrow streets heading away from the river. We passed an elderly couple. As soon as they were out of earshot, she came out with it. "Espy called. He changed his mind and said I'm still in. I got a dressing-down anyway, but the upshot is I've got seventy-two hours to set Tábori and make the exfiltration happen." Mindful of how the tight lane running between stone walls made an echo chamber, she paused until a cyclist passed. "Thought you'd want to know."

"I already did. Well, sort of."

"He called you?"

"He didn't tell you? I called him." I beamed with boyish pride. "My first encrypted call."

"…What? What did you do?"

"Direct intervention, Spy Cam. I told him it sucked and drew a line in the sand." It took me a beat to realize Nova had stopped in her tracks. When I turned back, her look was anything but happy.

"That's out of line."

"Espy thought so, but—"

"Screw Espy, you were out of line. What do you take me for, some withering damsel clutching her bodice, hoping the big, strong knight will swoop in and save her?" She made a street check and continued. "I fight my own battles. This is my career, my war, and one thing I don't appreciate is interference from an amateur. No, don't step closer. Do not mansplain this to me. You might end up in the hospital, I swear. Dammit, you have no business intervening in Agency politics. You don't know what—or who—you're dealing with. Or what house of cards you could be upsetting. God damn, Pike. You would have talked to me about this first if you had half as much sense as you do ego."

I watched her sharp breathing settle before I spoke. "On the plus side, you're done with me in seventy-two hours."

"Do not—not—try to cute your way out of this." Nova stormed past me. I kept up. The alley reverberated with brittle silence and the military cadence of our soles. We came out on Boulevard Georges Clemenceau, broad and tree-lined, illuminated by bars, restaurants, and the early promise of nightlife. Nova plopped down on a bench outside a snack bar, a skeevy hole-in-the-wall.

"May I?" I gestured to the space beside her.

"So now you're asking."

"If nothing else, I am trainable." I checked for chewing gum and sat, reflecting on the curious balance of power between us. A blink before, Cammie was the newbie producer proving herself to me. In the next blink the dynamic had flipped, and I was the spy trainee, the accidental joe, learning the ropes in her world. "So, you think I'm cute?" She rotated her head ninety degrees to regard me. "You warned me not to cute my way out, and I thought, 'Thank God she can see that I'm more than social subversion and brutal good looks.' Cute is something we can build on."

"You're doing more digging than building." But Cammie suppressed a smile when she added, "Food Boy."

"I overstepped. I apologize. Believe me, I wasn't trying to be the man-savior." Say it, I thought, say it. So, I did. "I didn't want you to go."

She'd softened, inching toward a truce. "Thank you." But Nova turned away, staring across the boulevard instead of at me as she spoke. "Remember I told you the Agency has office politics like everyone else? There are so many minefields. A thousand ways to sabotage your career. Eventually I'm going to get posted somewhere else, and I don't want some rumor to shadow me."

"About not handling Espy yourself?"

"About you and me having a thing." She made another slow pivot to me to make sure that registered, then regarded the street again.

"But we don't."

"We don't."

"Not that there's a hard-and-fast rule against it—if there were a thing. You're no longer my employee, right? We're coequals. One, an international woman of intrigue, and the other, an iconoclastic mustang too wild to be tamed."

Her laugh flew out spontaneously. She covered her mouth like she wanted it back. Then she reacted to something across the boulevard. "He's right on schedule."

"Who is?"

"Our fixer for this trip." Traveling shows like mine hire a connected local who cuts red tape, gets access, and greases skids for production. She indicated the man in the tan sport coat approaching a travel agency, which was closed and dark.

"Our fixer?"

"At least as far as anyone suspects."

"You mean to say this wasn't about taking me on a nice walk?"

"Something you need to know about me, Pike. You never really know."

The lights blinked on inside the Toujours la Tournée storefront. I made to get up. Nova stayed settled on the bench. "Park it and get a lesson in tradecraft."

The man appeared in the front window, showing no awareness of being watched. He took out a cloth to clean his wireframes, put them back on, then pulled down a cruise poster on the right side of the glass. "We're clear." Nova and I dodged traffic across Boulevard Clemenceau.

thirteen

Emil Dard greeted Cammie Nova joyfully, making *la bise* for each cheek. I towered over the little man, but I felt as if he were looking down on me as he offered a bland hello.

"Sorry I didn't tell you I was bringing anyone," said Cammie.

"No matter. I saw from your signal that he was all right."

She indicated her Nats cap. "Lets him know I wasn't your hostage."

"Understatement," I said.

We settled into chairs around a table with travel brochures neatly fanned atop it. I scoped the grinning families and active seniors forgetting their miserable lives, cheating spouses, and maxed-out credit cards in sunny escapes. "I imagine those don't hold much interest for a globetrotter such as you, Chef Pike."

"Oh, you've seen my show."

"I have." A neutral answer and indifferent stare that unsettled me. But Emil Dard was a study in the nondescript. Clean-shaven and unassuming behind clear wireframes. Could be forties; could be fifties. Brown hair cut neatly to the ears. A hint of crow's feet and signs of sun and gin. A presentation that would make him difficult to describe to police. Therefore, the exemplary spy.

"Emil and I have a long and happy history. Nothing we can talk about," added Nova, "but I already feel better about things now that he's involved."

In his refined French accent he said, "This is buttering me up for the impossible things you will ask me to do. Again." The two chuckled at unspoken classified memories. Cammie told me later his legend as a tour organizer not only provided natural cover to be our fixer, booking *Hangry Globe* venues and accommodations, his contacts at airports, customs, hotels, vacation rentals, and the seaports were exactly what she needed for this mission. Nova laid out her grocery list. She spoke without notes, and he took none.

"This is top priority, Emil. I need to track down a Hungarian oligarch who is supposed to have arrived recently for a vacation. The only probable destination I have is South of France."

"I am hearing supposed and probable. Plus, an area roughly one hundred thousand square kilometers."

"That's why I need my best joe." She briefed him on Ignaz Tábori but not the exfiltration mission. That was Need-to-Know, and I figured he was experienced enough not to ask. After she gave the HA number of the oligarch's Gulfstream, she said, "We are already sifting digital and banking footprints, but I'd like you to track signs of arrival and settlement. Useful ancillaries are his wife, Ilona; his daughter Lily; Ágnes Sipo, his mistress who may be in proximity; and his daughter's piano tutor, Henrietta Papp. Do you want me to spell these so you can write them down?" He smiled. She continued. "If they are in a villa instead of a hotel, you might check piano rentals; the daughter is a prodigy."

"Did he bring security?"

"I assume so, but I'm not sure."

"I'll see if anyone made any hires from the local personal protection agencies."

I knew enough about logistics to chime in. "He'd probably need wheels for that size crew."

Dard agreed. "I'll also check limousine services that specialize in armored vehicles."

Nova said, "That's plenty to get us started."

"Clear enough, as ever. I'll need twenty-four hours."

"You've got twelve." To drive her point, she added, "If that."

"*Les Américains*, always in such a hurry." And we were. I stood to go, but Nova settled her back against the rattan chair. Emil Dard studied her. "But apparently not terribly rushed at this moment." I sat.

"There's another reason I wanted to see you, Emil. I wanted to ask you about Thorvald Grepp." Dard had mastered affecting blankness, but when she spoke the name, the tells surfaced. He cleared his throat and took off his glasses to clean them again. "Do you much mind?"

"Thorvy. Well, Thorvald and I broke up. We have been apart for about a year now." One corner of Dard's mouth fluttered briefly like a tic, then settled. Nova knew about the split. She briefed me afterward that she knew when the two of them—assets she had cultivated separately, and later brought together on missions—had become lovers. She knew from how her two joes tried to hide it. That effort was always the give-away. Their relationship tightened their teamwork, but she kept an eye on them. Emotional ties carried high incendiary potential. Indeed, the last time she worked with the couple, their friction was palpable. Cammie pulled them, lying that Langley had called off the operation. She brought in new operatives and, to her knowledge, Emil and Thorvald were none the wiser.

"I'd heard you went separate ways. Whatever happened with Thorvald?" I had done enough interviews to admire her nonchalant approach. For once I knew something the travel agent didn't. That his ex had killed my guest in Paris two days before and that she was back-door interrogating.

"Thorvy changed is what happened. Because he was from Oslo, he got assigned to infiltrate a white supremacist group in Norway. Over time, he bought into his own legend and turned. Thorvald joined them and became part of this group. This was not like the Thorvy I loved. He kept trying to get me to join, too. And it was not for me. The hatred. The racism."

"Why did he want you to join? I mean besides to have you with him?"

"Because I was a spy like him. You see this group of his was an organization of spies who gave up working for governments and became outliers, united by their skinhead ideology."

"In my analysis work in McClean, I tracked endless failed attempts by ideologues to form stateless spy networks. It's a by-product of how the world has changed. America First, Brexit… Alliances got crushed. Look at the suspicion we get from old friends."

Dard nodded. "It's as if someone took a jigsaw puzzle of the world and gave it a shake."

"Know what we nicknamed these stateless clandestine start-ups? Coverts Without Borders. Generally, they cratered due to lack of funding and because organizing stateless spies is a lot like herding kittens. The white supremacist angle was new, though." Still sounding casual, she inched deeper in her questioning. "Did Thorvald's group have a name?"

"They call themselves Første Stamme." He spelled it for her. "In Norwegian it means 'First Tribe.' Alluding to the 'pure race' before the immigrants came."

"And they're unaligned?"

"As of last time he and I talked. Thorvy—how do you say it?—bought the T-shirt. He was excited about the prospects. A faction with deadly skills out to carve its own turf, disrupting the CIA and FSB in equal measure. He told me, 'Think of us as an ISIS caliphate, but of mercenary spies.'" His demeanor darkened. "Who are, unfortunately, neo-fascists."

"Is there some way you can find out more about Første Stamme for me? Where they operate, who else is in it, especially the leadership?"

"Are you asking me to contact Thorvald?" The money question, and Emil Dard asked it himself.

"If you know where he is, I'd like to know. To keep up to date, you see. Don't let him know who asked."

If Dard deduced what she was up to, he never let on. He remained stoic. "I do not know, but I will try to find out even as I do this other research. I will need to make contact with a cutout I know in Orange. He was also recruited by Thorvy but soon quit the organization." He stood. "If there is nothing else, I now have a long night ahead of me. I have confirmed your setup tomorrow at the Aigues-Mortes castle. Let us agree to meet after your video shoot."

Dard and Nova worked out the logistics of their meet, and we all made our *bon soirs*. Out on the sidewalk we both looked in and watched him. He had his back to us, bent over his desk making calls. Or dealing with the pain of a wound that wouldn't heal.

I watched the man and knew the feeling.

OUR STOMACHS WERE GROWLING after the meetup with Emil Dard, but Nova couldn't justify squandering the night in a restaurant. Not with sand hemorrhaging from the hourglass Gregg Espy put in her head. My suite had a galley kitchen, so a solution was for the SSO to set up her war room on my coffee table while I handled our meal. I found a market that was still open and snagged part one of the ingredients I needed: potatoes, spinach, olive oil, butter, herbs, onion, and peppers. By the time I returned, Nova was cursing in French at some unfortunate bureaucrat on the business end of her cell phone. Our evening was set. I cooked; Nova spied.

After steaming the Ratte potatoes, I skillet roasted them in clarified butter along with melty onion, peppers, and herbs. I kept the spinach on deck for sautéing in olive oil at the last moment. Nova finished one of her dozen-plus calls and appeared at the counter separating the kitchen from the living room to watch me slice a tuna steak on the bias. "What a cute paring knife."

"More than cute. My mother parted with two hundred fifteen bucks she could ill afford to make it my graduation gift from the Culinary Institute. It's a Carter Apprentice Wharncliffe. Forged Hitachi white steel blade, Arizona ironwood handle. It's my cherished pal, and it does the job."

"How in hell did you find fresh tuna at this hour?"

"Doggedness. All the *poissonniers* were closed, but I couldn't bring myself to go with canned tuna. Not when I'm effing cheffing for you." That scored a laugh, her momentary liberation from task mode. "Improvisor that I am, I found a seafood restaurant and sweet-talked them out of this baby. They refused to let me pay. It only cost me the handsome tip I insisted they accept and ten minutes posing for selfies with the line cooks and waitstaff. Hope you like seared extra rare; it's the only way."

"I do." Cammie looked puzzled when I pierced a slice of tuna with a fork and waved it back and forth over a lit candle. "What are you doing to that fish?"

"If I tell, are you sure I wouldn't be too chefsplainy for you?"

She tilted her head and squinted at me. "How would the flame end of that candle feel going up your nose?"

"Allow me to share. You see, I can't get a char on this electric range. So, I'm going with something I learned from an octogenarian master chef. I visited his cabin on a stream outside Lyon, and this is how he cooked the fish we caught that morning. He told me something I'll never forget. 'When the kitchen gadgets inevitably let you down, a true master resorts to the raw flame.'"

89

"I'm impressed. But as hot as it is to have a celebrity chef personally cook my meal, why go to all this trouble?"

"Because I enjoy it. I haven't had a chance to cook for someone else since…" I pumped the brakes because the next word was Astrid. "… Anyway, I hope you like *salade Niçoise*, even though I am violating the traditional recipe. Call me a rebel." Cammie scrutinized me in a way that made me feel like I was over that flame. I diverted. "Besides, I need to make up for awakening your ire. When I came in, I got a PTSD flash hearing you scald whoever that poor French bastard was."

"US alliances are still strained. The good news is my badgering is paying off. I'm getting a lot more cooperation and more reporting. That includes some false Tábori sightings, but that's OK. At least everyone's engaged."

My old mentor's preparation was a hit. She toasted with sparkling water, "To the raw flame." Our meal came with frequent interruptions while Nova made and juggled calls. One was her hourly check-in with the Open Source Enterprise in Reston, Virginia. The DNI facility was monitoring for social media posts from Tábori's family to slurp photo shares that might reveal location coordinates.

"I can't fault you for effort."

"Thanks," she said. "We're monitoring everything possible. Here's how desperate I am. I even check the *Hangry Globe* website in case Mrs. Tábori posts any more come-ons to you."

That got my attention. "Excuse me. For a second I thought you said our oligarch's wife was coming on to me."

"Pike. Do you ever read your fan emails?" Nova opened the show's official web page on her laptop and did a search. "Here, look at all these. I'm not sure whether I'd classify Ilona Tábori a fan or a stalker."

"Stalkers usually send bathroom selfies. You see a lot of strategically dabbed whipped cream." I pointed at one of the shots. "Oh God, look at this one. Mrs. Tábori, a kitchen selfie—in lingerie—beside her attempt at my croquembouche recipe. Even for an amateur, a pathetic try at the classic towering pyramid of glazed puff pastry. Or else Salvador Dalí baked it."

Nova scrolled through more of Ilona Tábori's emails. All were accompanied by selfies in bathing suits or skimpy tops that left little to the imagination. "How did you come upon these?"

"Because it's my job. The reason Ignaz Tábori initially said he'd come on the show is I learned his wife is such a fan of yours."

"Bet he doesn't know how much." I flicked my brows and spread my arms. "Although really. Who could blame her?"

"You make a point."

"I do?"

"Yep. Cheesy peignoir selfies. Probably into fixer-uppers."

Before I could respond to her dig, something popped into my head. "Any recent posts?"

"None since they left on vacation." She saw my grin. "What?"

"Humor me." Nova watched me log on to my computer and key in Ilona Tábori's email address. "'Subject: Would Love to Meet You Soon!'"

"What are you doing?"

"The logical thing. If Mrs. Oligarch is hot for teacher, maybe I can bait her into answering this and reel in her billionaire hubby. Don't worry, I won't tip our hand, just start a dialogue. A dialogue of irresistibility." I kept it short. Mentioned that I would love to meet her when her husband comes on my show. Bookings are tight, so please answer ASAP. "Send?" I tried to read Nova. "Something wrong?"

"Yeah. I wish I'd thought of this. Send."

"Who are you calling Food Boy now?"

"Gloating. So attractive."

I had started busing dishes when my email chimed. "Automated away message from Ilona Tábori. 'On vacation. Not checking emails for three weeks.'"

"It was a nice try." Nova opened the Côtes du Rhône she had avoided to keep a clear head for work. We settled side by side on the couch and enjoyed a moment of peace and the play of the breeze rustling the palm beside the balcony. Her phone lit up. A text from a private caller consisting of only four numbers. "Emil Dard confirming tomorrow's live drop."

"All that from four digits?"

"Only one mattered. You have to know which it is."

"I felt for the guy today. He's still wounded about his old lover."

"May I say? I appreciated your discretion."

"You mean not blurting that I watched his ex put two bullets in my guest? And wreck my best shirt? Give me some credit. Emil has enough tormenting him."

We clinked glasses and held eyes over our rims as we sipped. She broke that off and studied her glass. "It's a dangerous thing when people in my business get in relationships. Everybody's human, the heart has a mind of its own and all that, but it's a recipe for disaster. You know what field romances do? Cloud judgment. Feelings compromise objectivity. You have to be strong. It goes nowhere good. And for a woman doing this work, the relationship thing is a minefield every day."

"That doesn't sound like a detached observation."

"Oh, hell no." She topped off my wine. "I transitioned to fieldwork after being a TA, a targeting analyst at Langley. Forget the century we're in, the intelligence community is stuck in Cold War values. Old boys' club and military thinking. They're too savvy to say overtly sexist things, so they do it in code."

"Imagine, spies using code."

"The code for analyst is 'gal.' Nice, huh? Now imagine what it's like if you're me, and you're Black, too. So now this former analyst has to prove things. It's not enough to be talented. I need to work harder, be smarter, and shoot straighter. Know what they used to say when I was doing my field training? 'This one's sexy enough to be a swallow.' That's trade jargon for a seductress who lures male spies into honey traps."

"So, it's not enough to categorize you. They also need to sexualize you."

"How did you get so evolved?"

"Don't put me on a pedestal. I just do my best." I tried to measure how far to go with this thread. "Mind an indelicate question?"

"Ask it. I'll let you know."

"When Gregg Espy canned you today, a move defying logic, I wondered if, maybe you two had...you know. History."

"That this was payback? Not that simple. It's not that he made a pass at me once on a trip and I declined. Which is what happened. Or that he's paranoid that I'm out for his job. Which he is."

"Why isn't it one of those?"

"Because it's something else."

"And you're not going to tell me."

"Everybody has a secret they can't share. This is mine." Cammie found my eyes and locked in. I struggled to remain stoic. Desperate not to be seen, I reverted to form. Joke deflection.

"You missed an opportunity declining his come-on. Nobody rocks a lambswool cardigan like Gregg Espy."

The wind kicked up, and she stared out at the thrashing palm fronds. "In my business you never go there. You have to be strong. Sometimes you meet the perfect person under imperfect circumstances." She raised her eyes to mine. "Don't you agree?"

I considered briefly. "You are still talking about Emil and Thorvald, right?"

"Of course. Who else?" This time Cammie didn't look away. A wavelet of heat passed between us. I felt it. I know she did, too, because she suddenly held up a staying hand, set down her glass, and rose. "Time to go." While gathering her materials she made her excuse. "I'm operating on two hours of sleep. I need to crash." I waited by the door. She met me there and we stood face-to-face. "Thank you for the workspace and the grub." Then came the loaded afterthought. "And the company." She swayed toward me an inch. I swayed toward her. For a charged moment we stayed like that, each teetering closer then away, then closer again.

Until she shook it off. "Definitely time to go." Mindful of the old-boy culture she suffered, I left my hand on the doorknob and said good night.

OUR PARTING LEFT ME with an ache. Two nights before, I protested too much there was no chemistry. I sure wouldn't invest if it weren't there and weren't mutual. After the moment Cammie and I'd had, it definitely felt reciprocal. At least until Nova flipped the switch and left. Like she said, imperfect circumstances. Probably best to leave it there.

Easier said.

What was it about Cammie Nova that kept me off balance? Back to Espy. Back to when he warned me about her knack for playing the inner political game. He called her an artful manipulator. He also told me to watch my back, but I wasn't ready to buy into that. Maybe that's the greatest manipulation of all, that she fosters a bias to side with her without asking for it.

But that was on me, not her.

Then again, she did dangle the carrot about getting to the bottom of how Astrid died. By definition, dangling a carrot is manipulation, true. Unless it was a promise, not an exploitation.

I was whipping up a dust devil in my own head. To quiet it down, I busied myself cleaning dishes—in between countless phone checks for messages from Cammie that never came. I retreated to the couch and opened up the research she had prepped for my (hopefully) upcoming interview with Ignaz Tábori.

No wonder Putin loved this Hungarian oligarch. Tábori was replicating Vlady's kleptocratic moves in a friendly country, by the numbers: have the autocrat appoint you agriculture minister; use your position to create a monopoly by nationalizing farmland and, in exchange for kickbacks, let your rich cronies buy up huge parcels using illegally directed billions of EU stipends; then hide your dirty money in overseas LLCs under bogus company names. Meanwhile, the hardworking local farmer gets driven off family land. Nice guy. I couldn't wait to meet him so I could hand him his ass.

More phone checks. More no Nova.

I surrendered to the minibar, cracked open some Jameson, and fired up my Kindle to a Philip Kerr I'd started, but even Irish whiskey and a German sleuth couldn't turn off the noise.

———

A FOREIGN CITY AT MIDNIGHT is a tonic. I glided down streets dank enough to match my mood, steering my face into the soft bite of drizzle. For me, walking lightens the tare weight of my soul. Probably the right brain taking over. I get relief. Well, often enough.

I was still waiting for it. That night Cammie did more than stir my feelings for her. When she got into how we all had secrets, I almost told her mine. Not because the look she gave me felt like a polygraph but because that's how connected I started to feel. I wasn't there, though. Maybe if I had opened up, Cammie would have stayed. Maybe if I'd switched from wine to Jameson back then, I would have let her in. Didn't happen. But, damn, I came close.

The drizzle became a spray that became a shower. I circled back with a quickened pace, pulled my hat low, and flipped my collar up. Half a block from the hotel, I spotted another night crawler coming out of the lobby. A woman in a Nationals cap.

My first instinct was to call out to Cammie, but the determination in her stride made me hold back. Plus, I'd had enough to drink that I didn't want to be the wet souse slurring in the lane. When she swung the opposite way from me, I almost followed her. But that felt seedy. So, I stood in the rain watching her until she rounded a corner. I was about to seek shelter in the hotel when movement caught my eye. It was a blur in my periphery, but I swore I'd seen someone pop out of a dark alcove and go after her.

No hesitation this time. I followed.

fourteen

Was I being paranoid? Did I really see someone, or were shadows and whiskey feeding my imagination? When I peeked around the wall at the corner, the street stretched out in a straight line. It was empty except for Nova. I waited, watching her grow smaller as she went. Then I saw him. A man appeared from behind a tree trunk and strode in her direction. I speed-walked, keeping myself against the wall until I reached the sycamore he had emerged from and watched.

Poor light and weather made it hard for me to form a picture of him. Everything stood in silhouette against the glistening pavement. All I could tell was that he was big and moved like he carried some muscle under his black leather coat. When I gauged fair distance, I came out from hiding and followed at a matching pace. I had my phone on me and wondered if I should call or text Cammie. But what if the man wasn't tailing her but was merely a fellow tortured soul out for some cleansing movement? A text might lead to the embarrassment of explaining what the hell I was up to.

She made a right turn at an intersection. The man held back, sliding under an awning at a darkened bistro. I stopped, too, using a sidewalk billboard as cover. Euro Circus Coming Soon to Place Lamartine. Nova reappeared. She had reversed course, doubling back to take what would have been her left turn originally. Was she lost? Evading? What? I didn't get a much better glimpse of the man when he came out from under the canopy and continued his tail. Only enough to confirm physical power in the way he moved. I thought back to that snub-nose PPO Harrison tried to give me and wished it were in my pocket.

Nova had stepped up her pace and moved with authority through the alleyways toward familiar ground, passing the Café La Nuit, where I'd done my Van Gogh segment that afternoon. It was closed, and the staff was tilting chairs against outdoor tables to help the rain slide off. When she hesitated rounding a corner, I turned my back, hoping my own ball cap and wet coat would make me nondescript enough. When I looked back, she and the man had vanished.

In a panic I double-timed to the corner and sprinted up Rue des Arènes, skidding to a halt. There she was. Inside the front window of a wine bar. Nova stood by the front door hanging her drenched cap on a hook atop her raincoat. The bar was crowded, one of the few open at that hour. I watched her wave a greeting to someone at a back table. It was the man who had been tailing her.

While she moved to the rear of the house, I eased up closer to the window, hiding behind the potted palm outside the door. When she got halfway, the man stood. The guy was mid-fifties with close-cropped salt-and-pepper hair. Seeing him with his coat off, my assessment was correct. He was in shape. Not like a gym rat. More like a guy who didn't let his muscles go to shit with middle age. The sort you could see playing company softball or forward for his neighborhood basketball team. Which meant, without consciously thinking about it, American. To confuse me further, these two hugged. Then pulled apart to smile at each other, then hugged again.

The hug stung me in a way it had no right to. But I couldn't help gawking. Nova had her back to me, and the man who I feared was going to ambush her had his chin over her shoulder, smiling with his eyes closed. When he opened them, I retreated a step for camouflage behind the palm. I got enough sense of fleeting eye contact to worry that I might have been clocked. Instead of risking a confirmation peek, I turned away from the window, blended in with a group of college drinkers, and hoofed off with the herd. At the corner I looked back. Nobody was watching me.

I strode to the hotel, a wet dog wondering what the hell I was up to. And what was she?

My walk had begun seeking relief. What I ended up getting was clarity.

After what I'd seen, and saw myself doing, I wondered if I should dial it back from Cammie. Keep things purely about the show or the exfiltration. Look how I had tangled myself up flirting with the notion of a relationship. Also, I wanted to honor her stance about field relationships inviting complications. Last thing I wanted to be was "that guy."

Plus, I needed to face reality. At some point this operation would be over. Cammie Nova was a career spy, not a TV producer. She would be gone, and I'd land back where I started, pre-mission. Should I make the emotional break now? If I did it would honor her boundary and spare me a world of torment.

Choices are tough, man. They eat you up even when they're the right ones. Or because they are. If I did let go, it wouldn't be easy. I wouldn't cut off an ear or suck down a tube of titanium white, but it would be rocky.

Sometimes clarity bites.

fifteen

HANGRY GLOBE
Season 4, Ep 4
V.O. for Aigues-Mortes Opening
by Sebastian Pike

With a name like Aigues-Mortes, the place shouldn't be much of a tourist destination. Translated from the French, it means dead waters. Is it me, or is that sort of off-putting? Uh, yuh. It got its somewhat skanky name from the fact that this medieval town, a forty-five-minute drive from Arles, sits on a vast stretch of marshes and ponds no human should ever drink from. Dead water? Hmm, no thanks, I'll take a glass of your finest piss.

In spite of the name, tourists do flock here. By the thousands. There's lots to see and do. Starting with touring those marshes that meet the brackish tides of the Mediterranean. That's where a microscopic variety of algae (Dunaliella salina, if you're trying out for Jeopardy!) turns the ponds pink. The sea salt dries into a delicate crust that gets raked into mountains of fleur de sel, that stuff you bougies snap up for twenty-seven dollars from Williams Sonoma. Take it from me, though—as salt goes, it's worth its salt.

100

But the big ticket in Aigues-Mortes is the castle. Imagine Disneyland but built in 1302. That's when the walls surrounding the medieval town still thriving inside were completed.

Once a launch post for the Crusades, today it's not so medieval. In fact, it's kind of touristy, but in the way European towns put their T-shirt and pizza joints inside six-hundred-year-old bordellos, so I'm cool with it.

You had me at castle. I'm glad I came, and you will be, too.

But don't drink the water.

THE NEXT MORNING'S *Hangry Globe* segment started early and was designed to be short. Nova crackled with the tick, tick, tick of the seventy-two-hour clock DSA Espy had put on booking the oligarch. So, we were all about getting to the castle in time to wrap the segment and meet Emil Dard at the nearby live drop he had set up. The two of us had a production van to ourselves riding down from Arles. I took the wheel to help Nova stay glued to her encrypted screens and oversee progress of the Tábori hunt. The previous night weighed heavily on me. I tried to come up with a way to back-door test her on what I had witnessed. So much for disengaging.

We had traveled deep into the Camargue, France's sprawling delta where the Rhône met the Med. Cammie finished a call and swigged some coffee. I looked at the expanse of rice paddies passing my window and let out a theatrical yawn. "Man, I'm glad we don't have a cooking demo today. You don't want me near cutlery; I hardly slept. How did you manage?" I gave her a side-eye, nice and casual, so it wouldn't seem like I was studying her.

"Me, I was totally lights out. Don't know if it was stress or the wine, but I crashed as soon as I got back to my room." She raised her cup to her face and held it there. "Slept right through to my alarm."

"The rain didn't wake you?"

"There was rain?"

I marveled at how easily she lied. And brooded over why she had. Wasn't I the MVB on Team Spy Cam? If she'd gone out to meet a joe, why not loop me in? If it was a date, none of my business. I'd let go of that, right? Well, it seemed not. But still, why the commando-style tail from the guy that made me fear for her safety? Unless they were into some sort of role-play, which, go ahead and keep that to yourselves.

"Pike, you missed the turn." I had flown by our exit at Bouches-du-Rhône and had to circle back. Now Nova studied me. "You OK?"

"Never better." I could lie, too.

The castle shoot fell into the category I liked to call "hose and *adios*." Which basically meant, grab video and move on. No food? No interview? No problem. Quickies like these were rare necessities, usually reserved for short layovers and host hangovers. I generally played them for comedy.

The crew got to the castle ahead of us and was already set up in the town's main square, Place Saint-Louis. I would owe Emil Dard a handshake when we met up afterward. In the throes of his urgent to-do list, somehow our fixer still managed to book six mounted riders in full knight regalia. These folks were local medieval reenactors. My function was all about dress-up. The lead knight supervised outfitting me in a costume all my own. Throughout the donning of a tunic, cloak, and helmet, cameras rolled as I spouted *Holy Grail* dialogue. Sadly, I'm known for that. The crew calls it my Python Tourette's.

However, I must confess that when it came time to mount up and ride with the others, I stopped clowning and bought into the cultural appeal. It didn't hurt that they gave me a smart horse that knew the drill and made me fit in like one of *les lances fournies*. When the parade ended, two knights offered to help me down. When I was sure I had audio and a camera on me, I called out, "Ni!" and clomped off alone, disappearing behind a shrubbery.

HOSS THE ROADIE STOOD WAITING for me and Nova when we came out the castle gate facing the salt marsh. The big guy gripped our two Pinarellos by the seat posts as if they were kiddie bikes. Cammie took hers with a casual, "Thanks, Hoss. Off to do some location scouting."

"Looks like you'll have the whole path to yourself. The dude in the panini shop says the salt harvest doesn't happen until August or September."

"We'll be back before then." I mounted up and followed Nova, who was already crossing the packed-dirt track that cut across the grass border wrapping around the old fortress.

She waited for me to catch up at the water's edge where the trail ended in a T and joined a boardwalk cycleway. Emil's instructions were simple. Go right at the boardwalk and stay on the wood all the way around the pond until we came to the salt lot. "You OK on the bike? Not saddle sore?"

I peered over the tall reeds that rimmed the marsh. On the far side, salt mounds gleamed like mirages underneath a pair of red construction cranes. "Brave Sir Robin, saddle sore? Let's ride."

Nova caught up and pedaled beside me since we had the whole path to ourselves. "Check out the flamingos." The flats to our left were dotted by hundreds of them. "It's like they're posing for *National Geographic*."

"Know what a group of flamingos is called? Not a flock, not a gaggle, but a flamboyance. Why? Because flamboyant is what they are. They get their name from the Spanish *flamenco*, which means flame, thanks to their color."

"You are too weird. It's like you're reciting your first draft of a voice-over."

"See, that's why I need you as my producer. Flamingos are now definitely in for the VO."

"You seem to know enough about them."

"I made myself an authority. When it comes to voice-overs, I wouldn't make it up if it weren't true." She laughed. Cammie Nova got the jokes.

"All right, smarty, why are they pink?"

"They get that from chowing down on the brine shrimp that lives in the pink water. Astute question. When I write the VO, that one's going in. Ask me another, anything you like."

"Now you're showing off."

"Relentlessly."

"Do flamingos mate for life?"

"That would be your swan. Your flamingo is a serial monogamist. But only for a season."

"How male."

"You project unfairly. The male and the female bond in their exclusive sexual relationship by mutual choice after a ritual dance."

"Sounds like some dance."

"Oh, count on it. It's fueled by a veritable monsoon of hormones, pheromones, you name it. A potent cocktail of all the chemistry that makes two lovebirds go daffy with desire."

Nova coasted and stood on her foot pedals to look at the pond teeming with all that energy. "Must be tough. To lose control like that, I mean."

"You're a flamingo. Do you care?"

She got a funny look and resumed pedaling. "Makes me wonder. Can the male deal with the absence of his partner if she leaves him?"

That took me aback. "You mean…at the end of the season?"

"Or whenever it happens."

"That would be crazy. Even for a flamingo." We arrived at the saltworks. Although the pale pinkish hills of salt were remnants, set dressing left for tourist selfies, they were impressive.

"But suppose it did happen," she said. "And the female flamingo took off."

"Why the hell would she want to do that?"

"I don't know. By her choice."

"Choice?"

"Or by necessity. Birds, you know?" The plant sat idle. But the gate's padlock dangled on its chain, and the entryway yawned open for us to pass through. Once inside, we stopped for Nova to get her bearings. Or looked for secret signs only a handler would recognize from her joe.

Me, I was stuck on her question about leaving. "I guess the male deals. But here's the thing. Flamingos probably don't do a lot of thinking that far ahead. They groove to the power of that sweet mating dance and take every day as it comes." I was talking to myself. Her mind spun elsewhere.

"Something's off. Our signals protocol was for Emil to leave a pétanque ball right there in front of that modular office." Nova began a mad scroll of messages, from her expression to no avail.

"Do we give him a grace window? In my experience the French are charming as hell, but punctual? Not so much."

She surveyed the grounds, too. Nova also unbuttoned her blazer, a tell that she was carrying and concerned.

"Maybe the ball rolled." I coasted over to the modular, dismounted, ducked my head under it. I shook no, then hopped up its aluminum steps for a better view. "There. Got him." Nova biked down to join me and followed my eye line.

Emil was standing with his back to us in the center of the yard on the far side of a salt mound. I cupped my hands to call out, but Cammie grabbed my arm to stop me. She set her bike on the ground. "Stay put."

Nova jogged to the near side of the mound, reconned, drew her weapon, and slowly circled toward Dard. When my sole crunched a grain of salt behind her, she spun, braced to fire. I shrugged. How the hell was I supposed to stay put with all that going on?

She continued around the pile, and I shadowed her. On its other side we stopped, stunned. Emil Dard had not been standing with his back to us near that mound. His head was sticking out of it. He was buried up to his neck in salt and had a bullet hole in his forehead. The stainless steel pétanque ball was lodged in his mouth.

sixteen

Nova rotated, alert for threats. Or for anyone who'd find us with a mutilated body to explain. I watched her, seeking cues. "You're going to have to tell me what we do here."

"We get the hell out." Cammie looked at her dead joe. There was nothing to do for him. But there was something to do. "After we search him."

The tool shed hasp was no match for the metal bar I scavenged. We each grabbed a shovel and started digging. When we excavated the body from the salt, Nova went over him expertly: pockets, shoes, full pat-down. She gave me the rundown without looking up. "No message on him…no gun…no papers…no wallet. Only his wristwatch, a pen, and car key. Pro job."

"If you're a sociopath and a sadist."

Nova indicated the Mercedes Metris across the lot. "We'll take his van and search it somewhere else." She pocketed the key, then slid one of Dard's socks over her hand to pry out the pétanque ball without leaving fingerprints on the steel. His mouth was empty except for loose shards of broken teeth. That ghoulish image, combined with the meaty tunnels where his eyes once lived, telltales of torture, forced me to look away. I almost lost my breakfast but held it down. A voice inside me pleaded for her to be done. Nova said, "One more thing."

I shadowed Cammie on her slow arc around the saltworks. She came to a stop at a wooden telephone pole strung with overhead lines coming from the office trailer. "Chalk on the wood," she said.

"Those little quotation marks?" I'd read about signals like this.

"It flags his backup dead drop." Her jargon struck me as unfortunate, considering. She pivoted another 360 security sweep of the grounds and strode toward the pole. "There should be a hollow metal spike pushed into the soil with Dard's message hidden inside."

"Again, not the time to be Mr. Smarty, but you don't use email because…?"

"Old school is more secure, operationally. We could share info digitally, but that involves more logistics. And more eyes and hands that can compromise. With ground-level assets, this simply works."

Nova took a knee under Dard's chalk sign and brushed away grains of salt, exposing a rawhide shoelace looped through a metal eye on top of a black disk. She pulled it and extracted a metal spike about three-quarters of an inch in diameter. After examining the milled screw top to make sure the O-ring was still sealed, she stood. "We're history."

As we hustled our bicycles toward Dard's van, a macabre reality gripped me. Two bodies in four days. I've gone my whole life seeing corpses only on TV or from afar in war zones. Or in churches reposed on velvet. Now death had slithered up close and ghastly. The farewell embrace of the drunken Frenchman in Paris. And now this. Poor Emil. The little man had been desecrated during torture. My limbs went weak, a mix of trauma and repugnance. I paused for one last respectful look back. Emil Dard was human. Who did that to another human?

I found out when two men darted around a tractor and grabbed Cammie.

The first one wrapped up her torso from behind while the other dove for her legs. Before he could get to them, Nova smacked her boot into his face. But the other attacker held firm and bucked her backwards, neutralizing her feet by keeping them off the ground. I sprinted to help but before I got there, she shook no. Cammie wrestled her right arm loose and tossed the dead-drop spike. It landed at my feet. "Run!"

I snatched it up but hesitated. She yelled, "Dammit, Pike, go!" I raced back to my bike, my insides shredding with every step. I got there and halted. She told me to book, but I couldn't. Not after I saw what they did to Emil.

I lobbed the spike into the crawl space under the modular office and dashed back to help her. I only made it halfway. Someone tackled me from behind. Someone heavy and strong. My attacker pinned me to the ground while another one pulled a cloth sack over my head. Two sets of powerful hands grabbed my upper arms and yanked me to my feet. I struggled to get free, but their grips were vise strong. I called to Cammie and got a fist to the gut.

My legs gave. I gasped for air. From inside the coarse black hood, I heard tires crackle across *fleur de sel*, then skid to a stop. Car doors opened. I got shoved in. Car doors slammed. The vehicle roared off with me wedged in the back seat between two walls of muscle and bone.

seventeen

I fought nausea. Either from getting my bell rung or the driver's erratic wheel work. To a soundtrack of horn blasts and foreign profanity from the front seat, I tried to keep from retching inside my hood. "I'm gonna be carsick" earned me a sharp elbow to the ribs. One of my captors strong-armed the back of my skull and bent me forward, jamming my head down. I figured we must have come to a populated area where chauffeuring a man with a sack over his head might attract the wrong kind of attention.

I focused on trying to memorize the turns like I'd seen on cop shows. After too many left and right lurches, I lost count and gave up.

The course changed anyway. A long acceleration followed by the road smoothing out ended all the crazy stop and go. We were getting on a highway. A new flavor of sickness rose as I wondered where they were taking me. Out in the country to finish me off? Or a long circle back to the saltworks to mess with my head before they pack me like gravlax, too? Even though I couldn't see through my hood, I closed my eyes to calm myself. Panic wouldn't help anything.

Tell that to panic.

My cranial horror show kept spooling a GIF of Emil Dard's fucked-up body. I didn't want to think about what they'd do to me. But it was

Cammie I kept coming back to. I recognized my nausea wasn't motion sickness but worry about her. And what she might have to endure.

Best push that beast aside. All it did was roil my gut. Inside my suffocating hood, I tried to see something else.

I flashed on my misspent life, tempting fate with everything from dirt bike racing on the Henry Hudson Parkway to playing Russian roulette on a drunken dare, and wondered, How the hell did I end up battered, bruised, and captive in a carload of murderous kidnappers? The well-duh answer was agreeing to go for a roll in the hay with the Central Intelligence Agency. So much for Most Valuable Bystander. My own fault. I could have said no. Why didn't I?

Was it Cammie Nova? Was it patriotism? Was it an attempt to perform CPR on my wounded spirit with some latent 007 fantasy? I guess they all contributed. But I knew the real answer. And I remember riding along doubled over, starved for oxygen inside my hood, and concluding that if those suffocating breaths were to be my last on earth, when judgment came, I would stand tall behind my reason.

I was there because I wanted the truth. The truth about Astrid.

The drive went on and on. I couldn't tell the exact duration, but at least an hour, probably more. Discomfort and fear made it endless. The hood did nothing to filter out the cigarette smoke. God, the smoke. Conversation around me was minimal. Only the occasional "Merge here" or "The A7, see?" in French, but accented from elsewhere. One voice came dipped in Nordic. From another, hints of Central Europe.

The A7. I remembered seeing it on a map but couldn't concentrate enough to place it. Some spy.

A slalom of lane changes bounced me off the immovable goons on either side. But then an "*Ici! Ici!*" from the guy next to me preceded a sudden swerve right and a "*Skit…knulla mig*" from the Nordic on my other side. "Shit…fuck me," in Swedish. I'm not consummately multilingual, but years of globe-trotting did one thing. Taught me all the curse words.

The driver ramped off the A7 back into herky-jerky city driving. Horns. Brake stomping. Hard turns. I wondered what the end of the ride would bring. And would the bullet come before or after eating the pétanque ball?

The car braked after a sharp ninety-degree right. The driver killed the engine and opened his door. Both rear doors popped. The man on my right exited. "Let's go," said the one on my left. I arched my back to stretch out the kink, but two pairs of mitts hauled me out and onto my feet. My nose caught a familiar funk. Restaurant garbage that needed picking up. Somewhere overhead a George Michael song sent down a thunderstorm of megabass.

A metal door bonked open. I got ushered inside a piss-stinky room. Acoustics told me indoor stairwell. My own and three other pairs of shoes slapped up one flight of concrete steps, then through another metal door. Instead of urine, this area reeked of cooking, heavy on the onion and rancid oil. An apartment hallway, I guessed. One of my escorts rapped a two, one, two rhythm. A door opened immediately. I got shoved inside.

A CHAIR SCRAPED LINOLEUM. They muscled me into a seat. George Michael filtered through a closed window like the singer was hooded, too. Or singing from the afterlife, my preview of coming attractions. Muttered conversation, possibly Hungarian. Someone pulled the sack off my head. After all that darkness my eyes watered at the exposed bulb hanging over the kitchen table. The lone man facing me across its chipped enamel top scrutinized me in a way that felt belittling. He wasn't a hardbody like the others. Fleshy and nearly middle-aged, he bore the pouched eyes of a poor sleeper or grad student. The naked hundred-watter reflected on his waxed, shaved head. He looked past me. In a Norwegian accent, he said. "You better have something for me, Béla."

Movement from behind. One of my kidnappers stepped to the man at the table. I could smell his odor as he passed. He was the gut puncher who kept elbowing me. The bruiser handed over something. My heart sank. Emil Dard's dead-drop spike. Béla returned to his post by the door. The Norwegian drummed the table with the point of the black metal tube while he stared at me some more.

Since he wasn't talking, I did. "What's this all about?" The drumming stopped.

"Do not fuck with me. This would not be the time to fuck with me." He lingered on me long enough to satisfy himself that the warning sunk in, then unscrewed the cap of the spike. I'd never seen one. I paid attention while he tapped out a rolled slip of paper about the size of a fat doobie. While he examined the document, I took in the room. It was small and minimally furnished. The bed was pulled out from the convertible sofa, so I figured, studio apartment. I swung a look over my shoulder to get the odds. Three men stood with their backs against the wall near the door. Going by voices, I had counted four in the car. Maybe the other was posted outside.

"This is encrypted." I turned front. The boss man tossed the curled scroll on the table like an accusation. Then he set a pistol down next to it. The gun made a clunk on the hollow metal. "You will tell me things. Understood?" The man glanced at the paper again and flexed his jaw. "Where is the Hungarian? Tábori." Hearing him speak the name shot ice water through me. My brain synapses plotted an instant triangulation: Emil Dard said his ex joined some Nordic fascist group. Emil Dard's ex shot Victor Fabron. Victor Fabron was passing information about the Russian mole. "I asked you, where is Tábori?"

I saw no point in denying. I played my cover. "Wish I knew. I've been trying to get him on my show. Did you know I have a TV show?" Pale gray eyes narrowed. A wolf deciding when to rip at my throat. The threat felt imminent. I talked faster, trying to defuse it. "It's a food and travel show, and the Hungarian minister of agriculture is, well, he's a natural for my audience. I was all set to fly to Budapest to interview Tábori the other day, but his staff said not so fast, he'd left on vacation." When I realized I was this close to busting myself, I went full stop. Too late. My interrogator seized on it.

"So now you're meeting the Hungarian here? In France?"

"I…um…have set no meeting with the Hungarian. Not here. Not anywhere." Instinct told me to shut the hell up about Tábori and Provence. "His office told me he was gone for three weeks. Wouldn't say where. End of story."

"So, you do not have any idea where he is."

"Nope. None. Zero."

"And you claim you are simply a television host, some cook."

"Chef. And author. I do a food show. With travel, as I mentioned. And culture. That's why I'm in France." I felt relieved to be approximately truthful. "I already did a segment in Arles. And this morning, at Aigues-Mortes." I flashed on Dard in the saltworks and scrambled to edit. "In the castle, the castle."

"Then what were you doing at the saltworks?"

"Location scouting. I thought…" Viewed with skepticism, I faltered. "…cool location."

"You thought? Or was the idea from your—what do you call her?"

"I call her a Gypsy," said Béla. "She looks to me like Gypsy or Black, or whatever."

The man behind the table sparked to this diversion and clucked his tongue at Béla. "Her name is Nova. Sounds Mexican."

"Or mongrel," suggested his pal, who then howled like a dog. That got them all laughing and kicked off a round of racial slurs, most of which were foreign slang I didn't understand. But hate requires no translation.

Talk of Nova rekindled my panic. While they catcalled and made racist slurs, I swept the room in vain for an escape route. Béla and the other two blocked the door behind me. The only window, above the sofa-bed, was too far away. I'd get back-shot before I reached it. Their grab-ass subsided. Gray eyes settled on me.

"Does our talk piss you off?"

"I'm sorry?" I feigned distraction.

"Your face got all…" He mimicked cartoon tension. "Do you find our views upsetting?"

"Is this multiple choice? Because upsetting's too soft. What's 'execrable' in your tongue?" From behind, Béla bear-pawed the side of my head. I crashed to the floor, toppled chair and all, jarred, but conscious. Béla and his partner hoisted me upright and planted the four legs where they'd been.

"You would understand if you saw your pristine homeland infiltrated by mongrels. For you, in America, the Blacks were already there, already a problem." I tried not to let my disdain show. It didn't work. "There, I see it all over you. Fuck you. Shove your harsh judgment up your *drittstøvel*. You don't know what has been lost. What the brown people have dirtied. I do." The man lit a cigarette. I heard his guards relax against the door.

"Back when I was small, we would watch the news at dinner and my *pappa*, he told us that this ethnic cleansing we saw in the Balkans, it must happen at home. A sovereign nation has God's right to enforce its purity. The purity of its own tribe. *Pappa* said, 'They gave land to the Jews to have their country, what do we have?' I'll tell you what we have." He flung an arm toward the window. "Filth coming from North Africa. The Mideast. Our land is no longer our land. We don't know our neighborhoods anymore. They're selling falafel in Oslo. Shawarma in Bergen. But these scum, I can do away with them. A battle without borders, our own caliphate. Do I bore you with this?"

"No, keep going." Every sentence of hate manifesto was time I was still breathing. Besides I'd heard all the talking points. But the cultural appropriation of caliphate, that was a twist. Give your neo-fascist hatred an exalted brand, and suddenly it's *Skinheads Gone Wild.*

"The time is right. The world is in flux. Russia is a weakened gangster stronghold. NATO has its head up its ass. The Chinese are obsessed with Taiwan. Americans are divided and disrespected. Your intelligence structure is obsolete. It is a joke, you agree?"

"Hey, don't ask me about intelligence stuff. I'm a TV chef."

The wolf man's smile sent a shiver across the table. "I ask only once more. Why were you in Aigues-Mortes?"

"I told you already, location scou—"

His palm slammed down on the table. Everything on it jumped. "If you were location scouting, why did you and the mongrel dig this up? This thing that an enemy spy left?" He brandished the dead-drop spike, then set it down on the curled paper beside the pistol.

"Spy? She's no spy. She's my producer."

Soft raps at the door. Two then one then two. Béla spoke in a low tone. "Lesage?"

"*C'est moi,*" came the small voice on the other side.

Béla let him in and closed up. The massive guard appeared even bigger beside the sallow little man carrying the square black attaché. My interrogator moved his gun and the encrypted paper aside to make room on his table for the briefcase. "You're late."

"My kid's birthday party."

"You saw my text?"

"My kid's birthday, Sigurd. I came right after." Lesage snapped the fasteners on his briefcase and opened up. The lid blocked my view, but the Norwegian, the one he called Sigurd, glanced inside with approval. I thought, this couldn't be good.

Lesage took out a heavy-duty electrical cord and handed it to one of the door guards to plug in. Then he set about fussing with coiled wires in the innards of his attaché. Sigurd reached into the case. "This is new." He pulled out a yellow Taser.

"*Oui*. Is new from United States." The meek man continued his set up while the Norwegian examined the stun gun and turned on its power. "Careful with that."

Sigurd fired two darts at Lesage. He screamed and dropped to the floor, writhing. The shooter quickly thumbed the safety to switch off the power and signaled Béla to deal. The Hungarian plucked the darts out by the cords, careful not to touch the tips. While he and another thug hoisted Lesage to his feet, I remeasured my chances for making a break to the window.

"When I call, you come."

"Yes, *oui*, of course," he gasped out between breaths.

The man with the wolflike eyes replaced the spent pulse cartridge with a fresh one from Lesage's briefcase and stood to address me. "Locked and loaded, right?" He fired.

The probes pierced flesh right through my shirt. A vicious jolt made me shake in pain like Lesage. But this time, Sigurd didn't switch it off. I tried to count the seconds. That dimension no longer existed. There was only the hurting until I blacked out.

eighteen

I came to sitting upright in the chair again with no idea how long I'd been unconscious. My chest stung, and my shirtfront looked like two smokers had stubbed out their butts on me. Then I felt something odd. A bulge around my waist. Some kind of belt. Then I noticed the cord. It ran from under my shirt to Lesage's black case.

"You are now going to tell me the truth. Yes." Sigurd, the wolf, sat on the edge of the table only a foot or more away, looming over me. "Skip your bullshit. We both know why you were at the saltworks. I only want one answer from you. Then you will be released." With two ways to read that word, I didn't like where this pointed. "Listen carefully, you don't want to fuck this one up. Are you listening?"

My tongue had dried to the roof of my mouth, so I nodded.

"Tell me about Glinka."

I honestly did not know the word. Person? Place? Thing? Code name? For one tick I felt relief. Ignorance would let me answer cleanly. "I have no idea what you're talking about."

"No idea."

"No, sir, and that's the God's truth."

My interrogator said, "Light him up." Lesage flipped a switch. A swarm of electrical current encircled my waist. My muscles squeezed. My own body, invaded by a predator's claw, pulled and twisted. My skin burned. I howled. After a few seconds the unassuming Frenchman switched it off. The man with the wolf eyes sat casually on the table, swinging his legs to and fro. "This apparatus that you are wearing. It is called a stun belt. The device was invented to assist judicial police in keeping unruly prisoners in order. As you learned, it is adaptable to other purposes. Unlike the Taser, its effect is all-encompassing, *ja*?" He snatched a handful of my hair and raised my head to his face. "Tell me about Glinka."

"I did tell you."

"That was the low setting."

"Please, no more."

"It is up to you, you see." He let go of my hair. "I'll ask you again."

"You can ask, but I don't know. You want the truth, I'm giving it to you."

"That is a terrible answer." I tried to get up. To my surprise nobody stopped me. They didn't need to. Lesage zapped me again, this time upping the amperage.

I crash-landed in Hell. Dante's full nine, an environment of doom. The current shuddered me head to toe. A searing burn entered my kidneys and fanned out in a technicolor firestorm of brushfires and volcanic eruptions. My muscles contracted until I felt as if my body was trying to strangle itself. I doubled up. My gut twisted. I retched, but nothing came. Not even a scream.

I awoke. Squinting at them through a greasy haze, my captors looked cowed. Even Béla lost his swagger. But the wolf man seemed inured to another man's suffering. This guy must have worked psyops, the way he kept toying, teasing out the terror. "Glinka," he said in a flat voice.

"I'm telling you the truth. God damn, I don't even know what a Glinka is. I never heard the word before now." I could feel sweat drenching my shirt. All I could think of was the high conductivity of salty liquids.

The Norwegian instructed Lesage. "*Le plus haut.*"

"But that level will stop his heart."

"You hear that? Last shot, pardner." The cowboy slang sounded absurd in his Nordic accent. Hollywood had fed American idioms to a Scandinavian monster.

"I. Don't. Know."

"Giving you ten seconds to rethink. Pretend your life depends on it."

"But I don't—No! I'm telling you I don't know!" I watched Lesage lower his head to the case to apply the next dose. I braced myself, held my breath, and squeezed my eyelids tight as they would go.

"Don't close your eyes, you piece of shit. Look at me while you still have time to—"

A flash bright as lightning penetrated my eyelids. An piercing explosion rocked the room. My heart jumped, my ears pounded, and my head felt ready to split in half. Was this from the electric shock? Somebody tripped over my leg and hit the floor, but I heard no sound. Then I did hear three distant pops muffled by the throbbing of my ears.

I forced my eyes open but couldn't see for shit. My vision was milky and stung like driving into the sunset. I stood but lost balance and fell. Underneath me one of the thugs struggled to get up. Béla or the other, I couldn't tell which. Escape, that's all I wanted. I cleared my eyesight with hard blinks. I saw a body on the linoleum. Béla's partner. Blood chugged out of a hole in his chest. A hand grabbed my shirt. I spun and swung wildly, a miss. Cammie Nova stood over me, barking commands I couldn't make out. Clutching her pistol in one hand, she tried to pull me up with the other. But I scrambled away from her, crab-walking the kitchen floor toward Sigurd's overturned table. I swallowed to clear my ears. Nova's shouts came from faraway, dampened like George Michael.

"Pike, it's me, get up." I reached the table and stopped crawling. "That's right. Let's go. Now!" Nova got me to my feet, bracing me so I wouldn't fall again. My equilibrium was still trashed from the electricity and her flash-bang grenade. Walking backwards she fired her SIG Sauer through the open door. Red spray from Béla's shoulder painted the wall as he spun and went down in the hallway.

"Go, go, go!" Nova dragged me across the room and hauled me up on the bed. We tramped across the mattress. Shards of glass bounced around our boots. Nova kicked out a jagged remnant of the window, then guided me to sit on the sill, training her gun on the empty room.

In the alley, a few feet below, Emil Dard's van waited, engine running. I swung my legs over the sill. Hands reached up from the Metris's roof and helped me down. Nova dropped beside me and dismounted onto the blacktop. The man who'd helped me out the window fed me below to Nova, who stood near the reeking dumpsters. I needed to cling to the roof rack but managed to land on two feet. The van's side door was open. Cammie stuffed me in the middle row. As she slid the door closed, the man who helped me down jumped in up front and peeled off.

He burned rubber onto the street. I cast a look back as we roared past the entrance of the apartment building. I glimpsed Béla on the move and told Nova, "The guy you popped in the hall is up. I saw him and another dude booking out the front."

"I only winged him." Nova flicked a look back. "Aafeen, headlights just came on." The man at the wheel acknowledged and cut a left. But it was a one-way, and he had to abort to avoid an oncoming car. The maneuver sent me flying. Nova snagged me and started to undo the stun belt. I winced and she continued more gently. "Almost off. Oh, man... Look at you. How are you doing?"

"Better now." I felt overwhelmed and fought back a meltdown. "Damn, Cammie, I thought they got you."

"So did they. They messed with the wrong lady. One dead, one in custody. Not talking."

"Not yet, anyway," said the driver. He had a French accent.

"Pike, say hi to Aafeen. He's with DGSI. Aafeen scrambled to meet me when I tracked your cell phone here."

I had no idea where here meant. I checked the GPS. Marseille. "Hi, Aafeen."

"Hello, Chef. I will get you out of here or not be able to face my wife. She loves your hangry show." A broad smile appeared in the mirror. "I, too, am a fan."

"Not as big as I am of yours at this minute."

"Ha ha, *merci*. Hold tight."

We roared up a hill on Rue Gribal. The next street was the left Aafeen wanted, and he braked into his turn. Our headlights swept a wall covered with graffiti. That road was another one-way, with cars parked on both sides, which made it tight, but traffic was wide open ahead. The French spy accelerated through the amber cast of streetlights. "Anything?"

Nova and I twisted in our seats in time to see a pair of high beams round the corner and continue on our tail. "Yes. Not sure it's them." Taking no chances, Aafeen braked hard to make a sudden left. A bullet punched through the window next to Nova's head. The glass spider-webbed.

Aafeen stomped the gas. "Anybody hit?"

"No." I indicated to Cammie the fat hole in the headrest in front of me. Nova and I turned to see if the car stayed with us, knowing it would. The pursuer steered wide and scraped a parked car. The fender bender knocked one of its headlights cockeyed. It kept coming. "Still with us," reported Nova.

This time Aafeen fishtailed a right, yet another wrong way on a one-way. A car was coming at us mid-block. He steered between it and a brick wall, scraping the length of the van on my side. Another cross street. He spun onto it, testing the Metris's rollover limits. From then on, he took every turn he came to, tracing a square of lanes and alleys. "Now?" he asked.

"Nothing yet."

We came to a major street, Avenue Général Leclerc, from the GPS. Aafeen busted a red light to cross it. Traffic was two-way, crossing us from both sides. He wove through it, alternately mashing the brake and flooring the accelerator. At an on-ramp, he hard-righted to protesting horns, nearly getting T-boned on my door. Aafeen punched it and gobbled pavement, wailing onto the A7. Air whistled through the bullet hole on Cammie's side as we gained highway speed. I shouted to be heard. "Aafeen, what's your wife's name?"

"My wife? She is Fadia. Her family also came from Algeria." In the midst of his getaway, pride.

"Lose those bastards, and I'll come over and personally make you and Fadia tagine."

"Deal, Chef."

Nova finally got the shock belt off. I tossed it in the back. "Your timing was perfect."

"Once Aafeen and I located which apartment you were in. The rest was up to the stun grenade."

"Sure lives up to its name. If they need a testimonial, just say."

A grimness fell over her. "I think they got Emil's spike." I nodded. "Why didn't you run like I told you? Why'd you come back?" I let my look be my answer. Nova answered with a tender look of her own. She took my hand in hers. "Ass."

"Maybe you'll forgive me when I show you this. When I was crawling on the floor instead of getting up like you wanted…?" I pulled a scrap of paper from my pocket. "This was inside Dard's spike."

"Get out."

"I snatched it up. Heroically, I'd say."

"Give it up for the Food Boy."

Up front Aafeen chuckled. "Food Boy."

She took the paper from me and held it up to the headlights behind us. It resembled a cash register receipt filled with rows of alphanumerics. "I'll decipher it soon as we get in the clear." She raised her hips and slid it in her jeans. "Did I mention, nice job?"

"Valiant would go a long way after my ordeal."

"Seriously? You get yourself kidnapped, and now you're fishing for an accolade after I saved your sorry skin?"

"A Presidential Medal of Freedom would be a start."

"I'm sure. How about I buy you a nice, soothing massage instead."

"Happy ending?"

"Pike."

"Skip it. Add a mani-pedi, and we have a deal."

"Company," said Aafeen.

It was maybe a quarter mile back. But closing fast. A car with one headlight askew.

"Can we outrun them?"

Aafeen shook no. "I believe it's got a modified engine. What you Americans call a muscle car."

Nova leaned forward between the front seats and zoomed the GPS, calculating options. When she returned to the middle row beside me, she held a backpack she'd retrieved from the front passenger floor. "Aafeen was kind enough to bring some goodies."

"Tactical pack," said our wheelman with a smile.

One pull of the zipper, and out came a sawed-off side-by-side shotgun. She used the pistol grip to smash out the glass from the cracked window beside her. The whistle became roaring air.

Nova broke open the French banger, a modified Chapuis, loaded two shells, and closed up. Ready for business.

A loud thump walloped the door beside her. A slug tore an entry hole in the back of the drivers' seat. Aafeen groaned. His head tilted forward, and his shoulders sagged. The van started to weave.

nineteen

I froze. Nova acted. She lurched at Aafeen's seat back, stretching her body around it, and grabbed the steering wheel with the one hand that would reach. "Pike." Cammie, eyes on the road, her voice devoid of alarm. If she was freaked, she damn well sat on it. "Try to get yourself up there." She must have known I was still fried from my ordeal, because she kept it plain and direct. "Don't go all the way. Stand sideways between the seats. That's it. Now I want you to hook Aafeen by his armpits and haul him to the passenger side."

I heard an ominous sound. The pursuit vehicle's big engine drawing up. "They're coming." I didn't look but kept my focus. I popped Aafeen's seat belt.

"Good. That's it. Both hands.... Quickly." Tension in her now. I saw why. We were speeding toward a rear-end of the car ahead. "Aafeen? If you can you hear me, take your foot off the gas and help Pike."

Behind us the muscle car's rumble grew. While I wrestled with Aafeen I stole a look. It was four car lengths back.

The DGSI agent was alive but weak. He lifted himself enough to allow me to drag him over the hump and deliver him to the passenger seat. Getting his foot off the gas saved the rear-ender. But the deceleration helped the shooters close their gap.

Nova said, "You drive."

I climbed into Aafeen's place. Wet stickiness on the backrest leaked into my shirt.

"Get into the right-hand lane. Hurry."

The slow lane didn't make sense, but I did as I was told. I tick-tocked my eyes from the road to the mirror. The crooked headlight swept my hand on the steering wheel. Then the front grille of the Peugeot appeared in my side view. I made out the beefy form of Béla in the passenger seat. His wounded shoulder hung low. He brought the elbow of his good arm out the window to brace on the car door. A jumbo pistol darkened his hand. I gave it the gas.

Nova leaned between the seats and tapped the GPS. "When you hit this exit here stand on that brake at the last possible second and get off. They're going to go for a kill shot on you. They won't get it."

Cammie made a range check of the exit ahead, then slipped back again out of my sight. In the side mirror, I saw the chase car pulling even with our back tire. In my rearview, Specialized Skills Officer Nova popped up and swung her two-banger through the glassless window.

I flinched at one shotgun blast, then another. In my periphery I caught Béla's muzzle flash, but Nova's buckshot spray and the Peugeot's swerve threw off the killer's aim. His gun fired low and away. I stomped on the brake. The chase car, peppered by double-aught, flew past us. Its driver braked hard, sending the car into a tire-smoking 180 before it rocked to a stop pointing south on the northbound A7.

The exit came fast. I veered off at the last second, steering into a controlled skid down the off-ramp. I accelerated, correcting us out of a hairy zigzag, and sped on.

"Not bad skills, Chef."

Breathing again, I said, "Came by them naturally. Born in the back seat of a getaway car."

"Go right." I heard Cammie reloading shells. Snap, snick, snick, snap. "Stay on this road until we're positive we shook them." She knelt on her seat to face backwards while I followed the two-lane east. We were rising into some hills. The road took us through suburban retail. The *pharmacie*, *boulangerie*, and *boucherie* were closed at that hour, but light poured out of the chicken grill and a gas station.

Satisfied for the moment, Nova scooted forward into the seat gap to tend to Aafeen. "How much pain?" He wagged his head noncommittally. Every streetlight we went under revealed how much color he had lost. Cammie tore open his shirt buttons to see his chest. "No exit wound." She reached back and grabbed the trauma pouch from the tac bag.

"Hang in there, Aafeen. I owe you and Fadia a meal."

Nova sat him up and applied QuikClot to slow his bleeding, pressed a bandage over the wound, and wrapped some gauze around his torso to hold it in place. She worked fast, then returned to the back seat to resume lookout. A few kilometers up the gradual rise, we left behind a tidy shopping stretch and a sprinkling of modern apartment buildings. On the left we passed an automobile junkyard, a sign we were reaching the outskirts of civilization. Around a curve, the road darkened. Grasses and shrubs started showing up in my high beams. Something caught my eye on the dash. "Uh-oh."

She whipped her head to survey the road behind. "What do you see?"

"Low-gas light."

"No way. I filled it when I picked up Aafeen." Nova sniffed an air sample. "The big man's missed shot. Bet he nicked the fuel tank."

"I saw an open gas station where we got off."

She considered a beat. "See the roundabout coming up? Take it for a 180 and we'll backtrack."

I steered around the rotary and headed down the hill we'd just come up. In the distance, headlights appeared around the curve. It turned out to be a transit bus. But as we passed it, the Peugeot—the damn Peugeot with the off-kilter beams—was tailgating its bumper.

"Punch it," said Nova.

I hit the gas. In the rearview the chase car tried a U-turn. The road was too narrow. It had to stop and back up, giving us precious seconds. I said, "We can't outrun them on fumes."

"Take the next curve and pull into that junkyard fast as you can."

When I rounded the bend there was no oncoming traffic. I swerved into the wrong lane to give myself enough play to make the arc. Braking at the last possible moment, I made the sharp right and roared into the driveway. "Clear?"

"I didn't see any headlights. They must still be back around the curve. Go hard right. Kill the lights, coast, and keep your foot off the brake." We heard the Peugeot's big engine race by and continue on down the hill. "Park in that space between the wall and the SUV."

I drove along rows of cars and trucks, many of them smashed from collisions, most rusting in place waiting to be cannibalized for parts. The gap she picked was a tight squeeze, but I made a *Tetris* move, embedding us in the vast, dark lot full of junkers.

"Shiny Mercedes van like this is kind of a sore thumb," I said.

"That's why we're getting out." She leaned forward. "Aafeen, we're going to go do recon. Hang tight, we'll be back for you soon."

Nova met me at the rear of the Metris carrying the tactical pack and the sawed-off. I stood there toeing the dirt where a trickle of gasoline was growing into a pond under the bumper. The crescent moon reflected an oxidized rainbow. "From Béla's shot," I said. "You called it."

Keeping an eye on the road outside the gate, we hustled across the yard to the site office and work shed. Both were locked. A shaft of headlight bloomed on the street. We crouched behind a stack of tires. Only a motor scooter yinging by. Cammie tapped my back, and I joined her retracing our steps toward the van. She stopped a few vehicles away near a box truck, a ghosty castoff missing its rear cargo door. After a quick study of the area, she set the satchel and her twelve-gauge inside the hulk's cargo bay. "Give me a hand with Aafeen."

The wounded agent could barely walk. We supported him on both sides and propped him in the passenger seat of the box truck's cab. Her assurances that we'd have him out of there soon were met with drifting eyes. Nova led me back into the yard to an orphan quarter panel off an SUV. We each took an end and propped it sideways across the box truck's cargo bay to create a barrier. "Up you go." I put a foot on the rear step and got in. "Now lie flat." While I went prone on the dirty floor, she backed away to study the setup. Satisfied, she started to climb up with me, then changed her mind and hopped down. "Back in a sec."

Nova grabbed her weapon and something out of the tac pack and jogged to our van. I peeked over the improvised barricade to watch. She squatted near the Metris's rear bumper, then pulled out what looked like another dead-drop spike. Her back was to me, so I couldn't make out what she was doing, but the specialized skills officer got very busy with her hands. After a long minute, she pushed the spike halfway into the ground, hustled back, and joined me in the dark space.

"What was that about?"

"Field Survival 101: Tactics and Cover. Maybe we lost them, maybe we didn't. This is how we prep." Nova laid down on her stomach beside me, arranging the shotgun between her head and the fender. She unholstered her SIG and set it between us.

"Well, I'm giving five stars on the exit survey. 'Best barricade since *Les Mis*—Sebastian Pike, *Hangry Globe*.'"

She chuckled. "You always do that. Make me laugh and calm down."

"You? Need to calm down? Sometimes I think I ought to check you for a pulse."

Nova peered around the side of the barrier for a road recon, then eased closer to me, speaking quietly. "Good idea to keep our voices down now." She was so near I felt her breath on my face. Her summertime scent ambushed me. I thought, Who gets a flutter of intimacy hiding from killers in an auto scrapyard? She covered the light from her screen and checked her phone. "Making sure my ping to the cavalry is still hot. Response Ops en route. Boots on the ground before the bad guys wouldn't suck."

"Or in time to save Aafeen." I turned to the dark interior of the cargo hold and looked at the end wall. The man who got shot rescuing me bled on its other side. "What's your guess?"

"Hard to know. Time's definitely a factor."

"Enough dead people," I said. "No more."

She shook her head slowly. "Worst part of the job." As if she'd startled herself, Cammie stiffened and gripped my arm. "That was stupid. It isn't about the job. Losing someone is the worst part of anything." We listened while another motorbike passed. When the night returned to crickets and frogs, she said, "I apologize, that was shitty of me. And unempathic. Especially after your loss. I'm shoveling myself deeper. I should shut up." She took back her hand.

"Don't." I didn't think, it just came out. A blurt because for once I didn't feel like someone was sticking their nose where it had no right being. I didn't want to overthink it. And I didn't want to shut her down. I felt strangely comfortable talking about it with her. "You're not digging a hole."

"You sure? I'm not crossing a line?"

"I'll let you know. But you get a free pass. You did save my life tonight."

"So far…"

"Don't take it personally if I call time out, though. It's not something I talk about much. Correction: never."

"Tonight's not the night to solve the year you just had. Cut yourself some slack, you're still processing." If she only knew. Her hand found my arm again. "The important thing? I promise we'll try to get closure for you."

"I'm counting on that."

"You can." Cammie searched my face a long while. I studied hers in return. Our silence and our closeness charged the inches between us same as the night before in my hotel room. And once again, we hesitated. The desires were mutual, the permissions, strong. We wanted this. But we held there, wavering on a precipice. Why? I couldn't read Cammie's thoughts, but for her to succumb meant crossing the line she'd drawn against problematic entanglements. As for me, it was a delicious fear. Wanting her. Fearing the complications that would follow. And the confessions.

But in her eyes, I saw trust. The power of that moment was that I was only alive to feel it because of her. I drew closer. Without hesitation she eased nearer to meet me.

Then we heard the rumble. The muscle car.

twenty

We shot up to peek over the barricade. One of the Peugeot's head-lights filled the driveway; the cock-eyed one streaked across the fence during its creeping approach into the junkyard. Cammie and I ducked down again with our gazes fixed on the sky above the barrier. I put a picture to every sound, a lot like listening to *Reacher* on a TV in the next room. Nova gripped the shotgun in her left hand, her right was splayed flat on the wood floor. I could feel her body against mine, every muscle coiled to spring.

The car pulled all the way in and stopped. From twenty yards away, the idling of the powerful engine vibrated the chrome trim on our bor-rowed fender.

One of the car doors opened. When it closed, a tinkle of broken glass followed. So, the door that took the buckshot. Béla's side. Béla the indestructible.

Tires crunched grit. The Peugeot was on the move. Prowling slowly. The ambient hue inside the rear of our box truck changed from white to red. Taillights. It was moving away. Cammie knelt, surfacing for a glimpse. I mirrored her, keeping low and sitting back on my heels. Béla, the limp-ing, twice-wounded lug, moved with the car, using it for cover—and as a walker. He was hanging tough, but this guy was in bad shape. His shirt and half of his face were darkened with blood. The pistol looked heavy as a kettlebell in his hand. The big man leaned on the far side of the car as it trolled the row of vehicles, hunting for the van, gunning for Nova, Aafeen, and me.

At the end of the line, the Peugeot stopped. The driver waited while Béla tested the padlocks on the doors of the office, then the workshop. When he hobbled back, they reversed direction. The killers were heading toward us.

We dipped down. I could hear Cammie's sharp nasal breathing. It was steady, more like focus than fear. I searched for a calming thought. It came.

I felt glad I was with her.

Light swept across the ceiling of our cave. The Peugeot braked outside the mouth of the cargo hold, waiting. The rumble increased the shuddering of our fender's loose trim, making it buzz like a cicada.

"*Qu'est-ce que c'est?*" Even in a whisper I recognized the voice of my kidnap driver. "*Va voir* (Go see)." More sound pictures. Heavy footfalls approached, one foot dragging. My heart galloped. Nova readied the sawed-off.

Only feet from discovery, the driver whispered, "Béla." The footsteps halted. "*La camionnette. C'est la bas* (The van. It's over there)." Béla turned and began to shamble away. Then came his clotted, wet cough and a moan followed by the unmistakable sound of a body hitting the ground. The other door opened. The driver's shadow darkened the cargo bay as he eclipsed his headlights. "Béla?" Nova peeked. So did I.

Béla lay face-planted, his pistol in the dirt a foot away from his body. The driver moved in a crouch toward him. He was hefting a Desert Eagle. The semiautomatic pistol dwarfed his hand. He paused and gave a toe nudge to his fallen partner. Béla rocked but didn't respond. "*Merde.*" The driver stood to make another scan. Nova and I sunk down.

We heard running and rose again. I glimpsed the driver working away toward our Metris, using the junk cars in between for his stealthy advance. Once he got there, he made an approach that spoke of commando training: flattening against the van's body, rising up fast, leading with the .44 Mag, clearing the blown-out side window, clearing the front seats, clearing the rear.

With the van secured, he squatted between vehicles, letting the shadows absorb him. The man was patient. He studied the lot, listening, seeing, wary, ready. If you didn't know to look for the muted glint of brushed chrome from his Desert Eagle, you wouldn't know he was there. The two of us remained statues inside our cube of darkness, giving the killer no motion to detect. The only sound came from the megabass rumble of the muscle car idling before us. But for that, he would have heard my heart thudding.

After a minute, maybe two, movement. Our hunter emerged from his hide, staring at the spike Nova planted. Driven by curiosity, he made a tentative duckwalk to the rear of the van. Keeping his weapon up and ready, he reached down with his left hand and pulled the spike out of the dirt.

The explosion ignited the pool of gasoline by his feet. A whoosh of fire enveloped him. Nova leaped from the truck, shotgun up, charging at the screaming figure dancing inside the blaze. His left arm, now a stump at the elbow, arced a Roman candle of flame. But he stubbornly clung to the Desert Eagle in his right, trying to get a bead on her through the mirage of heat.

Nova blew him down with two blasts, one sending his gun sailing and the second turning his shirt into swirling bits of flaming confetti.

I stood for a better look. That's when I saw Béla hauling himself to his feet, gun in hand, eyes on Nova. Her back was to him, unaware and reloading.

Cammie's pistol was still on the floor in front of me. I grabbed it, hollered her name, and squeezed off three shots at him. Two missed, one bloodied his ear. Béla shook it off and turned unsteadily to aim at me.

When the gunshot came, I pushed a hand in front of myself, a defense reflex. But Béla never got a chance to fire. A dark blossom spread on his chest. He dropped his gun. Then flopped backwards into the side of the Peugeot before he collapsed on the ground.

Reloaded, Cammie raced over keeping her sawed-off trained on Béla. She tossed aside his pistol. But Béla was done.

I jumped down from the tailgate and startled when I landed beside Aafeen. The DGSI agent was kneeling in the dirt, leaning on the truck's metal step where he had braced for his shot. Aafeen had passed out from the effort, but the MAC 50 was still in his hand where he had lashed it with his blood-soaked gauze.

twenty-one

Through the sliding glass door behind Gregg Espy, I watched the dawn sky deciding what color to become. Trust me, there's nothing like thinking you'd never live to see another sunrise to make you relish God's spectacle. While the director of special activities studied some incoming on his secure iPad, I let my gaze float through the window beyond him to the familiar silhouette of my Paris bodyguard, Kurt Harrison. The paramilitary protective officer walked rounds with his M4 among the olive trees and umbrella pines in the acre behind the safe house. He stopped to chat with another sentry, PPO Ortiz, who had been the first responder at the junkyard the night before. Over the tan stucco wall of the villa, the hilltops outside Marseille were gaining definition under the pinking clouds. God's spectacle. Pinking clouds. Who talks like that? A dude who's blissed out not to be tortured and hunted, that's who. I sipped more coffee and parked my mug on the glass coffee table beside its mate. Nova's had grown cold. She stood inside the open kitchen door in a hushed cell conversation.

I made a study of the layout. Much like the bedroom where I'd napped a fitful hour until the DSA arrived straight from Istres-Le Tubé Air Base, the vibe was vacation-rental generic, towels and toaster oven included. Clean and airy with bare white walls and beige floor tiles that made everything echo up to the vaulted ceiling. A small villa on two acres of woods in a neighborhood of rustic clones. Secure, nondescript, easy to quit in a hurry. Airbnflee.

I checked out Espy and wondered how many hidey-holes like this he'd been in over the years. Debriefing joes. Sweating traitors. Listening to field officers bawl to go home or beg for another chance after shitting the bed. "This time I can break him, I know it." Maybe I've read too much le Carré and Herron. Not possible. I started looking around for pinhole cameras.

"Care to join us, Officer Nova?" Espy's tone was undisguised ball busting.

Cammie ignored him. She took ownership of the time she needed to wrap her call before she settled beside me on the couch. "That was European Hospital Marseille. Aafeen is out of surgery. It went well. His prognosis is good for a full recovery."

"So are his chances for a chef-cooked home meal to help him regain his strength."

"Glad to hear he's OK. And that DGSI came through for once." Espy got to his own agenda. "We decoded that dead-drop message from Emil Dard you managed to rescue." He directed a congratulatory acknowledgment to me, ignoring Nova. "Dard says after you left him at his travel agency, he contacted an old friend who knew his ex-lover—"

"Thorvald Grepp," said Nova.

"Are you briefing me? Seriously?" What was up his ass, I wondered. "Dard's old friend in Orange that he reached out to was named…" Espy referred to his iPad. "…Claude Portal. Dard says—said—Portal recently quit a group called Første Stamme. Spelling it for you, F-O (with a stroke) R-S-T-E…"

"…S-T-A-M-M-E. I'm briefed." Nova, shoving back. "Emil told me. I asked him to find out what he could about their members, since his ex became one. I wanted to find out how this group connected to our mission and whether they were a splinter cell or a consequential entity."

Espy acted barely tolerant of the interruption. He resumed. "Dard's dispatch says his friend promised a list of names and said he'd get back to him. I ran Portal to see what we had." The DSA tapped his iPad and showed it to us. "Claude Portal." The screen displayed an ID photo. "This dates back to when he was an agent with DRSD." For my benefit, he added, "One of the umpteen French intelligence agencies."

"That's our Peugeot driver." I looked from Nova back to Espy. "He was the *Ghost Rider* flameout she blew away last night."

"So, Claude Portal was active Første Stamme, not ex-Første Stamme," said Nova.

"Bastard set up Dard to be tortured and killed," I added, from their non-reactions, unnecessarily.

"More show-and-tell. You said they called the guy who interrogated you Sigurd?" Espy swiped to another photo. I felt a chill when I saw it.

"Oh yeah. And I'd call 'interrogated' kind of benign. That asshole and his Peter Lorre minion juiced me more than an MLB starting lineup. That's definitely him."

"Affirm," said Nova, who'd seen him only for a literal flash when the man broke for the door, plenty for a trained observer. PPO Harrison slipped in, assault weapon tipped down. He leaned a hip against the wet bar and became part of the background scenery. I forced my eyes back to Espy's iPad and Sigurd's ID shot. Straight into the lens. Compliant, but with something speaking through those gray eyes. Something lethal that dared you to look away.

"Full name, Sigurd Ringstad. This is his personnel photo from when he was with NIS." He was addressing Nova but translated again for me. "Norwegian Intelligence Service. Like Grepp he was once attached to their E14, a top-secret branch that runs highly classified covert foreign ops." He half turned toward the wet bar. "I asked Harrison to join us because he has firsthand knowledge of Ringstad."

"Sorry to say." The security officer stayed planted against the sink. It all seemed casual, but I had to admire Espy's stage management, letting things unfold, easy as dealing from a loaded deck. "I got deployed to Pakistan during the bin Laden hunt. Orders were to liaise with an E14 cadre Ringstad was in. Dude taunted me the whole time. Woke up one morning and found broken glass in my boots. Couldn't prove it was him, but I knew. Next night his sidearm goes off and a slug hits the wall this close to my head. Ringstad claims it was a misfire, then laughs. The beatdown I gave him bought some space, but I kept myself on alert. Let's be real, I grew up knowing bigots. But Ringstad. Man, Sigurd Ringstad, we're talking full-metal fascist. And not only toward Black people. We got tasked with flushing out undercover Sikh terrorists. One day he drags this local teen into a cave and chokes the kid with his own turban because he won't give up his dad as Khalistan. When we found the body, Ringstad walked off saying, 'One less Paki.'"

I whispered, "Jesus."

"You lucked out, Chef. Man would have killed you and sat back to play Wordle."

Nova asked for Espy's tablet. She swiped through the identity photos and bios he had collected based on names he got from Dard and me. "There's no shortage of exes here," she observed. "Portal was ex-DRSD...Ringstad is ex-E14, and Béla Czibor..." She tilted the screen to let me see the human target's ID pic. "Béla was ex-AVH, Hungarian secret police. Adding them up, we've got ex-agents from France, Norway, and Hungary."

"Don't forget the motorcycle killer from Paris," I said.

"Right, make that two from Norway." Cammie held out the pics for my review. "Any of these the guy who you surprised in your hotel room?" I didn't get the best look at him but shook no. "Then we assume there's at least one more from this group out there. That's in addition to Thorvald Grepp."

"Let's keep focused on Ringstad, shall we?" Espy, curt as a New York waiter, delivering more smack to Nova. Her expression stayed flat, but her shift on the next cushion made me reflect on their "history," as she called it, and how it leached toxins into the meeting. "Last night when Ringstad questioned you—"

"'Questioned?'" I couldn't hold back. The way he was going at Cammie made me want to serve up the same to him. "Gregg, my man, have you been listening? Wanna see the burn near my kidneys? That Viking turned my skin to crème brûlée."

Espy winced. "What did he want to know?"

"First thing he wanted, he wanted to know where that Hungarian oligarch was. Ignaz Tábori."

"What did you tell him?"

"The truth…ish. I said I had no clue but that I was trying to get him on my show."

"And he bought?" Espy's tone was dubious.

"Not a bit. I gave him the song and dance about missing him before he went on vacation, but I never let on I thought he was in the South of France."

"What else? Think of everything, big or small, don't edit."

"Well. They wanted to know about Nova."

"Like what?"

"Mostly they focused on her ethnicity. They were all, was she a Gypsy or Black or Mexican? Then they went off on a round of slurs. Locker room shit."

"But nothing about her being in the trade."

"Ringstad asked if it was she who took me to the saltworks, so I assumed they already figured that out. They even knew her name."

"OK, then what?"

"It got uglier. This was when they decided to play a game of let's air-fry Pike." I finished off my coffee to wet my tongue.

"Ringstad didn't do all that for no reason. What did he want?"

"He wanted to know about something called Glicka."

"What did you tell him?"

"The truth. I told him I had no idea what he was talking about. Oh wait. Glicka or was it Glinka? Yeah, Glinka. My answer got him more pissed and got me more zapped. Do you have any idea what it feels like to have some maniac insisting you're holding back, and you can't make him believe you have no clue? Thank God for Nova and her flash-bang, otherwise I'd have been beef jerky." The room was cool, but I felt perspiration beading on my forearms. "What is a Glinka?" No one answered. "Anybody?"

From the DSA, "That's strictly Need-to-Know."

"I need to know. I earned that." I persisted. "What is a Glinka?"

Espy relented. "Not what. Who. Arkady Glinka. Trusted member of Putin's inner circle. He's Vladimir's accountant, but much more. Inner circle inner circle. Like family."

"Like Tom Hagen in *The Godfather*?"

"Close to. But Putin doesn't know that his consigliere is our asset. He doubles for CIA. For me."

Of course, I was already there. "He's the exfiltration subject."

"Who is suddenly being closely watched by Vlady's personal security unit." Espy picked up his iPad as a visual aid. "And from the pissed-off encrypted signal I just got from Moscow, Glinka says Putin has quietly launched a forensic audit of his books. More bad news."

That didn't make sense to me. "Who cares? Why would an audit be a problem?"

Espy stunned me by lashing out. "Spare me your rookie-know-it-all horseshit. It means he's under deep suspicion. What else would it mean? If that's the first move, it's a matter of time before he is compromised.

And, if that happens, he will not only be in personal danger, but our intelligence networks will be, too. Arkady Glinka is in a knowledge position. He knows names and methods of our key assets. If they break him—correction: when they break him—it would be catastrophic for us. We lose intel and we lose the lives of patriotic men and women." He glared at SSO Nova. "That will not happen."

"Sir, we're working this hard."

"Bullshit. Three days playing with yourself, and nothing to show but lost time, dead joes, and our chef nearly catching the bus. Times two."

Nova shot to her feet and shouted, "That is bullshit." PPO Ortiz, who was patrolling out back scrutinized her and moved closer to the picture window. Harrison signaled him off. "That is so FUBAR I can't believe you said it."

"Officer, you can be insubordinate, you can be loud, but it doesn't change facts."

I raised an index finger to ask for the floor. "First of all, ironic you call this a safe house. Second, rookie know-it-all that I am, doesn't the fact that we're hitting resistance indicate we are onto something? Ergo, traction? Even the way they served up Emil Dard at the saltworks was a message of intimidation. And am I the only one who sees the involvement of Béla, a former member of the Hungarian secret police, as a sign that our Hungarian oligarch might be around here?"

Newbie conjecture or not, I could see Gregg Espy embracing my logic. "Maybe. But that also points out another negative. You two might have blown your covers."

"Doubtful," said Nova. "Let's play this out. Best case, we are blown with Ringstad and his crew. Første Stamme's pedigree is all ex-NATO and ex-EU, not Russia. All my experience as an analyst says they're acting more like an aspirational cell than a bona fide entity. Sir, they didn't even have the resources to take us out last night. Ringstad fled, and all he had to come at us with was Portal and Béla."

"Who was so perforated, he could barely stay on his feet," I added.

Nova continued pleading her case. "I say we do have traction. And I'm betting our cover is still intact. At least with the Russians."

"Enough to bet your life?"

"You gave me a deadline. Let me keep working it. That sound like a yes to you?"

Espy didn't reply. Instead, he turned to me. "What about you?"

"I'm with her." My instant answer, no reluctance.

"All right. OK. I'll green-light you to continue." The DSA rose to leave. "Don't make me sorry. We need to zero out on this like yesterday."

twenty-two

Espy departed in a small caravan with Harrison and Ortiz, leaving Nova and me in the care of other security officers, seen and unseen. Not wasting a second, SSO Nova sequestered herself at the dining table to get her first read of Emil Dard's entire decoded message. Her concentration was a nonverbal cue to give her space, so I planted my aching self on a chaise longue out on the veranda. I reclined there under the arbor and chilled, listening to the larks and finches and breathing off the residue of the previous night's trauma.

My Zen interlude lasted a full minute before the toxic meeting with Espy elbowed into my peace. It bugged me, especially witnessing the boss man land cheap punches on a subordinate. Maybe the DSA was still pissed about Cammie refusing his hotel key one night, or whatever. But why did I get a taste of the lash? Gregg Espy was a man so insouciant he could probably study autopsy photos while he enjoyed a good steak with the properly paired Cabernet. My innocent question about Putin auditing Glinka made him snap and serve me a ration of bile. Was that about ego? The cook daring to challenge the spymaster? Or in my naiveté did I trample on some sensitive turf? I could be charitable and say that Espy was simply in anal pucker mode. People freak out at crunch time. But after his dressing down, I didn't feel especially lenient. I was starting to see the DSA as an adversary, not an ally.

I checked myself right there and hoisted a yellow caution flag that read: "Do not get dragged into office politics." But wait. Aren't my revered George Smiley novels rife with intramural intrigues? You bet. Know what I love most about those books? None of that is happening to me.

Emil Dard had left Nova a short list of contacts he was waiting to hear back from, and she had already called most of them on her encrypted cell by the time I got back inside. "No sightings or leads yet, but I have a few more to try." Cammie used her foot to push out one of the chairs for me. "If there's anything you shouldn't hear, I'll boot you."

"Nice. Someone's been taking charm lessons from Gregg Espy."

Nova suppressed a grin. "Park it and mute yourself."

"Warm invitation like that, how can a guy say no?"

After exchanging countersigns for verification, the friendly at the Regional Customs Directorate in Nice asked if Cammie could phone her back in five. The woman was in her office and wanted to take the call off-site. Minutes later, sounds of a light breeze and the ubiquitous buzz of motor scooters came from Nova's speaker and echoed up to the villa's rafters. The woman spoke quickly, saying she only had a few moments. But she was prepared. No Gulfstreams from Hungary landed in the region within Emil Dard's requested time frame, and none had come in from any other country matching the tail number of Ignaz Tábori's G650. Because Hungary and France were within the EU-to-EU Schengen Area, neither Tábori nor his family would need to show passports, therefore no official record of entry. Same for the daughter's music tutor. Cammie and I looked at each other, bummed by that dead end, when the customs contact surprised us.

"However, one of the names on Emil's list arrived via commercial carrier. Ágnes Sipos." Nova picked up a pen. The oligarch's mistress had indeed come to the South of France. "Mademoiselle Sipos didn't need to show a passport either, but I found her name on the airline manifest. Her ticket was booked by a travel agency, which also had arranged a limousine to her hotel, the InterContinental Carlton in Cannes."

Cammie took down the info for the limo service and thanked the woman for her extra effort. "Anything for Emil. Please give him my love." Without a blink, Cammie said she would and hung up. She immediately called the hotel, pretending to verify the address for a floral delivery to Ágnes Sipos. The hotel clerk singsonged, "*Un moment, s'il vous plaît.*" After a pause he clicked back on and apologized. "That party had a reservation but did not check in."

Her call to the limousine company mirrored that. Ágnes Sipos never met her ride at the airport. Cammie speculated Tábori had arranged a secret backup hotel for her, to which I said, "This is why I'd never cheat. Look at the expense this oligarch's going to just to keep his wife from finding out about his mistress."

"Or to keep people like us or the tabloids from tracking her." Nova tapped in the number of Emil's final lead. While it rang, she reopened Dard's coded message to follow the script of his instructions. "*Bonjour,*" answered the man. "*Crosière pour la Vie.*"

"*Bonjour*, is this Monsieur Fauré?"

A slight hesitation, then a cautious, "Who wishes Monsieur Fauré?"

"I am a friend of the Teddy Bear from Arles."

"Very well." He sounded more relaxed. "Go on."

"Do you have some information about a cruise package my friend was interested in?"

"I do." We heard a door close on the other end. "If you wish to have a look at the vessel, it recently arrived from Portofino. You will find it docked at Port de Cap-d'Ail. You know it?"

"Yes, near Monaco."

"Look for the *Pavana*." After he spelled the name for her, Monsieur Fauré wished safe travels and hung up.

We looked at our watches in tandem, calculating driving time to Monaco.

twenty-three

The GPS in our Citroën said we'd get there before lunch. First thing, Nova called the DSA to apprise him of the tip. Savvy of her. Toss him a crumb and buy some relief. Since my kidnappers stole my cell, I used the encrypted replacement Espy issued me at the safe house to call Latrell, who was still in Arles. I didn't want the crew to sit idle or wonder where the hell we were.

My DP led off by asking where the hell we were. I told him still scouting, which was truth-y. "When I didn't hear from you overnight, I thought, you better not be shacking up, all I can say." He laughed while I made a check of my driver, who didn't act like she'd heard. "Joke, Chef. You there?" Sidestepping, I asked Latrell to take the crew out in the field to shoot some scenics we could cut into the episode. My team excelled at that kind of assignment, but I gave him a list of suggestions anyway, mainly to make myself feel like I was staying engaged with my day job. The Museum of Ancient Arles and Provence, Moulin de Daudet, the ancient coliseum, and a short drive north, the Pont d' Avignon. "Just don't sing it. I don't need an earworm."

"Cool. I also thought I'd go back to Aigues-Mortes and shoot the saltworks." My insides took a drop, but I said fine.

Cammie appraised me. "How are you?" She bordered on affectionate. "I mean, how are you holding up?"

"All in all, I'm elated not to have a hood over my head."

"Sarcasm, Basty's first line of defense." She'd never called me that before. Cammie must have overheard Astrid's pet name from my friend Eva on the Paris shoot. Coming from Nova's mouth, Basty sounded jarring. "You don't have to be stoic with me. I want to make sure you are up for whatever comes. Yesterday may look like a day at the beach."

"As long as you have my back, I'll be fine. You were a goddamned machine busting me out of Ringstad's little day spa. And the way you went to work on Aafeen's wound right in the throes of our escape? You saved his life."

"What can I say, I was raised in a family of overachievers. In my house you paid a high price for mediocrity. So, this lady brings it." The smile she gave me was a heart skipper. It made me think about the kiss we almost had. I'd been thinking a lot about that, wondering if it was a thing of the instant. Danger triggering foxhole hormones. I felt her studying me. At last Cammie said, "I hate when people ask, 'What are you thinking?'"

"Me. Too. The worst. I want to tell them to sod off."

"But what are you thinking?"

"I'll make an exception because it's you, and you did save my life."

"You can stop saying that now."

"I was thinking how totally hot you looked in badass mode."

"Get real."

"Major turn-on. Tossing flash grenades, making lead fly...oh, and wielding that shotgun walking away from those flames like you were Linda Hamilton in *T2*." She frowned and chewed her lower lip. "I'm sorry. I reveal too much?"

"No, it's the Sarah Connor ref. I always pictured myself more like Shuri in *Black Panther* or Charlize Theron from *Mad Max*."

"Well, there's a peek behind the Cammie curtain. Clearly, you've given your alter egos a fair amount of thought."

"It's how a girl psyches up. Badass ain't easy." We laughed. It felt good to let down.

"Is that the hardest part for you? Of being a spy, I mean."

"Mm, Pike the interviewer surfaces." She sucked her lower lip again. "Hardest part… Not the danger. Know what it is? It's training myself to broker my feelings."

"You mean shut them off?"

"No, to compartmentalize them."

"So that you won't feel?"

"So that they won't betray me." She dipped her head, satisfied with that, and turned the page. "Think over what I asked you about whether you're cool with what might be coming. This could easily get more hairy."

"I'm in."

"Be sure. I mean it. I don't want to see anything happen to you, all right?"

I wondered what else could happen. In the last forty-eight hours, hadn't I checked all the boxes? "This is me repeating I'm in. As long as you don't ask what I'm thinking."

WE FOUND THE *PAVANA* EASILY. "After all," I said, "how many fifty-six-meter Benettis could there be in this joint?" The joint being an exclusive private marina comprising the last piece of France before you hit the Principality of Monaco. I knew Cap-d'Ail as one of Astrid's ports of call and had web-searched the vessel on our two-hour drive, reciting its specs to Cammie from the shotgun seat. "'Sleeps twelve, VIP suite, three al fresco dining decks, Jacuzzi, outdoor cinema, fold-down transom that converts to a swim platform and Jet Ski launch.' And get this. 'Tinted under-hull night lighting.' Perfect for illuminating your wildest mermaid fantasies. I made that last part up. Price tag for leasing this baby? A mere one hundred sixty thousand euros. Wait for it: per week."

Standing on the wharf with our heels to the international border, I showed her the Google image that matched the gleaming white craft before us—a super-luxury yacht so ginormous, it needed to be docked against the seawall, an area shrewd marketers designated the Basin of Honor. It was late morning, early in the season, and the marina wore that aura of flat quiet unique to paradise in downtime. Plenty calming on a vacation, but we were anything but relaxed on our approach to the *Pavana*.

Sigurd Ringstad and his neo-fascist hate-mongers were at large. Damn straight I was on alert. It reassured me to watch Nova check out our surroundings with a practiced eye. On the drive she'd muted Radio Oxygène out of Saint-Tropez to give me a recon primer. Look for idlers. Who appeared to be playacting a little too busy? What was happening on boats in the nearby slips? Were any couples necking or taking selfies who weren't quite touristy? Or were mismatched? Was anyone dressed wrong for their surroundings or looking too jacked?

We reached the yacht. Nova paused to cock an ear toward the decks above. No conversation or music indicating signs of life. All was stillness except for the calming trickle of runoff from a drain meeting smooth water.

A flight of wooden stairs, glossy from polyurethane, led up to the main deck. Nova assumed the lead. Topside we were met by two men, obviously security. They weren't in uniform, but what else would you call their matching black polo shirts and khaki cargo pants? Kurt Harrison had worn the same getup that morning, except his polo was olive green. Also like him, this duo radiated a "don't mess" vibe.

"Excuse me, may I help you?" Polite words for WTF are you doing?

"Oh, hi," said Cammie as if she'd lost half her brain cells on the ascent. "We were just... Your boat is awesome. And so big. We were hoping maybe we could, you know, get a selfie on it? We wouldn't touch anything."

"This is a private yacht." A more overt WTF.

She kept her feet on the upper platform but leaned forward to peer up and down the deck, fore then aft. "Oh my, will you look at how posh? You have to tell me. Does this belong to Elton John? I saw a picture of him with Victoria and David Beckham at my nail salon on a big ol' boat like this."

"We must ask you to leave the property." He struck the confrontation pose. "Now, if you please."

We didn't have to look to know we were being watched on our exit along the wharf, but I turned around to see anyway. "Amateur," she said.

"You laugh, but they're waving us to come back." I side-eyed her for a reaction, but Nova didn't take the bait. Just kept walking without missing a step. "Not even tempted to look?"

"Tell you what. Save the fourth-grade practical jokes for when we're off the clock, and I'll laugh right along. Deal?"

"Deal. But you sell me short. That was junior-high-quality comedy, and we both know it."

At the end of the Basin of Honor, the walkway made a sharp left. Nova stopped there and boosted herself up on the low stone wall to get an elevated view of the *Pavana*. I joined her. "Think our oligarch could be aboard?"

"I can't see enough of the deck from down here. But those guards were ten percent too relaxed. You can smell it on personal security when the boss is around." We watched some more, then hopped down. A man's voice hailed across the water.

"Oi, Chef! Chef Pike, over here!" We searched for the source and spotted a deckhand waving from a bosun's chair suspended over the side of one of the other super-yachts.

Cammie checked her watch. "Think you can skip the autograph this once? Bigger fish and all that."

But I was already heading for the water's edge and calling back to the man. "Chipper, you layabout. You missed a spot." Across the marina the deckhand made a comical show of buffing a porthole, then rope-climbed up on deck and jogged to the gangway. "I'll make this short, but I can't diss him. He was crew on that rock star's yacht…you know."

I could see she knew. LED text practically scanned across her brow: "The *Thumos*…Athens …Astrid."

Chipper, a sunburned Aussie with wild blond beach hair, batted away my extended hand and clinched me in a bro hug. "I thought that was you. Except you're too good-looking to be you." He threw in a shoulder bump for good measure. I introduced Cammie. Chipper gave an approving "allo" and threw in a waist bow. "How cool is this, mate? It's been an age since…"

And there it was. The fog of discomfort formed between the three of us.

"I was totally rooted after it all happened. I tried to write you a note, I truly did. I didn't know what to say."

"No worries." To let him off the hook, I added, "I still don't."

After a few leaden seconds, Chipper clapped his hands together. "Come aboard for a coldie?"

"It's early in the day." I deferred to Cammie. "Besides, don't we have to—?"

"We'd love to," she said.

Chipper's yacht wasn't booked for a charter until two weeks off, so he had the run. When he doled out our beers, Nova asked if we could drink them on the upper deck. She took a swivel chair near the rail, overlooking the *Pavana* with an unobstructed view of three decks and several windows. I toasted her. "Nicely played."

She tried her gee-whiz routine on Chipper, asking if he'd seen any celebrities on that yacht. "None that I recognized, and I've seen the bunch—such as they are, am I right? That tub berthed about this time yesterday, and they flew off that thing like cockroaches when the lights go on. Three black SUVs. One for the swells and two more following behind just for their kits."

"They must be famous. Have you talked to the crew about who they were?"

"Not the friendliest lads, you ask me. A simple g'day, and they show me their backs."

While she surveilled the mystery yacht, my deckhand pal and I reminisced about the cruises we took together on the *Thumos*. Sardinia, Trieste, Malta, Barcelona… "You always treated me right, mate. Never like a lowly grunt, and that's dinki-di." He tipped back his 3 MONTS, nearly draining the bottle. "Confession. I saw you and the lady pass by before, and I hid so you wouldn't see me."

"If it's because of Astrid, don't feel awkward."

"Can't help it, I did. Then my conscience got me. I hung myself over the side on the chance you'd come back. As for Astrid, never knew her to be happier because of you." Kind words from Chipper, but the tidy bow the Aussie tied on the box was his perspective. Everyone else's, too. Because when outsiders get around love they project what they want to see and stick to it. But the thing is, they never know what's inside that box.

Before memory lane led to an unpleasant place, I asked about other crew members and what became of the yacht. But that question only brought the Aussie back to the death of its rock star owner and Astrid in the Zodiac explosion. "I'm of the belief it was a hit on Kogg."

I leaped to what Cammie told me in Paris. That the official story was false. But she didn't react. Her attention stayed on the *Pavana*. I said, "The investigation said it was his bag of crystal meth."

"Yeah, the 'shake and bake' verdict. Shake this." The Aussie demonstrated air masturbation. "Kogg drank but, except for the bedtime spliff, no drugs. Remember Cedric, the first mate? Before it happened, Cedric claims he heard some dude getting heavy with Kogg. Cranking the volume up to eleven about him getting cold feet on some deal they had. The dude telling Kogg to grow a pair or some bad shit would rain down on him." Nova swiveled and reached for a monogrammed bar napkin. A casual way to put eyes on this conversation.

"Cedric's no bullshitter," I said. "Did he tell that to the police? Did you?"

"Naw, I only heard this recently from Cedric. He's working down the coast in Menton, and we had a brew. Said he was too scared to talk about it. Scared of the rough types who'd started hanging around the old bucket."

I knew that up close. Kogg had the same working-class appeal in Europe that Springsteen, Seger, and Mellencamp cultivated in America's heartland and Rust Belt towns. He even branded himself with a stage name to evoke hardness and blue-collar machinery. The German rocker took it a step further. "Kogg loved his biker fans. Rock and roll, right?"

Chipper's beach hair wagged no. "These guys weren't everyday bikers. There was a...guess you'd call it...skinhead entourage aboard. Fucking barnacles, you ask me."

Nova was already swiping the screen of her phone. She found what she wanted and held it out to Chipper. "This guy look familiar?"

"Yeah, him. He was most deffo one of them. King shit, this one was." I didn't need to look. It would be Sigurd Ringstad. "How'd you know?"

I said, "Somebody I met."

twenty-four

Our visit to the marina office turned fifteen precious minutes to ashes dealing with a starchy manager who refused to divulge anything about the *Pavana* or the whereabouts of the party that chartered it. The prig said that to do that would be indiscreet. Being an oligarch buys you a lot of discretion.

Sniffing a warm trail, Nova hatched a plan. From the parking lot she called her contact at the DST, France's Directorate of Territorial Security, and asked if they had traffic cams on the routes leading out of the marina. She figured they would, since Cap-d'Ail marked an international border with Monaco. Score one for Team Nova. They had cams and were happy to let her screen the video, but they would need about two hours to organize a session. I said that left us time for a quick trip to Menton. Cammie disagreed with that idea and got prickly about it.

"No way. Just because Chipper put this Cedric guy in your head, we are not going on a goose chase for him."

"Am I detecting a nastitude?"

"Hell yeah. We need to keep the main thing the main thing. Period." Nova's flare was a first. I knew how much pressure she was under, but the hairline fracture in her coolness showed me there was a human in there.

After the nerve-racking night she'd had and the heat she was getting from Espy, I let it go. But not my idea.

"Cedric sounds plenty main thing to me." I read her skepticism but went on. "It may seem like I'm angling to sidetrack into Astrid…and maybe a little bit of me is…but you heard Chipper. He all but connected Cedric to direct contact with Ringstad. How much more main thing can you get?"

"All right, fine." Nova checked her wrist. "But no matter what, we are at DST in two hours."

DURING THE TWENTY-MINUTE DRIVE to Menton, Chipper texted me back with Cedric Devlin's particulars. We found the career first mate, a man always in demand on the most extravagant luxury yachts in the Mediterranean, behind the counter of a car rental franchise. He had no customers, and we caught him reading a Patrick O'Brian paperback. The slim little man's face popped with joy when he recognized me. Then he quickly turned downcast as a second thought jerked his leash. I had seen that happen so often I named it Astrid Reflux, the sudden recoil when greeters realize they have to make nice around tragedy. Cedric tried to divert with a joke. "Sorry, we don't rent vehicles to show people. Not without a double deposit." But his attempt was a mask that slipped. Right after a back-clapping hug, he grew somber again and asked how I found him.

"Ran into that useless bastard Chipper. He said you might be here." At the mention of the Aussie from Kogg's yacht, Cedric's eyes flicked to the parking lot as if he expected a pack of jackals to follow in our wake. "Thought we'd surprise you with a quick hello as we pass through." I introduced Cammie, who waved briefly while perusing a local map over by the door. Cedric appraised her carefully. This man's demeanor had changed completely since I last saw him. Once quintessentially genial, he'd turned guarded and on edge.

He attempted small talk about my recent *Hangry Globe* destinations. When that stalled, his eyes reddened. "I feel bloody awful about Astrid."

"Thanks. She always liked you." The old first mate's lower lip twitched. "You all right there, Ced?" In my periphery, Nova's head rose out of her map browsing.

Cedric's bony shoulders started to wobble. He crossed his arms and held himself. "Sorry. My conscience getting me, I guess."

"If it's about being out of touch, don't feel awkward."

"It's not that," he muttered to his shoes. His head popped up and he shouted, "It's because I'm a goddamned coward." He sniffed, loud and liquid. Tears fell, matching the drips from his nostrils.

"Brother, you'll have to help me understand."

"I'm a coward because…because I knew there was going to be trouble. And I did nothing. I don't know what I could have done, but that's what I did. Absolutely nothing. Please don't hate me for that, please, I couldn't take it." He lowered his head and fought back sobs.

"We're cool, it's all cool." I stole a quick glance at Nova, who had set her map down, and I got to it. "Tell me about it. What do you mean you knew about trouble?"

He took a moment to settle. "You must have noticed when you were around. There started to be a lot of yabbos aboard. Body tatts and Speedos over cock rings sunning themselves or raising holy hell on the Jet Skis." He smeared wetness off his cheeks and got a grip. "Very well, then. Clean breast, right? One night, this was before the…the incident, I walk into Kogg's stateroom to return the Beats he left in the cinema. You know how he rolled, no formalities, so no knock, I breeze in. What do I see but Kogg with his back flat on the deck and some bully boy's got a knee on his chest, holding a pistol to his forehead. The gorilla's yelling at Kogg not to screw up their deal or he's dead. Then the guy spots me and swings his cannon my way. I'm backing out like this." He held up surrender hands. "The fellow braces me and puts the gun right here." Cedric put two fingers under his chin. "Gives a nice shove to make sure I'm listening, and says if a peep of this gets out, he knows where to find me. I mumble no worries, and bolt. Ran straight down to my quarters, loaded my kit, and was straight off that gangplank and never went back."

"Any idea what the argument was about?"

"Even if I knew, I wouldn't tell. Not after what happened. But something over money. That's a guess, but a fair one. On the table in Kogg's stateroom—cash. And no small lot. Stacks like you see in the cinema. Stacks like the Manhattan skyline, high, tight, and squared. Right beside a holdall. That's what they call killing money. Why you think I jack-rabbited? I'm sure this had everything to do with what came down on Kogg." He held back sobs again. "...And Astrid."

I numbed myself to my own inner battle and spoke softly to urge him to keep him talking. "Why didn't you tell the police?"

"Because I'm a fawkin' coward. I still am. Can't you see? I'd have been blown to bits or something, too. I wasn't about to give 'em cause to come for me." I laid a consoling hand on Cedric's back and felt serrated spine and flop sweat through his turquoise uniform shirt. "No! Don't do that."

"Ced, I just—"

"Fuck you and your pity. I don't deserve it." He shook me off with a violent twist.

I gave him a hard shove backwards with both hands and shouted back. "You've got to let yourself off the hook, man."

He pulled himself away from where he'd landed against the counter and composed himself. In a voice barely audible, he said, "How can I?"

I saw him. I heard him. I felt him.

Nova handed me her phone. "Is this the man who threatened you?" I asked as I held out Sigurd Ringstad's picture.

He swept a low gaze to Nova, held on her, then settled back on Ringstad. Cedric squinted. Cedric stared. Cedric tilted his head to one side, then the other. "Mm. Can't say. Doesn't look familiar." His words lied; his face busted him. I didn't press, though. I had his answer. I didn't need his pain.

As Nova and I were crossing the parking lot, Cedric Devlin opened the glass door and called out another lie for good measure. "Couldn't make him out. It was dark, you see."

IN NICE THERE IS A NONDESCRIPT government building a block from the Place Toseli rotary with a basement suite for screening video. Since the November 2015 attacks, France had upgraded its network of security cameras. Improvements that gave the French military intelligence officer assigned to us access to digitized footage of all roads surrounding Port Cap-d'Ail for our review. They also gave me something to get my mind off my exchange with Cedric Devlin.

Thanks to Chipper, the search was less of a needle in a haystack. His recall of the approximate time of the group's departure from the *Pavana* narrowed the window. Within minutes of scanning video at quad speed, we got a hit on three black Range Rovers exiting the marina gates at lunchtime. Cammie muttered a "Good onya, Chipper," and reached over to squeeze my hand.

Our video technician, *Sous-lieutenant* Darroze, not only possessed local knowledge, but she also had total command of her studio. Her pro capability matched the best editors I had worked with over the years. When Nova asked her to track the motorcade to the next street, her fingers made efficient attacks on the keyboard and triple lutzes on her trackpad. The only delays came from slight buffering time when she called up a camera's video to load. "The spinning beach ball of death, yes?" said the *sous-lieutenant.*

Spotting the caravan filled our tiny control room with excitement. But we didn't dare celebrate for fear of a jinx. Except for the clacking of the keyboard and the white noise of cooling fans, all we could hear was our own breathing. I leaned progressively closer to the two monitors. One showed the image recorded by the street cam we were currently viewing, the other flatscreen displayed a road map with a blue progress overlay of the convoy's route. It inched like the smartphone worm of an Uber through the Avenue du Port roundabout, then west on Avenue du Trois Septembre, following that along Baie de Saint-Laurent. The blue line traced the convoy around the loop up the canyon and back down past a rest stop and onward, joining the bayside again. A seaside cam picked up the Range Rovers heading into the Saint-Laurent tunnel, one, two, three—and then out the other end—one, two, three. Yes, yes, and yes.

Then all the air hissed out of the balloon.

SSO Nova flicked bewildered looks from the screens to the *sous-lieu-tenant,* who was madly tapping keys, advancing footage, and selecting new video from up-route. Cam after cam of sunny streets, but no motor-cade. "*Quel est le problème?*" I asked.

The video specialist opened a new window on the monitor. Icons on it displayed closed-circuit camera locations on a map. And a big gap. "As you see, they drove into a null zone. There is little business or activity, making it low priority, so they have not yet erected CCTV coverage in this section of Èze-sur-Mer." She used a pen to point from the tunnel to an icon near a beachy area. "The next camera is *ici.* Port de Beaulieu. That is where I am now scrubbing the video to try to pick them up."

The DST agent began a high-speed scour through recorded street activity at various locations between Port de Beaulieu and Nice. I hung my head. "So close." Cammie got up to pace.

Sous-lieutenant Darroze took her task personally, a puzzle challenge she needed to solve. But she found no sign of the caravan on the major roads coming out of the surveillance gap. "In that null zone, there are residential side streets. It is possible they stopped somewhere in one of those neighborhoods. Or perhaps they took a back road up to the main highway, you see." Her cursor traced the bright yellow stripe of the A8 on the map. "I am sorry. After you go, I will continue to screen pictures from those cameras, I promise."

Nova managed to smile. "You did your best. Wonderfully." She asked her to rewind to the marina, hoping to capture license numbers from the vehicles. Darroze had called up the shots before she finished her request. We got license plates on all three SUVs. Nova offered a *merci* again and signaled me it was time to go.

I raised my hand. "Indulge me one thing?" Cammie shrugged. That placating look again. I pulled my chair up to the console beside the *sous-lieutenant*. "Can you roll it back to when they were *I said*, coming out of the rotary?" Balancing looks at me and the monitor, she scrolled backwards, making the cars reverse into the roundabout. "Right there. *Là!*" She froze the footage. "Almost. Can you rock it forward twenty-four frames?" The agent smiled. An American chef spoke her language. After precisely one second of video, another freeze. A stripe of sunlight hit the second vehicle. "Beauty. Now, can you punch in on the rear passenger window?" A few more keystrokes and the still frame zoomed into close-up. It showed a man in the back seat, but pixelated due to the digital zoom. "Maybe try toggling to remove shadows."

Darroze executed my instructions and enhanced the shot. Nova moved closer to view the end result. Although still grainy, the result was unmistakable. The man in the back seat was Ignaz Tábori.

I stood and made a *Price Is Right* model's gesture to the monitor. "Elvis is in the building."

twenty-five

Blitzed by the ordeal of the last twenty-four-plus hours, Nova and I needed a hotel to crash and regroup. Unfortunately, with the Cannes Film Festival only several weeks off, advance PR teams had already started hogging rooms. I recalled staying once at La Pérouse, a boutique on Castle Hill above Old Nice and far enough from the action of La Croisette to hope for vacancies. We scored its two remaining avails, small singles but with stunning views of the port and the Baie des Anges.

After a short break for combs and phones, I knocked at Cammie's room. "Why are you using the hallway? We have adjoining doors."

"It seemed kind of…" I searched and landed on "…presumptuous?"

Amused, she said, "It's a door, not a statement."

"I could go back for a do-over."

"Get in here and sit down. I had wine sent up. If that's not… presumptuous."

Nova had established her work zone at the only chair, so I sat on the edge of the bed. While she uncorked and poured, she gave me an update. "I got word on the plates. Unfortunately, the Range Rovers were not from a local limo service. They were leased by a private corporation in Luxembourg."

"Tábori tax dodge?"

"Oligarchs love to hide their money in shell companies. Pretty much untraceable. At least on our deadline. Also, *Sous-lieutenant* Darroze called. She came up empty on her extracurricular scavenging."

"Well, that sucks."

"Only mostly. All intel is useful. If Tábori's motorcade never reached Nice, it lets us know he's somewhere between here and where we lost him coming out of that tunnel."

"Great, roughly a half-million people. Let's go knock on doors."

She laughed and handed me my glass. "…And he's back."

"I have a report, too. While you were getting nowhere with your fancy intelligence contacts, I told Latrell to start a company move to Nice as soon as they wrapped scenics. Hoss the Roadie will pack up our hotel rooms and lug it here. They should arrive by midnight. If I were driving, eleven."

"OK, I've got to know." She sat and studied me. "Were you really born in a getaway car?"

"For a spy your lack of information is an embarrassment. Indeed, I did draw my first breath in the back of a speeding Chevy Impala pursued by New York's Finest. For that I thank my mother for her extramarital fling with a smash-and-grab jewel thief. Mom was Bonnie to his Clyde. Fortunately, they did not go down in a hail of bullets. He went to Dannemora for a five-year bit, my mom returned to her own prison, back home with my father."

She nodded to herself. "Makes sense. Now I see why you've spent your life on the move."

"Because I was born in a speeding car?"

"Because of what came later. At home, growing up."

"We all have our stories. Except the version I got of yours from the job interview clearly omitted a number of details, i.e., you lied."

"In the interest of national security."

"That was then. This is now when I am…what term did you use to describe me, 'conscious'?"

"What do you want to know?"

I wanted to say everything. Hell, we'd almost kissed. What I was most curious about was her relationship status. Especially after tracking her and that mystery man to the wine bar. But I knew better than to force that right out of the gate. I went for, "How about the parts that led you to spy life? And don't say you were born in the back of an Aston Martin."

"Simple enough. I got recruited while I was at George Washington University."

"Hold on. Your résumé said Howard."

"GW came after. A masters in police and security studies didn't fit my legend for your job interview."

"Again, you lied."

"Anyway, my story? They approached me because I fit the profile. High GPA, my dad was a defense contractor, and we moved around a lot growing up. LA, Boston, Paris, London, Seattle. That's a green flag for the Agency. Rootless, adaptable, resilient. Able to sever ties and move on. It also meant no long-term relationships." Now she was taking this where I wanted it to go. I sipped and listened. "But I ended up in one. With my Agency recruiter. We both worked at Langley, so we kept it down low. It was our business, and he…he was everything I ever wanted. At Tysons Corner one Saturday I saw him shopping for a ring."

"Oh." My heart sank. Nova was engaged? Back to keeping things at arm's length. "That's a happily ever after, isn't it?"

"Not done." Nova swallowed half her glass and drew a steadying breath. "One day my supervisors called me in. I sat and listened while they systematically laid out all they knew about my relationship. At first, I thought it was the usual due diligence the Agency does to vet lovers. But the more they talked, the more it became an exposé of his secret life. They had me listen to recordings of my fiancé working as a double agent for the Russians. They had surveillance video of him doing dead drops and brush passes. They had evidence of his online activities, texts he thought were encrypted, everything. God's truth? During that meeting, I hoped they were going to tell me he was having an affair. That would hurt, but this was worse."

"What did he say to you? Did he offer any explanation?"

"He was isolated in HVD, High-Value Detention. I never saw him again, and that's for the better." Her brow darkened under some internal deliberation before she decided to go further. Again, I waited for her. This was a tender place. She deserved patience and respect. "He did manage to sneak me a note. I don't know how he got it out, it just showed up. An envelope on the floor mat of my car. It was his apology offering 'redemption,' he called it.

"I was crushed. He didn't only betray his country and his fellow agents, he played me in a way that cut deep. Everything was a lie. The ton of bricks was that..." She battled tears and won. "...He never chose me. Oh, he did, but for professional reasons. He was the one Russia sent." She paused. When she continued, she sounded small and her voice quaked. "Do you have any idea what it's like growing up never being chosen? And then after you are, you learn you weren't? It went to all my biggest insecurities. Do you know what that does to you?"

She had talked herself out. I felt awful that my self-serving question delivered her into a world of hurt. Now she sat there searching me, totally vulnerable, wondering if I understood. But Cammie must have known I did because of our talk in Paris, the night she told me that she, too, knew loss. She was waiting for me to say something. Because I did know loss—and then some—I knew one thing: what not to say.

No platitudes. No sorrys. No advice.

When I answered I spoke softly, but it was the truth, and therefore loud and clear. "I know that insecurity. It's from having something happen out of nowhere that brings all your flaws front and center and puts them in your face, so that you wonder whether you are even lovable." The room was darkening, but the torchlight from the beach danced in her eyes. Something in my chest did a backflip, and I said, "So you know? I would choose you."

Cammie leaned forward to take my hand. I took her other. When she came forward in her chair, I leaned to meet her embrace. Our hug began tenderly. A gesture of warmth. But soon emotion fueled deferred passion. I stood and drew her up to me. We hugged tight like that, enfolding, clinging, magnetized, then found each other's mouths. Nothing tentative like before. This was primal and hungry. We pressed against each other, moving and swaying in flamingo time. She broke away from our kiss to put her lips on my ear for a breathless whisper. "Now."

twenty-six

A *brr-brr-brr* startled me awake. Cammie leaned over the side of the bed to grab her phone off the rug, exposing her muscled back and all, shared without self-consciousness. She held the pose for the call, mostly grunts of acknowledgment and instructions to check in with this point person or that in some alphabet-soup agency. Finished, she rolled back toward me. When she returned her cheek to its warm spot under my collarbone, I said, "HR might have something to say about this."

"Whose? Yours or mine?"

"Not mine, seeing how your employer is Uncle Sam."

I felt her smile grow on my chest. "Let's hear it for delayed gratification."

"Yeah, who knows what might have happened last night if we hadn't been interrupted by a team of killers. At least this time we didn't have to deal with gunfire and explosions."

She tilted upward, one brow arched. "Oh, trust me, there were explosions." Cammie nestled again and took my hand. "I want to know about this." Her fingertip traced a line across my left thumb. "Tell me where you got this."

I didn't need to look. "CULS-100. Intro to Kitchen Fundamentals at the Culinary Institute of America. The other CIA. In my knife skills demo for Mastering Classical Vegetable Cuts, I learned you don't showboat by holding eye contact with Chef." Cammie kissed it. Then she switched to my right hand and gently drew an oval on the palm, which did not feel at all unpleasant.

"And here?"

"In the restaurant free-fire zone we food slingers call Saturday night, there's no time to slip a pot holder on your dainties. That beauty mark came from a sauté pan I thought I was man enough to juggle. If I close my eyes, I can still hear the hiss." She put her lips to that one, too, then turned her attention to the flip side, finger-mapping a jagged pattern across three knuckles.

"This doesn't look like a slice or a burn. Let me guess. Shark bite?"

"Plate glass window. It's a long story about a short fuse." I offered a self-effacing smile. "I view all of these not so much as scars as lessons in humility."

"I saw that today." Not the humility. I knew she meant the short fuse. My shove.

"I wasn't proud of that. I want you to know, I'm not a hair-trigger guy."

"Yes, I know that."

"He...touched a nerve, I guess." When lovers talk about their pasts they talk about their wounds. Joy may be aspirational, but our injuries define us. Cedric held up a mirror. I lashed out at what I saw in it. He'd been tying himself in knots about running away instead of notifying the police. I'd been torturing myself with the same guilt but for a different reason.

Reader, when I told you the Pike-Astrid saga, do you remember I said that I was holding something back? Because you have been such a steady companion, let me give you the unredacted version, starting after Paris. Astrid went back to sea on the rock star's mega-yacht when it left dry dock. I had my own commitments and hit the road, too, but I performed all sorts of gymnastics, bending my *Hangry Globe* schedule to line up with hers for what we dubbed our Ports-o-Call Trysts. But they were more than that. I ached for her when we were apart, and the effort to meet defined labor of love. Until the unwinding started.

It began slowly at first, in Genoa. I met Astrid for one of our precious weekends, and she disappeared for two hours after lunch. Not the biggest deal. Plus, I respected her independence, so I didn't press her about it. But it evolved into a pattern. Astrid busted a dinner date in Barcelona; she needed to run an errand for Kogg. In Hamburg, she got a late-night text and went out. Kogg needed her to put together an after-concert buffet for his manager and the record label, she said. I'll spare you the blow-by-blow, but these new and sudden disappearances to service the rock star's impulses became more frequent. They popped up in Rotterdam, in Porto, in Haifa... Her manner had also shifted. Carefree Astrid grew more self-contained. Preoccupied. I'd say almost secretive. She talked less freely when we did talk, and our once-comfortable silences were simply silent.

I could no longer hide in denial. Not when I was cutting segments from my show to orchestrate our visits, only to sit alone watching lovers at surrounding café tables while she broke away to be with Kogg. Not when I had opened my heart, something I don't take lightly, only to feel it slowly drain. What I was afraid to face was my creeping belief she was having an affair with Kogg. Whenever I joined her on his yacht, I searched them for signs of that, but saw none. Nobody would accuse me of being passive, so I forced a conversation. Not about Kogg; I kept it open-ended. Was she having second thoughts? Astrid got defensive and called me needy. "I am," I said. "I need you."

After that it got better for a bit. Then her last-minute absences returned. It boiled over when she pulled the rug on an entire weekend. She needed to go on a spur-of-the-moment voyage with Kogg the next day. There I was driving to Heathrow, and she was scrapping the trip.

She said this was about duty. Duty meant she couldn't say no. I said, "You don't have any problem saying it to me." Astrid knew I was pissed and asked me to keep my flight and come along on the yacht. I said no. And that we needed to chill for a while. "Are you calling off our engagement?" The vulnerability in her voice, suddenly frail and innocent, bore a hue of early Astrid and tore at me. I can still feel the swirl of disbelief that, after all we had, the two of us were even having that conversation. By then I had pulled off into the kiss-and-fly lot near the airport to wait out the silence and her breathing. Finally, she spoke. "Basty, I'm not going. I will come to you right now to work this out. Screw the concert trip. I will come to you."

Every day I live with the bone saw of guilt that I didn't say yes, come back to me. Instead, I told Astrid that we should take some space and sort this out, face-to-face, when she returned. That she should go on her voyage with Kogg out of Athens.

"I can literally feel your heart. It got loud." Cammie's voice from my chest. "We don't need to get into what happened with Cedric now. You're still dealing with a lot of stuff." She gave me a free pass. It didn't stop the demons from clawing at the door.

It pained me not to self-disclose to Cammie. Especially since she had opened up to me about her ex. Some things are too hard to put out there. Once you give them voice, you don't own them anymore. But this was starting to feel like it owned me. I almost told her. I chose deflection. "Ever think that heartbeat's because of you?"

Cammie hoisted herself to hover over me, and we kissed. Her hand roamed and found me. I traced my hands down her back. Our kiss deepened and soon my untidy past got banished along with frets over a reclusive Hungarian. In a while new explosions came.

AFTER SHOWERING TOGETHER in her room, we split up to make our phone checks. Latrell was rolling out of Arles in the lead van of the *Hangry Globe* convoy. I gave him the name of the hotel our network's travel department had scrounged for him and the rest of the crew and said to watch his email for the list of scenics I wanted them to shoot around Nice and Cannes. He needled me, asking if we were planning any actual interview segs or cooking demos on this trip. I told him my auteur's vision for this season was silent film and to shut up and drive. Latrell was still laughing when I pressed End. After Nova finished checking in with informants and spotters and making rounds of classified websites, we strolled hand in hand to dinner.

"Please tell me you picked a place with no dress code," she said. Latrell had confirmed that Hoss brought our luggage, but at that moment it was in transit near Aix-en-Provence, so we had to set out in the clothes we'd worn for two days of dodging bullets and rolling in filthy trucks. Fine for where we were going, although I did stop at a vendor's stall on the way to buy her a lovely chiffon scarf to cover a bloodstain.

La Merenda held center stage of a side street in Old Nice. The twenty-seater was run by the chef-owner who said *au revoir* to his upscale restaurant gig one day and opened his own humble bistro. Now it's a darling of the gastro cognoscenti. We ordered starters of tomato tarte Tatin and beignets of courgette flowers that were golden fried and served with a ramekin of flaked salt for us to pinch to taste. We shared two mains, the *daube de boeuf* and the signature house-made green linguine with pesto. While I watched Cammie delight in the meal, I reflected on her ex, the traitor, and the nightmare he put her through. I had no idea until she told me, which made me remember the great lesson of travel. You never can guess what's going on inside people. Behind every face you encounter could be someone suffering from addiction, abuse, mourning, illness, you never know. So, meet the world without bias. Go easy, lead with a smile, open your heart. There's ample time to get jaded later.

"You're smiling," she said, taking a dip into the chocolate mousse the chef comped us. "I mean a for-real one. It's a good look on you."

"I have to admit, this doesn't suck."

"You deserve it after the year you've had. Wave me off if I'm poking a sore spot, but have you been able to experience anything close to joy since…you know."

"Hmm, joy? Me?" I set my spoon down. "Here we go. Talking about feelings."

"I'll let it drop."

"No, no, I'm being facetious. It's you, so it's OK. Besides, I can answer that in a heartbeat. Joy was the month I spent volunteering at World Central Kitchen for José Andrés. I went to Ukraine to escape—you know, take a head break—and throw myself into the grunt work of being one of the line cooks. My pal Alton Brown once confided to me how the simple act of feeding people who are truly hungry feeds your own soul. I never expected how much.

"I won't bullshit you and say it saved me. I'm not out of the darkness yet. But hot damn, it sure helped."

The face she gave me was full of wonderment. "I had no idea you did that."

"Nobody knew. That was the idea."

We took the Promenade des Anglais back to our hotel. Promenading seemed called for, and we did so, hip to hip, pulling each other as close as we could get. Behind us, the lights of Cannes cast a glow in the sky and dappled the bay. At l'Opéra Plage she paused to look up at the sway of the international flags on all the poles. When I looked up, too, Cammie lassoed the back of my neck with her new scarf and drew me into a kiss. We stood there locked in an embrace to the night music of lazy waves gurgling between the rounded stones of the beach.

Duty always an inch away, she responded to a text from a watcher she had posted at the marina in case the oligarch returned, then we resumed our promenade. "Tonight's been amazing. The sex, the company, the dinner." She circled to face me. "Did I mention the sex?"

"Not nearly enough. My ego is a bottomless pit."

"Not to worry. We're fabulous. Almost as good as the restaurant. Now that was a discovery."

"To you," I said. "I go there every time I'm in Nice. It's reliable. Predictably excellent."

"I thought your mantra was 'surprise me.'"

"Ah, but my alt mantra is, 'If you're going to violate something as inviolable as your mantra, make it worth it.'"

"Most convoluted mantra ever. Just sayin'."

"Every city has one restaurant that's my go-to. Here, it's La Merenda. C'mon, you travel. You must have yours, too."

"I guess I do. I like discovery, but I'm also a creature of habit."

"Aren't we all? As the famous French gastronome Jean Anthelme Brillat-Savarin once said, 'Tell me what you eat: I will tell you what you are.' My riff on that is, 'Tell me what you eat: I will tell you where you are.'"

About three strides later, Nova hit the brakes. "Chef? What does our oligarch eat?"

Implications lasered between us. Without another word, we race-walked to the hotel.

twenty-seven

I guess any room can be a situation room. Cammie sat cross-legged on her bed with a laptop, sifting through endless emails posted to the *Hangry Globe* website from Ilona Tábori. The corner chair was my base of operations. I used my CIA-issued phone to search restaurants in the area. Pinching and spreading to tighten and widen the screen, I scanned a map of restaurant icons, dragging east to west—Monaco to Cannes—the area Nova called the zone of likelihood. "If this works," I said, "I'm expensing tonight's dinner."

"If this works, I'm buying the next one. And I'll be dessert."

"Any hits?" I asked.

"No restaurant mentions, at least none around here."

"Recipe requests?"

"About a half dozen for croquembouche…"

"Makes you wonder what Freud would say about her obsession with an edible tower. 'Sometimes a croquembouche is just a croquembouche?'"

"And she offers you a recipe for her grandmother's paprikash." She scrolled and scrolled. "Oh, and a request for a surprise dinner for her husband's birthday, his all-time favorite. Ready? Rabbit in blood sauce. One word? Ew."

"Only to a plebeian. Rabbit in blood sauce is a classic. But I grant you it sounds better when they call it Lièvre à La Royale."

"This plebeian thanks you and Ilona Tábori for reverse spoiling tonight's fabulous meal." Nova closed her laptop. "Any restaurants jumping out?"

I handed her the side list I was keeping on the hotel notepad. "With hundreds and hundreds of restaurants, I had to narrow. So, I filtered for the high-end places, either Michelin stars or ones where I knew its rep or the chef. No tourist traps or dives." She studied my roster, which included Alain Ducasse's three-star Le Louis XV and the two-star Joël Robuchon in Monaco. Among multiples in Nice, I'd listed Flaveur and Le Chantecler, each of which had two Michelin stars.

Cammie made a tally and tossed the notepad on the bedspread in exasperation. "Maybe this wasn't such a genius idea after all. Your list is more like a directory. Are you even listening?" Only half. I was immersed in a map on my screen. "What do you propose I do, set up surveillance at two dozen restaurants in case Tábori happens to show up?"

"Or we could try this." I tapped one of the restaurant icons on the map. When its home page opened, I pressed the phone symbol.

"What are you doing? Who are you calling? It's quarter after eleven."

"Quality never sleeps. Or punches out." I got an answer on the first ring and held up a forefinger. "*Bon soir*, La Colombe d'Or? *Est-ce que* Gavroche Thénard *est là*?" I got a yes and winked at Cammie. "Tell him *je suis Julia Child*." While I waited, she flopped back against the headboard with her arms crossed, scrutinizing me. Soon laughter filled my earpiece. I got up to siphon off anxiety while I talked.

"Gavie, you dog. Who let you out of the kitchen?" More laughter, loud enough for Cammie to react to it across the room. "I know it's late, but I like calling to find out if they got wise to you yet and fired you. But remember, there's always a spot for you at Olive Garden, *mon ami*. Not cooking, though. I mean as a customer." The two of us enjoyed a few moments of back-and-forth, alternately roasting each other and reminiscing, ending with me brushing aside Thénard's gratitude for featuring him on the first season of *Hangry Globe.* "You'd better thank me. I almost didn't get renewed, because of you." That set him off on a string of mock cursing. I sat on the arm of the chair, chuckling. Cammie watched. I pointed to the phone and got to it. "Question, Chef. Are you still serving rabbit in blood sauce?" When Thénard asked if I meant then, I laughed. "No, I don't mean tonight. God, your toque must be too tight. I mean is Lièvre à La Royale still on your menu?" He said yes. I pumped a fist. "Excellent. I may feature it in a special I'm working on. One more thing. A favor? I recommended your place to a friend who's visiting, and I was wondering if he booked a reservation. His name is Tábori. Ignaz Tábori."

The wait wasn't long, but even a few minutes is a stretch when you're holding your breath. Chef Thénard came back with his answer. "He did? That's great to know. May I ask when?" Cammie could no longer sit. She hurried over to put her ear close to the phone. "One p.m. tomorrow. Wonderful."

Better than wonderful. Better than lucky. My riff on Brillat-Savarin's maxim turned out to be better than droll, it was detective work. A day after docking in Provence, our oligarch had arranged to satisfy his rabbit craving at the best place around to indulge it.

"Listen, Gavie, I know it's short notice, but I'm going to be passing through tomorrow. Any chance you can twist an arm, front of house, and squeeze a deuce for lunch?" Chef Thénard's "*mais oui*" sent Cammie into a celebration dance that almost knocked the phone out of my hand.

After I hung up, she hugged me, and we kissed. When things got serious, she drew back. "Hold that thought. I need to report this immediately to the DSA."

I feigned hurt. "Fine. Use me and make me feel cheap."

"Count on it."

twenty-eight

HANGRY GLOBE
Season 4, Ep 4
V.O. for Colombe d'Or Opening
by Sebastian Pike

What's the deal with Americans not eating blood? That observational nugget never made a Seinfeld episode, but it should have, dammit.

"Hellllo...Globin."

The truth is, as a culture, we are not sanguine with the sanguineous. At least not in our diets. The closest we ever get is a Bloody Mary, which, of course, contains no blood. Unless the bartender nicked a finger cutting up the celery. Cheers.

Seriously, why the aversion? Blood is what? Protein and water. Properly cooked, blood brings richness, texture, color, and flavor. As a thickener in sauces, it adds body like flour and less fat than butter.

The rest of the globe embraces blood in its cuisine. There's Oaxacan blood sausage, British black pudding (a mixture of oatmeal, fat, and animal blood). Polish blood soup is a delicious blend of duck blood and poultry broth. Swedish blodplättar is a blood pancake, not too distant from its French cousin, the sanquette, or cooked blood.

Relax, it's food.

Here's the recipe: In a skillet cook shallots, parsley, duck fat, and bread-crumbs. The secret? Add a dash of vinegar to the blood. It'll keep it from curdling. Save room for dessert! From Italy, it's Sanguinaccio dolce, a rich, creamy pudding made of chocolate, sugar, milk, and...wait for it... blood. Guaranteed to satisfy your sweet tooth.

Or fang.

NOVA AND I GOT SOME welcome deliveries overnight: our luggage, dropped off by Hoss the Roadie, and a custom G-Class Mercedes that had been driven down from a CIA motor pool in Milan and left in our hotel garage. The gun-metal-gray Brabus 900 would not only fit in with the luxury vehicles parked at La Colombe d'Or, it had a modified V-12 AMG engine with a top speed of 168 miles per hour and could go zero to sixty in under four seconds.

The souped-up SUV easily navigated the winding ascent to Saint-Paul de Vence in the steep hills above the Mediterranean. The message of its capability wasn't lost on me. This was no toy. It was an exfiltration asset. I swallowed hard at the certainty that shit was getting real.

I worked to appear as relaxed as the upscale day-trippers at the other tables on the patio. Adrenaline is not a calming influence. Some wine would take the edge off, but to stay sharp we stuck with sparkling water. I made a privacy check and kept my voice low. "Assuming we do book you-know-who, I'm itching to call him out on camera. Exposing his corruption. If I gave the Hungarian a blistering fucking hotfoot, would that jeopardize anything?"

"That's what you do, isn't it? Speak truth to power?"

"In spite of my aversion to that shopworn phrase, I do. Are you giving me a yes?"

"More than a yes. And let me put it in a way you won't find hackneyed."

"I did not say hackneyed. Shall we roll back the tape?"

"Shall we let me answer your question? Good. Go with your strong suit. Win another Emmy. Work your mojo."

"For someone who might be moving on, you're sounding a lot like my producer."

"We deal with that after we bring this home."

"Are you always this vague?"

She smirked. "Even my graduation picture from Camp Peary is blurred."

I ordered the *panier de crudités* to start. When it arrived, Cammie gasped. More than a basket, it was the entire Whole Foods produce section. Two heads of celery, a dozen radishes, each the size of a thumb, artichokes, squash, and the best bread you'd ever eat. "My God," she said, "this is humongous."

"Notoriously. I ordered it in case we need to hunker down behind something in a hail of bullets. Tactics and cover, right?"

Cammie took my hand. "Don't be nervous."

"Who said I was nervous?"

"You clown around when you get anxious."

"Profiling my behavior?"

"It's a calling."

"You think you have me all figured out, huh?"

"Pike, you're as transparent as Mrs. Tábori's nightie."

I pulled a face. "You wound me with your smug judgment. Oh, you laugh, but did you consider that maybe I'm only letting you see the surface? How do you know there's not a stone-cold lion in here, pacing at the door of his cage, itching to bust out and take down our prey?"

"You've got the jitters, don't you."

"Tied in goddamned knots."

"Just breathe." Even though she was all about taking it easy, Nova's hand disappeared under the tablecloth when two men approached from behind her. But she relaxed when the couple came into view. They were honeymooning fans from Carmel who wanted a selfie with the celebrity chef. I obliged, and they moved on.

When I sat back down, I adjusted my chair for a better view of the inn. "Gavie says our oligarch has reserved the entire dining room for his party. Personally, I like it better out here."

Cammie took a moment to absorb the surroundings in non-surveillance mode. "I have to say, it is stunning."

"This, for me, this is the attraction of travel. You endure all the heavy lifting to get somewhere—disrupted sleep, middle seats, delayed flights, revolutions, labor strikes, mudslides—but if you're lucky, you find yourself in a place that merges history, nature, and regional cuisine. It's sensual overload. Hear that? Water dribbling in a fountain. Birds out in the scrubby hills. And inhale that. Bougainvillea. Almost like honeysuckle, isn't it?" She didn't answer. "Something wrong?"

"Pike. He's here."

I arched back for a better view of the breezeway leading to the dining room. I had studied Tábori's pictures but didn't see him. I did spot two men in suits that screamed personal security being led by the mâitre d' into the private room. Moments later, one of the protection team emerged. The blocky bruiser disappeared into reception, then returned, cutting a path ahead of our oligarch. But Ignaz Tábori didn't go in. On such a lovely day at such a beautiful venue he paused to take in the terrace, sweeping his sunglasses across the greenery, Fernand Léger's ceramic mural, and the quiet murmurs of pampered diners shaded by white canvas umbrellas.

"Here we go," said Nova in a low voice.

Talons clenched my diaphragm. I slid my chair back and hopped up to wave. Because of Tábori's shades, I couldn't tell if he noticed me—and, if he did, whether he recognized me. Bad form to holler. I started toward him and made it to the middle of the terrace, but the Hungarian turned away and all I got was Tábori's back getting swallowed by the dining room. The door closed. I retreated to our table.

Neither of us could eat. We ordered two espressos and tried to figure out what to do next.

It wasn't like we didn't have a plan. Nova had worked out several. Among the leads was positioning ourselves in reception or at the front steps and act surprised when we saw the oligarch come out. I preferred enlisting Chef Thénard to act as go-between. I lied to him the night before, saying that I knew Tábori. Asking him to usher me into the dining room to greet my imaginary friend would be no big deal.

Cammie tinked her cup down. "He's out." I turned and caught Tábori leaving the dining room. A server directed him to the hall where the arrow pointed toward *hommes*.

"Nature calls billionaires, too." I rose. "Let's see if they unzip one fly at a time like the rest of us."

The squarish security guy I saw escorting Tábori moments before stepped in front of me. "Excuse me, *mon frère*. Pissoir."

"You must wait. It is in use." Denial, delivered in a working-stiff French accent I'd heard from restaurant dishwashers in rural Besançon.

"Not my first visit. I happen to know they have more than one urinal." I made to go around. He blocked me, planting his chest close enough to sniff the spearmint gum he was munching. My heart thumped, but I held my ground. The second bodyguard slid out of the dining room. This one wore a suit one size too large and his shirt had a broken button, a half-moon that barely kept his collar anchored. These two were not top tier, but their coarseness gave me pause about how far to push this. While I was mulling, the door to the loo opened and the Hungarian stepped out.

"Oh my God. Ignaz? Ignaz Tábori?" The guards tightened their blockade, but the cheery voice behind them eased the standoff.

"Chef Pike? Jesus, what are you doing here?" His muscle-by-the-hour parted, leaving room for their boss to pump hands with me.

"I'm in Provence shooting an episode. My producer and I came here to location scout." I waved to Nova across the terrace. "I'm truly bummed we crossed signals about getting you on the show. I heard you were set to do it, then your office said you were on vacation."

"I am." He inclined his head toward the dining room. "I have to get back in there, but I look forward to doing your program. First thing after I return to Budapest. Book it with my office. Enjoy your lunch." He disconnected and started back to his private room.

"Hey, here's an idea. Since we're both in the area, why not do it here in France?"

That stopped Tábori. He angled himself halfway toward me but didn't return. Instead, he closed the subject. "Budapest. Call my chief."

Our mission was riding on this, and I saw it walking away. My brain went on a rampage, frantic for a way to salvage this. The blocky bodyguard spit his gum in a planter and held the door open to let his boss back in. I heard a woman laughing inside the dining room and caught a glimpse of her face at one of the tables. And recognized my biggest fan.

I called out. "*Úr* Tábori? Would it be convenient for me to say a quick hello to your wife? She's so supportive of my show, I can't leave without saying thank you."

The oligarch appraised me, trying not to look like I was dog crap stuck to his shoe. But whether to move me along or to please his wife, he nodded. "That's very kind. But briefly."

The woman shrieked and sloshed her kir royale the instant she set eyes on me. She rushed around the table in shuffled kiddie steps, muttering high-pitched exclamations in Hungarian. After making such a big deal to her husband, I froze and blanked on her name. I bowed slightly. "A pleasure to meet you in person, *Asszony* Tábori."

"You call me Napsugár. That is what my friends call me. Napsugár. You say it."

"Napsugár. Is that because you are sweet?"

She cackled a ribald laugh. Just like her cloying fragrance, a mismatch for the refined room. "You hear him, Ignaz? The chef, he is funny and cute like on his program." Her husband smiled, barely. It occurred to me that his boisterous wife, not security, was what the private dining room was about. "It means sunbeam. You call me that, you call me Napsugár, yes?"

"Yes."

"Yes! Oh, this is so unexpected. Oh, Chef Pike, can you join us for lunch?"

Her husband answered for me. "No, Ilona." At least I got her first name. "Chef Pike has already eaten. He only came to thank you for your support before he left." The look he gave me said to wrap it up.

"Yes, you send many kind emails…. Many, many emails."

Her cheeks reddened. "I send pictures, too."

"Yes, how could I forget the pictures? I replied to you, but I got your away message."

"You wrote to me? I must look at it! Did you see my croquembouche?"

"I'll never forget it."

"I love croquembouche. So festive. So tasty."

Here's the love-hate thing about me. Well, one of them. I love it when I get a devious idea. I hate myself when I put it in action. I figured I'd deal with the self-loathing later. "I would love to make a croquembouche with you, Napsugár."

"Bake with me? You would do that?"

"It would be my honor. And we will…if I am able to shoot a segment with your husband."

"You're coming to Budapest?"

"Sadly, it looks doubtful. Due to scheduling." I took her hands and avoided the glower I knew I would get from the oligarch. "I had hoped we could shoot it now, here in Provence, but Úr Tábori says that's impractical."

"Ignaz?"

"It's all right, Napsugár. This is your vacation." I let go of her hands and started to leave.

"Ignaz? Chef Pike himself would cook for us."

At the door I stopped and turned. "And bake. With you as my on-camera sous chef."

Ilona Tábori spoke her husband's name once more. This time not as a question. And her tone carried the gravity of ultimatum only known to the long-married. One word that tallied the balance of their emotional accounts. "Ignaz."

When I stepped out of the dining room, our lunch table had been flipped to another party and Nova was standing in the breezeway. "I was starting to wonder if I should toss another flash-bang in there. Well? Tell me."

"It's on."

"Seriously?"

"For tomorrow."

"Holy crap. You are amazing." She hugged me, then pulled back and wrinkled her nose. "What's that smell?"

"Eau de Napsugár. The fragrance that saved our mission."

twenty-nine

After all the days of anxiety, of hunting, of searching, of retribution, of hoping, and of battling, a mere four hours after contact we were back down in Nice setting the stage for the operation. To gear up for my role, I made a walk-through of the kitchen of le Vide. The hip brasserie between the Ópera de Nice and Place Masséna was closed to customers in order to prepare for the next day's segment with guest of honor Ignaz Tábori. For his inconvenience, the restaurateur went home with a fat check written by *Hangry Globe* producer Cameron Nova. Everything looked workable. I inspected the salamander, the lowboy, and the induction range, then prowled along the pass trying to find a camera angle to tie in the house. When Cammie stepped over, I told her, "I could get used to this."

"Good kitchen?"

"I mean the budget. Four years on basic cable, I've never been able to buy out a location. I wish to thank the intelligence services of the United States government. Do I send a note, or is the CIA recording this?"

"Sh." Latrell and Hoss came in lugging light stands and tripods. "Easy."

"Oh, right. 'Cause then I'd have to kill them." A crash inside the walk-in was followed by a barrage of cursing. Nova followed me over for a damage appraisal. A middle-aged guy, bald but for a horseshoe of gingery side hair, knelt on the floor using the sides of his hands to corral the ooze from the two dozen eggs he'd dropped. Muttering another expletive, he arm-swiped gleaming sweat off this forehead. "How'd we end up with George Costanza as our Food Sarge?"

Chuck Ludik felt wrong on sight when I'd first met him in the pantry an hour before. The guy didn't give off the culinary vibe. I had a sixth sense for that, and picked up none of it from the new Sarge. His résumé— a culinary degree from a community college and a stint as sous chef at a private country club—didn't blow me away; however, two seasons working prep on *Chopped* did. But could this be that same guy? This unhip, round-shouldered, goateed, short fella with a gut? Chuck looked more like the schlub who'd take your picture at the DMV, not the pro who could fire eight redundant versions of the same dish in proper sequence of doneness under pressure, revealing a succession of camera-worthy creations. Voilà!

Chuck Ludik had no Voilà! in him.

After the cleanup, I watched him prep onions. I needed three pounds thinly sliced for one of my recipes next day. First, I had to tell him to wash his hands unless he wanted to kill someone with the raw egg. "Thin, Chuck. The thinner they are, the better they'll caramelize." He held a sample up like the kid at the deli counter. I shook no. It was thick as a coaster. His next cut split the onion, mangling it. "I'll take this. We need to slice it, not perform a satanic mutilation." I got out my chef's knife and ran it on the steel. Instead of gutting the new Sarge from belt to brisket like I wanted to, I sliced an onion whisper thin. "Like that," I said, and walked off.

I huddled with Nova in the pantry. "I don't know where you found this guy, but he is not Food Sarge grade. He's the gym teacher who got asked to teach chem class."

She closed the door. "I hear you. Chuck Ludik is here for other reasons. He speaks Russian and is security trained."

"They let this saggy-pants dimwit have a gun?"

"Trust me, we get this exfiltration done, you won't see him again."

"Oo, I like the vague menace of that." I made crazy eyes. "Disappear him, Spy Cam, disappear him bad."

After the setup and food prep were done, Nova and I made plans with the crew to meet for drinks later. Immediately after they left for their hotel in the Old Port district, two familiar faces arrived: DSA Espy and the security agent, PPO Harrison. Tailing behind them were a half dozen other men and women. Like Harrison, all were dressed in civvies but unable to mask the paramilitary vibe. A handful more filed in and took seats at the brasserie's tables. But these folks didn't carry themselves like CrossFit junkies. They looked like everyday tourists, quotidians who wouldn't turn a head. Amused, I even recognized a few from the Colombe d'Or terrace, including the gay honeymooners from Carmel. Cammie noticed me noticing and smiled. "When it comes to security, we know how to blend in."

"Know what hurts? I really believed those lovebirds wanted a selfie with me."

Espy stepped up to us, all smiles, but put his attention on me. "Cool audible you called up on the hill today."

"Props to Nova on that. If she hadn't shown me the email pics of Tábori's wife, no way I'd have recognized her. That's how I was able to jump on it." The DSA didn't even give Nova a passing glance. A Zamboni maneuver, icing her same as at the safe house outside Marseille. Espy kept his attention on me. "Well, you picked up the fumble and scored."

"Assuming he shows."

"If he doesn't, we know where he's staying now. We slapped a tail on him from Saint-Paul de Vence to the compound in Éze he's leasing, borrowing, whatever. Never mind that. Let's stay positive. Cameron, I assume you have a plan?"

"Yes, sir. Crew arrives here tomorrow at nine to set for a noon lunch shoot with Tábori."

"Táboris plural," I added. "To make this happen, I promised the missus I'd show her the ins and outs of the elusive croquembouche."

Espy chortled. "Sounds like a Kama Sutra sex position." He chortled alone and seemed oblivious to that. "Continue, Nova."

"Chef Pike will sit for lunch over there with the oligarch, his wife, and his minder from the Kremlin to conduct his eater-view, surrounded by our cast of diners." She indicated the undercover tourists at the tables. "When that's in the can, he'll move to the kitchen to record a baking segment with Tábori's wife."

I covered my eyes with both hands. "We may actually even record it. Who knows?"

PPO Harrison spoke from behind, startling me. "We'll use that distraction to effectuate the exfiltration."

"When you say that, it sounds scary official. What am I supposed to do?"

"Chef, you will stay in the kitchen looking pretty and keeping busy. My team has this. We chose this venue for a reason. The kitchen is open but with obstructed views to and from the dining room."

"I noticed. I'm killing myself trying to frame a tie-in shot."

"Might as well stand down from that. The view to the back hall is also obstructed, but not enough. Overnight we'll install a curtain. The hall leads to a door that opens onto a one-way alley. We'll have control of traffic with a fake pothole repair crew. Once the Russian package exits, it's into a honeycomb of narrow streets, easily blocked by pulling our delivery trucks and vans across when the exfiltration vehicle passes. The various cross streets between here and the POD—point of departure—will be similarly cut off in the event hostile chase vehicles attempt an end-around pursuit."

"You've done this before, haven't you?"

"A time or two."

"Where are you taking him? Airport? Train? We're near the water. Speedboat?" All three stared, acting as if I had never spoken. "If you need me, I'll be in the kitchen. Looking pretty."

WHILE SSO NOVA AND PPO HARRISON convened a meeting to brief the two dozen operatives who would play the roles of diners, waitstaff, street maintenance workers, drivers, even sidewalk *flâneurs*, Gregg Espy sidled up to me while I was in the pantry, writing. "You busy?"

"Finishing the menu for tomorrow so my knucklehead Food Sarge can screw up his prep."

"It's a beautiful evening. Twilight in the South of France. Let's take a walk."

We slipped out the back door. I envisioned the risky transfer that would take place on that same spot the next day and got a flash of the yips I felt in a delivery room once, helping a friend. In a not-so-weird way, this echoed that. Anticipation. A countdown. Wheels in motion to an inevitable culmination. While I wrangled my anxiety, Espy busied himself studying a young woman strutting the sidewalk. "Is she one of our extras?"

"Extras. Hilarious." But the CIA man didn't crack a smile. "Never thought of it like that. Like we're casting a movie."

"I'm thinking *Mission: Impossible*. A lot of moving parts."

"Nervous?"

"Yes."

"Good. It keeps you on your toes." We reached the Fontaine du Soleil as the lights popped on, illuminating the statue of Apollo. "I got some good news. Arkady Glinka is wheels up from Moscow-Domodedovo. His Nice ETA is oh-one-forty. It's on."

"Ask a stupid question?" Still pissed at the blowback I caught from him when I asked about the audit, I asked anyway. "Why all this? Why not simply nab Glinka at the airport?"

"Because there is no simply when he has a security detail. Translation: thug minders. Yes, he's in Putin's inner circle, but with the suspicion that's been cast on him by leaks from his blackmailer, Vlady's FSO goons will be watching Glinka as much as they would us."

I couldn't seem to fill my lungs. "You mean Glinka's going to bring armed company to our segment?"

Instead of answering, the DSA waited for a couple swanked up for an opera date to pass, then walked me the opposite way, following the streetcar tracks up into Place Masséna. "Tell me how it's going with Nova." It wasn't a question, and my people sense told me this was the reason for the stroll at dusk, away from the others.

"She's evolved into a good producer." A weak reply, so I added, "Given time, she'll be a great one."

"Like I give a shit about that. Sorry to be blunt, but I have doubts about her."

"Yeah, I kinda got that. You made it a point on our drive the other day." After Cammie told me about Espy's rejected proposition, I took his smack talk with a grain of salt.

"Well, this is the deeper dive, Chef. Have you seen her acting suspiciously?"

"Gregg, she's a spy."

"Any unexplained absences, even for a few minutes?" When I shook my head, the DSA pressed. "I tracked your phone. You spent an hour at a marina outside Monaco."

"We were scoping out Tábori's yacht."

"One hour?"

"I ran into an old deckhand pal I knew from another yacht."

"Which one?"

"Not Tábori's. One from a while ago."

"Whose?"

"A rock star. Guy named Kogg."

Espy knew all about Astrid. All he said was, "Ah," then plugged onward. "You also went to Menton. Menton?"

"To see another pal from Kogg's yacht."

"Who?"

"His name's Cedric. Cedric Devlin."

"Interesting."

"Interesting, why?"

The DSA didn't elaborate. "You're visiting old friends while you were supposed to be tracking down Tábori?"

"Which we did. Successfully. So, what's the issue, Gregg?"

Espy kept steamrolling. "Nova have any meetings or encounters with people?"

"Not that I noticed."

"Flimsy answer."

"I'm not her nanny."

Espy tongued the inside of his cheek, thinking something over. In a decisive move, he got out his phone and tapped the screen a few times. "Let me get specific. You ever see this guy?" The picture he flashed was a street surveillance shot of the man who tailed Nova to the wine bar in Arles. This pic gave off a sinister vibe. A tough guy on the prowl looking for trouble in a foreign city, a wisp of exhaled frost vapor, the collar of a black leather coat turned up against the snow. "Any hits?"

Don't ask me to explain why, I only knew what I felt. An instinct to protect Cammie, right or wrong. "Nope," I said as offhandedly as I could deliver it.

"Look again. Memorize him. His work name is Farrel. A CIA contractor who is dirty. Recently gigged for the GRU in Ukraine recruiting locals to destabilize our ally. If you see him, steer clear and contact me immediately—and alone—meaning no Nova involvement."

My turn to be blunt. "What the hell?"

The spymaster stepped close, voice low. "We both know someone is trying to screw this mission."

"I vote for Ringstad."

"A given. But alone? And if not, who is working with Ringstad?"

"And by 'who' you mean…?"

"I've got my eye on a number of folks. But let's walk through the little misfortunes that have befallen this operation as related to Specialized Skills Officer Nova. Paris: one of our most trusted joes gets shot making a brush pass to you, on whose watch? Aigues-Mortes: Emil Dard buys it on a meetup with whom? Then a certain deep-cover celebrity chef gets bagged on that same live drop accompanied by none other than…?"

"I owe her my life."

"Yeah, yeah, the Ringstad rescue."

"Don't brush that aside. Cammie Nova saved my ass."

"Really? Or did she buy credibility? How did Ringstad manage to give the slip?"

"Training. You said he was with some elite Norwegian outfit. Cammie helping him makes no sense."

"God, you are new at this. One thing you either learn—or die—is that when things don't make sense, that's because they're not supposed to look like they do. That's what covert means. The best truth is only apparent. It hides the thing that fits inside the thing that doesn't fit."

"Sorry, but when did we go from *Mission: Impossible* to *Dr. Strangelove*?"

"You think this is a joke? Laugh at this. SSO Nova's fiancé was a Russian plant in the Agency."

"Who betrayed her."

Espy stopped walking. "She told you? Jesus H."

"People tell me things. It's why I score on my TV interviews. You should watch sometime."

"Then I guess she also told you her betrothed smuggled her a note out of our detainee interrogation site in Maryland."

"You know about that?"

Espy smiled. "Do now." I cratered inside. Espy tricked me into confirming Cammie's secret. The DSA dropped his grin. "Did she tell you what he wrote?"

"No. Why would she tell me that?"

"Funny. It's almost like she doesn't want you to know. And why would that be? Russian double somehow manages to get her a note from a secure facility? The possibilities, I'm afraid, are not endless." The commuter tram approached. He led me off the tracks. "Oh. That's top secret. That I know about her ex's note. Tell no one. Especially not her."

"Why are you telling me?"

"Two reasons. First, so you can alert me if you see her do anything off base. And second, to warn you. I'm ratcheting this up from the friendly tip I gave you in Paris. Do not trust her." He paused for emphasis. "I'll toss in a third, since she's confiding secrets to you, oh trusted TV interviewer. Whatever you do, don't sleep with her." Espy fixed me with an appraising gaze. "You didn't sleep with her, did you?" I shook my head until I realized how much I was overplaying. DSA Espy smiled. "Uh-huh. When you two are in the afterglow tonight, get her to talk about what was in that note from her so-called ex. You can brief me in the morning."

We reached a grouping of café tables where the plaza ended at a cross street. A blue Volvo V90 idled there. PPO Harrison at the wheel. Espy didn't get in yet. He stepped close again, invading my personal space. "Want to hear what I meant by interesting? Your pal Cedric Devlin was killed last night in his apartment in Menton. Neighbors heard screams and called the gendarmes. He had been tortured to death. By electrocution."

I blurted louder than I'd intended. "Ringstad! He's here?"

"We're cutting this close." Espy shook my hand. "Big day tomorrow." He paused at the passenger door before he opened it. "Chef? Watch your back. A man who works around knives should know that."

thirty

The *Hangry Globe* traveling company met for Crew Cocktails that evening at one of the open-air bars lining both sides of Cours Saleya, a landmark promenade that stretches for blocks through Old Nice. Middays, the pedestrian mall hosts the Marché aux Fleurs, one of the great culinary markets in France. Stalls run the center strip, selling fresh flowers and produce. After dark, it's a hot spot for couples and singles to shout over megabass and *oonce-oonce-oonce*. Floral fragrances by day; Axe body spray by night.

I was last to arrive at the pagan rite of bonding, coming straight from my unsettling stroll with Gregg Espy. Cammie was already there sandwiched between Latrell and Hoss at the far side of a pair of four-tops they had jammed together on the patio of Les 3 Diables. She and I traded perfunctory nods across a tablescape of beer bottles, wine glasses, and frozen cocktails the color of a Chernobyl discharge. We kept our acknowledgments slight to thwart gossip. It helped that the only remaining seat was eight feet away from her. The chair back pressed against my burn from the stun belt, and I shifted, trying not to moan. Cammie locked eyes on me for appraisal while I yelled my drink order over the homicide-by-karaoke of "Bohemian Rhapsody" pounding out from the indoor bar.

At first, I worried that her study of me was heat fueled, and it would give us up as a couple. But except for new the Food Sarge, who was pretty much clueless to everything but the Food Sarge, the crew must have guessed something was going on. After all, the host and the producer were staying in one hotel while they were lodged in another. Road Rules applied, though. If they suspected anything, they kept it to themselves. Nothing to see here.

My beer arrived. While I led the traditional group toast, the story in Cammie's eyes unsettled me. It wasn't heat. She was looking for tells about my disappearing act with the DSA.

Could she see how much Espy got into my head?

Try as I did, I couldn't kick him out. Even though I felt I could take Nova at face value, he'd embedded a pernicious nugget of what-if.

To quiet my brain, I discounted Espy. Not as a leader, but as a casualty of his profession. Suspicion was a side effect of the gig and fostered paranoia. All I had to do to prove it was play back the DSA's *Strangelove* spew, the pretzel logic of the truth hiding the thing that fits inside the thing that doesn't fit. But then I wondered, Could that paranoia be hiding an actual truth? Was Espy right to suspect a double on our inside?

I surveyed my crew. Nova apart, could one of them be working against this mission? Latrell, no. Hoss, no. Declan, no. Marisol—shit, now I was doing it. These were my peeps, my Globers. After years of laughing, having each other's backs, smelling each other's BO on the roadie bus, what was I thinking? The Food Sarge made a walrus beer belch. Hmm. The Food Sarge. Nope, scratch Chuck Ludik. Not just because he was inept. What-the-Chuck was too new.

What about someone else? Someone not in the traveling company? PPO Harrison. Talk about the potential to be hiding inside an apparent truth. Where did the paramilitary protection officer first make the scene? Paris. When things started getting deadly. Kurt Harrison, always

Johnny-on-the-spot. A little too cool. A little too present... I stopped. I was doing it again. If paranoia was a virus, suspicion was a bioweapon.

"Ready to go?" Cammie Nova stood over me. Everyone else had hit the pissoirs before making the trek around Castle Hill to their hotel.

"Yuh. Unless you'd rather tag in on the karaoke."

"I'd rather get alone with you." I followed her between tables and out onto the Cours Saleya. We passed a strolling accordionist who nodded approvingly at us, the two lovers. American tourists on a carefree vacation in Provence.

The apparent truth.

WHEN WE ENTERED HER HOTEL ROOM, Cammie started punching a code in the room safe. "I've got a bottle chilling in the mini-fridge but no corkscrew. Want to see if you've got one?"

Housekeeping had left the connecting doors open, and I went into my room to check the minibar. Passing the bed, I stopped. My toilet kit rested on the pillow. Odd. Why would housekeeping move it from the bathroom? I went in to hook it on the towel rack. It felt heavy. I unzipped the case and saw why.

Inside, I found the snub-nose PPO Harrison tried to give me on training day. The K6s was nested in its nylon pocket holster. I took it out and checked the cylinder. Loaded. Plus, there was a box of .357 cartridges in my kit. A note penciled on a sheet from my hotel pad said, "You never know." No signature.

A minute later, standing in the connecting doorway, I said, "Hey, look what I found." I held up a corkscrew.

I didn't tell her about the gun. If it had only been the snubbie and its ammo in that bag, I might have. But the note.

You never know.

If it had come from Harrison, wouldn't he have signed? No signature smelled like Espy. From my close-combat trainer, it meant a general caution; from the DSA, it grew more charged. I didn't buy Espy's lethal warning about Nova. But to bring up the revolver to her meant a deeper conversation than I had the bandwidth for. I wasn't proud of it, but I surrendered to the male strand of DNA of benign avoidance. I'd slip the K6s back to Harrison in the morning.

"Good timing. All clean." She stashed her bug sweeper. I opened the local rosé and poured.

"To tomorrow."

"You're a better chef than a sommelier."

There was enough cork in our wine to fill Sammy Sosa's bat. "Hotel corkscrews. You know."

"It's a poor workman who blames his tools." Cammie smiled and fished out some floaters. Her cell vibrated. "The DSA." She read the text and tapped acknowledgment. "Our man is en route from Moscow."

"So I hear." Her eyes narrowed. They stayed on me while she plucked a cork crumb off her tongue. "Espy told me. On our walk."

It gave her pause, but not much. "He told you before me? That petty shit." She sat with her wine and patted the cushion beside her. "Not bad enough the big dog's made a career of undermining me every chance. Now he's playing you against me because he can't stand to see it's all coming together."

"Why wouldn't he want that?" I sat next to her, and Cammie slid against me. Her familiarity felt natural. I leaned into the warmth coming off her.

"Because it's all happening without him. Espy is on the road to faded glory with none to show. His legacy is zip. A bland caretaker. He marginalizes me so he can claim credit. He wants a scalp before he rides into the sunset." She cocked an eye. "Still, that was a long walk just to tell you our man's airborne."

"All the better to mess with you, I guess." I hid the lower half of my face in my rosé, sloshing some on my thigh.

"What's with you? Are you tweaked about tomorrow? Don't be. If this goes according to plan, the crew will never even know it's happening."

"If."

"It will." Cammie set her glass down and squared herself to me for a reading. "What." I sat there, my avoidance no longer feeling so benign. She took my hand.

There's no discounting chemistry. Her magnetism drew me closer. Yet holding her gaze wasn't easy. I knew this was a moment to get right or regret. The sort of thing, if done wrong, a man carried forever into the dark hours. I've always been guided by Hemingway's maxim that what's moral or immoral is what makes you feel good or bad afterward. That's always been my compass. I saw no reason to ignore it. "Espy told me to hold this in confidence. But I can't live with myself if I keep it secret from you."

I told her everything he'd said. Nova let me download without interruption. Not when I shared Espy's suspicions over her joes who died in Paris and Aigues-Mortes, not when he speculated she and Ringstad might have a deal, not even his mention of her ex, the Russian plant. Although her mouth did curve downward at that one. When I finished, she closed her eyes a few seconds to process, then opened. "Did he say anything else?"

I nodded. "Three things. Cedric Devlin is dead."

"Oh no. When? How?"

"They got him last night in his apartment."

"Who got him?"

"He'd been tortured to death. Electrocution."

"Damn. Did you tell Espy Cedric may have seen Ringstad?"

"No. He was too busy making his parting shot. Telling me to watch my back."

"Again?"

"And he told me not to sleep with you."

Her laugh burst out, a cleansing release. I was too uptight to join in. "Aw, come on, that's funny." I wagged my head side to side, all the joviality I could muster. Still, I didn't open the can of worms about the gun. I wanted to be finished unburdening for the night.

Nova had other ideas.

"Let's circle back to what Espy said about my ex."

"Are you interrogating me?"

She chuckled. "Can't help it. I'm a pig after truffles. Espy. Walk me through the conversation about me and my ex. Every inch."

I dropped my chin to my chest to summon the exchange. "He initiated. He said your ex was a Russian plant. And then he got in a twist because I said I already knew."

"OK… Keep going."

"We got into the note your fiancé smuggled to you."

She jerked upright. "Whoa, whoa, whoa. You told Espy about that?"

"He, um, sort of knew."

"Explain sort of."

"He mentioned something about it, and I said something like, 'Oh you know about that?' and he was all gloating, 'I do now.' Shit, I'm sorry, Cammie."

"Son of a bitch took you fishing and hooked what he was after."

"He tricked me."

"All technique designed to throw you off. Here's a timely piece of advice from the Field Interrogation Manual: 'Never answer more than you are asked.'"

"Again, my bad."

Cammie pinched another of the endless flakes of cork out of my glass. "The good thing is you didn't hold back from me. I know what I'm dealing with now."

"I couldn't hold back. Not from you. We're past that."

"Are we?"

I smiled. "I've learned never to answer more than I'm being asked, so yes."

She cupped her fingers under my chin, and we kissed. An incoming email chimed from my room. I didn't want to budge from her, but on the eve of the mission, Cammie said I had better check. I returned in seconds grinning at my iPad. "Reply to my note to Ilona Tábori."

"What did she say?"

"No content, only a photo. You don't want to see it." But Cammie did want to.

Ilona's pic was similar to her others, except this was in a black lace teddy, with some areolae reveal. "Good lord." She handed the tablet back like she might catch something from it. When I closed Napsugár's email, I noticed I had something in my spam folder. Cammie read my reaction. "What is it?"

"Email from CDevlin_at_Sea. That's Cedric. Time stamped yesterday, a couple of hours after we left him. Subject: 'A Memory of Better Days.'" After two missed taps, I fumbled the email open to a photo of Astrid and me toasting the camera with glasses of beer.

"Something good, I hope."

I sat down with it. "Wow, I remember this. Cedric took it the weekend I met up with Astrid when Kogg's yacht was in Hamburg. Happy hour on the rooftop bar of the Blockbräu brewery. Poor Cedric must have sent it to make amends after our shitty visit." The moment it captured brought me a smile. A melancholy one, but at least a smile.

I shared the screen with Cammie. "It was a fun day. And a stunning view. Right on the Elbe. See the port?" I spread to zoom and enlarged the freighters and container ships across the river. But zooming in also brought forward the rooftop's background. My breath caught. At a table behind Astrid and me, far at the end of the deck, turned from the camera but recognizable, sat Cammie Nova.

thirty-one

Thunderstruck, my gaze darted from the iPad to Cammie, back to the iPad, then back to her. One was Nova in three-quarter profile, avoiding the lens; the other was Nova three inches away at the same angle, avoiding me. When I finally could speak, I didn't sound like myself. What words I summoned came out dry and abraded. "…What the hell?"

While I sat with my head spinning, Nova had been organizing herself. She must have been. She came off so centered. "This is not the time to discuss this."

"Christ, how can you even say that?"

"I'm telling you, this is not the time." No strain, all composure.

"Seems perfect to me." I held up the photo. "Not waiting on this."

"You have to. This feels like a sucker punch, I get that. And it breaks my heart for what it must be doing to you, but right now is when we need to avoid distraction and keep our eyes on tomorrow."

"The mission."

"Yes, exactly."

"Fuck the mission. I want to know what this is about." I whacked the iPad with a knuckle. So what if I shattered the screen. "What were you doing? Tailing me? Hamburg was, what…a year and a half ago? More? I want an answer. And don't tell me it was a coincidence."

"Pike, listen to me. Don't go over the top. This has to wait."

"Like when you and Espy held back Glinka's name? Meanwhile Ringstad turns me into a human light bulb."

"That was different."

"Damn straight. That was about your mole. This is about me. And, for who the hell knows why—you. And you're not talking. And calling it a sucker punch… That so minimizes it. I believed in what was going on here. Between us. But this? Can't you see how this knocks the ground right out from under me?" The room became small, suffocating. I got up to pace, shaking my head and hissing "sucker punch" to the rug.

"You know, since I was a kid, I've been into the whole spy thing. Why do you think I devour those books like crazy? Shit, when I'm in London, I even go to Ian Fleming's old barber shop in Mayfair. Call it geeky, but it's one reason this…little diversion…intrigued me. If you haven't guessed, the novelty's wearing off." I opened the sliding glass door. I needed air. "I'm not naïve. I know double dealing is baked into the job. And have I witnessed the full spectacle this week. The office intrigues, the information withholding, the backstabbing…the exploitation of the vulnerable…the death of innocents. I can almost deal with the culture of lies. But now, with us?" I crash-landed back on the couch. "Do you even know the CIA motto? It's from the Bible."

Cammie said, "'And ye shall know the truth—'"

"'—and the truth shall make you free.' I'd laugh if it weren't so twisted. I mean, what do we value if we don't value the truth? What's true is our core. It's who we are. What we believe. What we do. Rather than what we're willing to do. Now I've smelled a dumpster load. How expediency makes it A-OK with everybody. Like the real motto is 'Life is short, then you lie.'" A quivering inhale, and I downshifted. After I got myself composed, I turned to Cammie. "Where is the honor? What happened to principles? Who on God's wretched mistake called Earth are the good guys?"

We sat through a fragile silence. Then she spoke in a ragged voice. "Don't you think I'm one?"

"I want to. And I have thought that since we met. But then I see this." I lifted the Hamburg photo and plopped it back on the cushion.

Nova pondered another beat. "All right. It's against my judgment— but in the interest of clearing the air, I'll let you in." I didn't reply. I waited. "The idea of embedding in your show wasn't recent. I got it during your second season. The Agency is a bloated bureaucracy, so it was a tough sell. They gave me the go-ahead conditioned on two things. First, that I got some culinary training and second, that I shadow you and thoroughly vet you."

"You had me in your sights back then?"

"I told you; I am thorough."

"How long did you tail me?"

"Long enough to see who you made contact with, to watch you for criminal or clandestine activities…"

That one took me aback. "Clandestine activities? Me?"

"If our side could think of something like this, so could the bad guys. This had to be ironclad. That's as far as I go."

"One more thing."

"You're not dropping this, are you."

"The crystal meth verdict. Was all this how you found out Kogg didn't do drugs?"

"Please, take a breath." She put a hand on my arm. I didn't pull away. By coming clean Cammie had settled me down. "Didn't I promise to dig into all that, after? It still stands."

I believed her. Not just because I wanted to, I needed to. "Sorry I went off on a rant."

"Totally understandable. That picture was a shock. I'm sorry, too. For your upset."

"It freaked me out to think you were, I dunno, up to something."
Thank Gregg Espy for planting that seed. "I can't stand to be lied to,
including by omission."

"Don't you think it eats me up not to tell you everything?"

"Have you told me everything?"

"Of course not." We laughed. I felt lighter by a ton. Cammie inclined
her face toward me and raised her eyes to mine. "Are we going to be OK?"

"You mean the mission?"

"I mean us."

The rhyme of that moment, its curve back to the last conversation I
ever had with Astrid on a different eve of peril, almost became too much
to bear. Enough to make me examine my role in my life's infinite loop. If
I'd learned anything during a year of rumination since Athens, it's this:
be careful of the words you leave people with. Life is short, death is a
prankster. This time I would do it better. "We're going to be OK," I said.
Then I closed Cedric's picture of Astrid and me and Cammie. "All I ever
want is the truth."

"And you will get it. Promise." We found our smiles and kissed.

EVEN THOUGH THE LUNCH SEGMENT was booked for noon, at eight thirty the
next morning my crew was already adjusting LED panels and ring lights
for Ignaz Tábori's interview at le Vide. Cameras were white balanced and
batteried up. Spares were getting charged. Latrell set two tripods for his
Gemini A-cam, one in the kitchen, one at Tábori's dining table. Marisol
would rove. Declan set up his audio shop on a breakfront against a far
wall. He tested the three wireless mics the Táboris and I would be wearing. Check, check, and check. His backup fish pole leaned in the corner.

In the kitchen I tasted the redundant main course dishes the new
Food Sarge had prepped from my pissaladière recipe. The onions were a

little thick but would do. The air carried the tang of something burning. I heard cursing. Chuck Ludik discarded a tray of burnt choux pastry into the garbage. "What's your oven setting, Chuck?" I refused to call him Sarge.

"Supposed to be three-seventy-five, from the recipe."

"What. Is. Your. Setting?"

Ludik waddled over to the oven and peered at the thermometer. "This shit's all Celsius. I've got it at two-thirty, give or take."

"Three-seventy-five Fahrenheit converts to one-ninety-five-five, my man. Back it off." I plucked a dead chou from the trash. "And these aren't only burnt, the tops are like alligator skin. Switch the pastry bag to a Wilton 1A Round tip." What-the-Chuck's response was to silently mouth Wilton 1A. I hollered to the ceiling. "Hoss?"

"Yo," came from the back hall.

"Come show our culinary producer what a Wilton 1A Round tip looks like."

Espy and Harrison arrived together an hour later. The crew, alert to strangers, cornered me to ask who they were. Nova intercepted and told them the minister of agriculture's advance security. That pretext provided cover for the logistical business those two would be up to. Cammie also spared me from telling my folks another lie.

She ushered her DSA aside with a professional greeting and status report. "A few food glitches but everything else is good to go."

"Pour a bowl of muesli for all I care."

I tried to lighten him up. "Careful, Gregg, don't make me hangry."

"Like I give a rat's ass about that, either." He beckoned us to follow him into the private dining room. When we got there, he closed the glass door. "Dispatch just came in. Our Agency ops in Russia detained the blackmailer."

"That's great," I said. "So, the pressure's off."

"Let me finish. The blackmailer set it up with a courier to deliver a sealed message to the Kremlin in the event he didn't check in. It's a matter of hours before Putin is tipped off about Glinka. By three o'clock his own security team will probably kill him. If we're lucky. Worse, he gets flown home for an old-fashioned torture party in which he'll give up every secret he has. Including all our agents. We do this today or the shit storm's coming and coming hard." He pressed Nova. "Anything at all from Tábori confirming?"

She answered with a head shake. "How about our package? Did Glinka arrive on schedule?"

Espy barely tolerated the effort to acknowledge. "Would I be here if he hadn't?" He flung the door open. We followed him out into the brasserie's dining room.

"Chef Pike." PPO Harrison chopped air toward the breakfront Declan was using for his gear. "What's this here?"

"Audio department."

"That goes away. We'll need unobstructed access to the back hall."

"Woop." Nova held out her phone. The screen lit up with an incomer. "Budapest area code. Stand by." She stepped outside to take it, leaving me alone with Kurt Harrison for the first time. The security agent reacted to my stare.

"Issue, Chef?" That little gun badgered my mind all night. I had locked it in the Brabus and wanted to tell the PPO to take it back. But Gregg Espy busted the moment.

"Let's not stand here with our thumbs up our cracks." He strode to the front door. Harrison and I followed him onto the sidewalk. When we got there, Nova was already pressing End.

Espy maintained his edge. "Let's go, let's hear it."

"Tábori's chief of staff. Change of plans. He wants to do this up at his rental."

"Did you tell them we were all set here?"

"I did, sir. He said one o'clock at his villa. Take it or leave it. I took it."

A hard silence followed, broken by yours truly. "Good answer."

thirty-two

Maestro Leonard Bernstein once said, "To achieve great things, two things are needed: a plan and not quite enough time." We certainly overachieved in the up-against-the-clock department. Unfortunately, our plan was in tatters. While the spooks regrouped, all it took was a few short words from me on my way in—"Strike and load"—and the pace inside the brasserie shifted from orderly engagement to controlled chaos. I held the light panel at the main dining table while Latrell unscrewed it from the stand. "Company move to our guest's residence." I didn't know the reason for the change of venue, so I joked it off. "Guess he didn't find le Vide sufficiently oligarch-y." As I passed the LED to Marisol, I said, "We're wheels up in one hour, so none of your usual fiddlefarting."

"Yes, Chef!" She shouted it like a skittish Gordon Ramsay contestant, volleying my playful sarcasm right back at me as she hustled off to pack up the gear.

Espy, Nova, and Harrison had isolated themselves in the glassed-in private dining room where they could huddle confidentially. Tense words were flying when I opened the door to let myself in. Everything paused until the knob clicked, then the assault on Nova resumed in full. Espy's voice lashed the air like razor wire. "Well? What is your contingency?

You're the specialized skills officer. Now would be the time to show some skills." *Au revoir* to Gregg Espy's collegiate cool.

"We're going to need to ad-lib, sir."

"Fuck me. You don't have a plan B?"

That was the first time I'd heard the F-word come out of Espy. I tossed out some levity to defuse the tension. "I'd cut her some slack. Seems to me this eventuality isn't even in the alphabet."

"Later for this." The DSA took out a menthol inhaler stick and sniffed each nostril, saying to Nova, "Right now let's assess ramifications. I'll deal with you at the postmortem."

If his threat intimidated her, she didn't show it. The SSO stayed pro and recited next steps. "We scrap all the logistical support. Eighty-six all our extras and floaters. Broom the fake diners, the fake street workers, the fake *flâneurs*."

"Affirm." Kurt Harrison stood behind us. We turned to the paramilitary protection officer. "And pulling the sniper."

I almost laughed, then caught myself. "There's a sniper?" Harrison whispered something to his collar and beckoned me to the window. A dude in a backwards ball cap two-finger saluted from a high floor across the street. I recognized him from the safe house in Marseille. A black rifle strap banded the floral print of PPO Ortiz's Hawaiian shirt.

The door jerked open. The Food Sarge blundered in, oblivious to his gaffe. "Hey, Cookie, the fuck am I supposed to do with all that choux pastry I got cooling?"

"Rest them another half hour, then load them in empty egg crates—and carefully." Ludik walked back to the kitchen, leaving the door wide open.

Espy pushed it closed. "Screw the damn food. Who cares now?"

"You should." I took a last look at the sniper and moved back to face the DSA. "If we show up without a credible meal presentation, our cover is in jeopardy, along with your man from Moscow."

Nova stood with me. "Pike's right. It needs to pass muster for the two most important fans this show has right now."

"And that would be Ignaz and Ilona Tábori. If they smell a rat, well…"

"All right, all right. But it all means squat if we don't have a mission plan now that ours augered in."

"We draw a new one." Nova pulled a chair up next to Harrison. "Kurt, let's see what you've got on the residence and start with that."

"I've got the site plan you asked me to pull from the Alpes-Maritimes property recorder yesterday after we tailed Tábori home from lunch." Harrison knew the crap Nova was taking from Espy, so he was clearly highlighting her fore-planning for the DSA's ears. He withdrew an architectural drawing of the house from a satchel and spread it on the table. "This is an exploded view. Three stories. We'll want to focus on the ground floor, I guess." He used a ballpoint to indicate each: "Kitchen, pantry, dining. Which looks like a great room leading out to a veranda. Hallway access off the kitchen and pantry leads to the rear driveway and garages."

"Plural?"

"Two-vehicle attached, here, connecting to laundry. Five-vehicle detached across the turnaround. This will give you a better sense." The PPO woke his iPad and brought up an aerial photograph of a walled villa with three buildings, two pools, tennis courts, and a putting green.

I leaned for a look. "Which one is Tábori's?"

"All of them."

"Looks like a resort. There's no business like oligarch business."

Harrison ignored my color commentary. "This is the main mansion we were looking at. Here's the offset garage. Over here is guest quarters-slash-hospitality for the upper pool."

Espy borrowed the tablet. "I'm not liking the setup. Too isolated."

"Exactly their idea." Nova pinched the photo to bring in the surroundings. "High position on the cliffs. Remote from the main road for noise abatement and security. Distant from neighbors, separated by scrub brush and rock canyons. No sight lines from above."

"Are those the three Range Rovers we tracked from the marina on the traffic cams?" I asked.

"Good resolution on the plates. They match." Harrison took back the iPad. "And that silver DS 7 and white SUV near the guesthouse? That's Glinka's minder team. We tailed them coming in from the airport overnight."

The implications struck me. "So, this isn't Google Earth…. This is from this morning?" Harrison cracked a rare smile.

Nova looked up from the screen. "Any confirmation Glinka is on-site?"

The security agent swiped to a new shot. Grainy and pixilated from enlargement, it showed a man in a light gray suit and white fedora stretching outside the guest quarters. Two men in dark suits flanked him. "May I?" She swiped back to the drone overview of the area. "I see two gated access roads off the corniche. So, Tábori's security detail had the sense not to box him in." Nova drew a circle in the air above the grounds. "Three-sixty of either walls or cliffs. I'm guessing no sight lines at ground level, either."

Harrison shook his head. "Probably not, which doesn't give us opportunity to provide cover fire, should you need it." He rose and headed for the door. "I'll dispatch a couple carloads of our tourists to recon for confirmation."

When the PPO stepped out, the Food Sarge pawed the door open before it closed. "Yo. Pastry's packed. Need me, I'll be on smoke break." He didn't hang around for an OK.

This time I shut the door. "Oh Specialized Skills Officer Nova? Given the heightened holy-crap factor of this operation, what say we cut that joker loose now?"

"Mm-no. Not yet."

"Why not?"

Nova directed her answer to DSA Espy and put a barb on it. "Because that joker is my plan B."

Through the glass, I watched Chuck saunter out. "Him? How?"

But my producer left to catch up to Harrison without answering.

AN HOUR LATER CAMMIE NOVA navigated another climb in the Brabus SUV, this time eastbound on the Moyenne Corniche, a two-lane sliver clinging to the cliff overlooking Beaulieu-sur-Mer. I couldn't tell if the corkscrew in my gut was tension from what might be waiting on the mountain in Èze or the steep Wile E. Coyote drop of the canyon out my side window. I closed my eyes to snap meditate.

My mission jitters were amplified because, when it came time to nail down the revised plan, Espy, Nova, and Harrison had dismissed me from their war room. While the big kids devised exfiltration 2.0, I got sent off to make sure the kitchen got packed for the move. The closest I got to a briefing came before we rolled. Espy cornered Nova and me. "I have strong misgivings. My gravest concern is execution and security without our full complement of assets. No Harrison, no Ortiz, no snipers, no road control. But this is our only shot. We can't re-create these circumstances or timing to get Glinka out. The bottom line is this: it's all on you two. Don't fuck this up."

The DSA's version of a pep talk.

"Pike, it'll all go fine." I opened my eyes. From behind the wheel Cammie was reading me. "Think of this as utilizing what that master chef told you to do when everything in the kitchen breaks down. We're resorting to the raw flame."

"But why? Do you think Tábori and his gang are onto us?"

"Doubtful. They'd pull the plug entirely. My guess is that Glinka's security team from the Kremlin doesn't want him in an uncontrolled venue."

"Which makes me bug about the crew. It's one thing to set up a video segment in a brasserie and the deed is done in the back alley. But now you're asking me to take them into the lair of the hairy beast."

"You heard Espy say what happens if we don't get Glinka out—and right now." I noticed that time she didn't reassure me about my folks being totally out of harm's way. "It's on, and it's all good."

"I'll have to accept that on blind faith since you decided not to share the plan."

"It's not that we don't trust you." She reached a hand across the console, and I took it. "But except for Glinka, we're the only ones up there who know what's going down. If you know the hows, you may react and give them away without realizing."

I could buy that as operational procedure. Probably enforced by Espy, which was why I didn't personalize against Cammie. Yeah, she had lied to me, but for a higher cause. I trusted her. Besides, there was a long list of people who had lied to me one way or another on this mystery tour. Espy, slinging whatever BS worked to sign me up and keep me in. Then there was Sheila, lying about rehab; Rayna, lying about her mom's stroke; Cedric, pretending not to recognize Ringstad. The irony? Ringstad was one of the few who hadn't lied to me.

There's someone I left off the roster. Me. Hadn't I adjusted, bending myself around digestible falsehoods? Like the others, I claimed mission motives. Maybe I didn't drink the Kool-Aid, but I had for sure sniffed the bouquet. It gave me no absolution, only a justification. Every secret needs a fortress of lies and an army willing to defend it. I accepted that, but it was an awkward embrace.

"Almost there." Cammie, pulling me out of my head. "Here's what I need from you. Once we get inside, help me get access to recon the house.

Three things we look for: One, is Glinka there? Two, what level of security is in force? And three, identify escape routes."

"Got it. But a question. With our original plan scrapped, how is Glinka going to know where to go and what to do?"

"That's our weak spot. We've only had sparse communication with him. He's only aware to be alert for instructions from me. Meanwhile, you go about your cooking and your oligarch eater-view. And when it comes time, do exactly as I say, without question."

"Because I'm so good at that." I slid my gaze to the side mirror as we took a hairpin. Like a train rounding a bend, I could see both crew vans keeping pace behind us. My little traveling family, blissfully unaware, thinking they were off to shoot a segment like any other day. I hoped Nova was right. That they'd never know what was happening right under their noses. I didn't want to envision the alternative.

OUR INSTRUCTIONS WERE TO BYPASS the main gate and enter the east entrance, which sent us up a steep rise. A hundred meters along we came to a chain-link gate latticed by mocha-colored vinyl strips to block prying eyes. "Not a lot of grandeur."

"Service entrance." Nova pointed to the wooden housing for trash barrels beside the rack of empty water jugs. She reached for the call button on the metal stand outside her window, but before she pressed it, the gates swung inward, pulled by two men in dark suits with single earbuds.

The sight of these men, sleek professionals, sparked a klong in my solar plexus. "These dudes aren't anything like Beavis and Butt-Head at the Colombe d'Or yesterday."

"Those yahoos? Rentals Tábori engaged from a local agency with a B-team rep." I gave Cammie a look. "What. I ran a check on them after your encounter yesterday."

"Wonky is as wonky does."

"Basic due diligence. This crew would eat Beavis and Butt-Head for breakfast. These are FSO agents; Federal Protective Service. First-rank paramilitary elites from Moscow." On our walk the evening before, Espy had referred to them as thug minders. One look made me seriously consider asking if we could turn around and just go. Cammie, ever attuned to my rookie butterflies, said, "Hey? Nothing to worry about." My stomach growled, and we both laughed. A third suit, a severe guy made more so by his black unibrow, beckoned us in, military-style.

Passing through the security gate, I marked it as a border crossing, a point to turn off all the outside noise needling me for attention: Astrid baggage; Nova feelings; Espy's mind games; Ringstad's torture session; the corpses of two joes and one old friend dotting the French map; and yes, Russian thug minders. My focus needed to be on making a *Hangry Globe* episode without distractions. It was literally showtime.

Our production vehicles weren't allowed up to the main property. Not yet. Although we could see the roof of the main house topping the rise, we were directed to pull over and park all three vehicles side by side on a blacktop holding area. Nova and I unlatched our doors to get out, but one of the guards gave a short whistle, held up crossed arms to us, and shook no. The agent with the unibrow appeared in Nova's window, arriving from behind. "Please wait in the vehicle until you are directed to step out. Thank you."

"What's up? Are you breathalyzing today, Officer? It's a little early for me." Unibrow gave me an impassive look and moved to the far van. "I hope there's no strip search. Every fifth day I go none-derwear." I stage-winked at Cammie. "Pro travel tip."

"Nice to see you're not nervous or anything." She looked past me. "I can't see through Hoss's van, but it seems their detail is going full rummage on Latrell's." Nova didn't act rattled. Instead, she craned high in her seat to survey the grounds. My heart leaped up against my Adam's apple at a sudden oversight.

My .357. It was still in the door pocket. If they found that snub-nose, it could burn the whole mission: busting me, busting Nova, busting everything we've set up. Not to mention what might happen to us—and my innocent crew—as a result. I worked to appear nonchalant. "Spy Cam? Do you think they're going to toss everything? We'll be here all day."

"Their clock. Their call."

"Getting hot." I took off my ball cap, folded it in half, then pressed it down inside the door pocket on top of the snubbie. I wondered, Should I tell her about it? I decided I'd test her degree of anxiety. "Are you concerned about anything they might find? Meaning, I assume you are, you know…packing."

She smirked and arched the brow I was getting used to seeing. How could Cammie be so blasé? I let my eyes drop down and to my right. The gun was completely hidden by my hat. Safe—as long as their search wasn't too thorough. Knuckles rapped my window. I powered down the glass.

"Please step out, both of you, and stand over there."

Nova signaled me to comply and got out. I opened my door but couldn't get up. "Ha, duh." I tugged at my locked seat belt strap. All I got back was the flat stare of the FSO agent. I unbuckled and moved away to lean against the front grille with Cammie, trying for casual. Then came a cold blast of dread.

Our Russian disappeared, squatting beside my open door for a look-see in the pocket.

thirty-three

"*Arrêtez*. You stop this right now." Everyone did stop. Ilona Tábori charged down the driveway from the upper. Napsugár, spitting fire, gold lamé sandals slapping blacktop. "Cease. What is this insult you are doing to my guest?" The FSO man rose up from my open door in response to the oligarch's angry wife. "Chef Pike, I am mortified for this trouble." Both agents looked to their leader, Unibrow, for guidance. Ilona Tábori filled in the blanks. "You. Yes, you. Tell your men to stop this and let these people up. *Immédiatement*." Then in Russian, "*Pryamo seychas!*" The lady even clapped twice. "Now. Or would you rather I involve my husband—or your man from the Kremlin?"

Unibrow processed the situation. He didn't look pleased but signaled his team to stand down.

"Chef, I am mortified by this. Please accept my apologies."

"No harm done, Napsugár."

"Oh, listen to you. And the accent, it is perfect." She leaned in to offer European air kisses, beaming until her gaze landed on Nova. "Who is this." Not a question. Nor a veiled reaction. Napsugár put it all out there, especially when she sniffed a rival to her fantasy narrative.

"Hi, I'm Cammie." Nova read the moment and went submissive. "Chef Pike's told me all about you."

"Cameron—Ms. Nova—is my producer. She's here to make everything go like cream today."

"Anything you need, let me know, *Asszony* Tábori."

"Hmm. This one. Her accent is not so good as yours." The oligarch's wife addressed Nova like house staff. "You will find the kitchen through the garage. Go up now and you will see. Be careful not to scratch anything with your equipment. All is new." She crooked an arm for me to take and guided us up the rise, leaving Nova and the others to drive.

As we ascended the incline, the belle époque mansion revealed itself top to bottom as ships do approaching over the horizon. First the upper floor of three, the lid of an elegant box with blush-pink walls accented by white cornices. Then the middle story, carrying the same color scheme, but studded by white plaster balconies spilling cascades of painstakingly trimmed bougainvillea in vibrant magenta. The full reveal came at the crest of the drive where palms and cypresses framed the ground floor, replete with curved white awnings and turn-of-the-century lampposts with opaque globes.

"Nice curb appeal."

"But Chef, this is the rear of the house."

I took the lay of the land, but not because I was impressed by the grandeur. My appraisal was about escape routes. My eyes tracked across the concrete to a strip of Belgian block paving stones on my right, the start of the lane I'd seen on the aerial photo. According to the drone shot, the drive flanked the main house, running between a ribbon of grass and the steep rock cliffs that transformed a mere mansion into a fort. At the other end of that passage, on the west side, would be one of the swimming pools and guest quarters. To my immediate left was the attached garage. Our crew vehicles made semicircles around me and Ilona Tábori before they backed in, side by side, presenting rear doors for unloading and loading.

And, knowing SSO Nova, poised for rapid exit.

Behind me the three Range Rovers we video tracked from the Cap-d'Ail marina reflected midday sun. Against the detached garage sat an Opel service van from Connexion Côte, a new arrival since the morning flyover. Nearby, a man in blue coveralls and paper booties crouched at a cable junction box, unimpressed by the doings. "I apologize to have a workman present. We lost our Wi-Fi and cable this morning."

"With *Hangry Globe* on tonight?" I called to the cable guy. "*Plus vite, monsieur.*" The man barely looked, a very French dismissal. "Always nice to meet a fan." Midway to the garage, some little nothing prodded me to take a second look, but the repair guy was head deep in his van's cargo bay.

Hoss knew the gig and made sure to be inside first to unroll vinyl mats to protect the terracotta flooring in the kitchen. Our hostess was pleased. "When do we cook together?"

"I think we should do Napsugár's segment first. What do you say, Cammie?"

"Before the interview, sure…" Nova made a show of flipping through her rundown, but she had already worked this out with me. "I suppose we could do that. You and *Asszony* Tábori have your fun here in the kitchen, then we will shoot lunch and the interview with *Úr* Tábori…. But where?"

I played my part. "Dining room?"

"But I'll bet this house has many other beautiful settings. *Asszony* Tábori?"

"Ilona, please."

"Ilona, while the crew sets up the kitchen would you excuse us to go do some looking?"

When Ilona hesitated, I said, "Standard location scouting while you go get camera-ready." She was cajoled enough to agree.

The dining room would have been perfect. I didn't care where we shot, but Nova and I looky-loo'd the ground floor, starting with the living room and its commanding view of the Golfe de Saint-Hospice. We stepped through the French doors onto the balcony, not to see if the tip of Cap-Ferrat would make a nice background but to eyeball the parking area near the guesthouse. We leaned over the balustrade and found what we wanted. The silver DS 7 and the white SUV that brought Arkady Glinka and his minders from the airport were still there.

Nova looked relieved. "Now the study."

"This way, madame." Both of us had memorized the architectural drawing Kurt Harrison secured, and soon we arrived in the front hall-way. She held up a forefinger to signal slowing down as we approached a corner. We stopped to listen. Nova pointed a forefinger ahead, and we rounded the turn coming face-to-face with an imposing pair of Russian security agents. The nearer one put up both palms. "*Stoy.*" He had receding sandy hair combed forward in bangs that didn't reach his forehead. His companion stood taller. He was bulkier and more weathered thanks to deep facial creases and a chinstrap beard. Maybe Chechen, if they were allowed in Russian security. That one, Beard, held both hands at the lapels of his suit coat in the classic ready pose for a quick draw. "*Vozvrashchat'sya.*"

"Speak English?" Her question was pure stall; their message didn't require translation.

"He say to go back. You go now," said Bangs. Beard's hands stayed against his chest, but his right inched slightly inside the coat. Even more than the others at the gate, these two breathed paramilitary lethality.

Muffled voices came through the closed door they were guarding. I recognized Ignaz Tábori's from meeting him the day before plus the You-Tube videos of him I had watched for research. His companion laughed, then rattled off a flurry of Russian. Glinka. The mole who brought us there. I had no idea how he looked. What could his voice tell me? Baritone, measured and carrying gravity, kind of like a nature documentary narrator. I shifted forward an inch for a better listen. Immediately Bangs shoved me. Five fingertips that hurt like pokes from five ski poles. By reflex, I raised forearms to protect myself. In a lightning flash the agent seized my wrist with one hand and my elbow with the other and leveraged me to the carpet. "*Da*. Going back now," I said into the deep pile.

WHEN CAMMIE AND I WERE ALONE in the dining room, I flexed my sore wrist. "You can check the box for assessing the level of security."

"They're probably ex-Spetsnaz, Russian Special Forces. The elite of the elite get the highest-level protection assignments, meaning Putin's pal. Anyway, we got our confirmation the package is on-site."

"And I got a timely warning to reconsider using my interview to hand the minister of agriculture his ass."

"Don't you dare pull back." Nova looked freaked. She tensed and bored her eyes into mine. "I can't believe you'd let that pair intimidate you."

"Maybe because you're not the one who got manhandled. This place is crawling with Russian killing machines."

"They're no match for you. Stay tough. Use your words." She lowered her voice to an urgent hush. "You told me you would give Tábori a 'blistering fucking hotfoot.' Don't let the thug entourage cow you. Do it. I not only need you to do it, I am relying on it." Hoss rolled a cart of electronics in from the kitchen so she spoke in subtext. "Am I clear? *Relying.*"

Her whispered message couldn't be louder. My interview was part of her plan. "Got it."

"Be an asshole."

"In other words, be myself."

I checked progress in the kitchen. The escalating tension of setting up for a cooking segment usually buoyed me. Not that day. I wanted this done, and soon. All the motion, all the micro-crises, and all the brain tugs—like my director of photography quizzing me about options for pick-up shots—only tested my patience. Or anxiety, to be honest about it. I couldn't fault my little cadre of pros. They were only doing their jobs, unsuspecting of my ulterior mission. Chill, I thought, and forced an unfelt smile. Tough when What-the-Chuck Ludik only made things more tense. The Food Sarge had left our contingency doubles for the main course, pissaladière, back in Nice at le Vide, a bonehead move. "Show me what you did bring, Ludikrous, before I serve your severed head on a bed of lettuce."

"You don't have to be an asshole."

"No, but you make it feel so damn good." Ludik led me over to the lone pissaladière that did make it. "Lucky for you, flatbread travels. Listen carefully. Eyes, please? Before I shoot the dessert segment with Mrs. Tábori, slide this in the oven at low temp—one hundred four—just to warm it. When it comes out, give it a tiny spritz of olive oil. Only a whisper, so it catches the light on camera. Got that?"

"I'm not an idiot." Chuck backed away, nearly colliding with Hoss, who was gingerly rolling in a utility cart bearing the four-foot-tall pyramid of stacked choux pastry for the dessert demo. Nova jumped between him and the croquembouche, averting a Three Stooges moment.

Ilona Tábori breezed through the dining room doorway. She had freshened her makeup and changed into a crisp white blouse with a yellow sweater draped over her shoulders and knotted. The Hungarian Martha Stewart. "Ignaz says he will be finished his meeting and ready for you in the dining room at two thirty."

Nova approached her. "If I may, Ilona."

"Is there a problem?"

"No, a modification. I would prefer to shoot your husband's segment on the veranda instead of in the dining room."

I swung over from the island where I was rearranging my utensils. "But the dining room is more spacious. Plus, we can control the light.

And it's close by the kitchen to facilitate…" I trailed off, finally getting Nova's wide-eyed signal to back off. "On the other hand, the veranda is picturesque. Eye candy. I bow to my producer."

"Smart."

"Very well, but don't scrape my French doors with your equipment."

"Wouldn't think of it," said Nova. "If you're set, Ilona, we should do your segment now."

Mrs. T. hesitated. "Chef Pike? A moment in private?"

The pantry was as big as most kitchens. I stepped in behind the oligarch's wife, and she closed the door. "I confess I am a wreck. I have entertained heads of state, captains of industry…once, even Mr. Josh Groban. I cook as a hobby and have dreamed of being with you on your show, but now. Now, I have stage fright. Look at my hand." She grabbed one of mine and folded it in both of hers. This skin sandwich was a bit more than a look, but indeed they were trembling.

I tried to slip free, but she clung tight. "You're going to do fine, Napsugár. We have this all worked out. You saw the croquembouche, right? I've got the pastry tower nearly complete already. All we need to do is a demonstration of how I make choux pastry that I will walk you through live, on camera. We set the batter aside, we take a couple of the pâte à choux that I've prebaked, and use them to finish off the tower. Done."

"You make it sound easy."

"Because it is. All you have to do is follow my lead."

"That is it. That is what I want. Lead me." She tipped forward to kiss my cheek but at the last second put her lips on mine.

I eased back before any tongue came into play. "Ah-ah, Napsugár, no dessert before dessert."

Nova studied us on our return. I signaled no prob and took my mark at the center island. Cammie joined me. "Hold still, what's this here?" She thumbed my lower lip. "Huh. Almost looks like lipstick."

Turned out, anxiety during the demo belonged to me. Knowing that my segment with the oligarch and his handler Arkady Glinka came next turned my usually adroit fingers into crane claws at the arcade. While helping my amateur sous chef add flour to the boiling water, butter, and sugar mixture, I lost my grip. Ilona Tábori cackled as the air filled with a white cloud. "Here's where we hop in our time machine, Napsugár. Oh, look, our pastry's already been baked to a golden brown." I reached below the counter and came up with a tray of finished specimens. Latrell panned the camera with us as we walked over to the nearly completed choux tower. "I cheated and started this croquembouche ahead, but I left a space for you to stack these and finish off the pyramid of goodness."

"I erected one of these once, but it drooped over."

I leaned into the lens. "That happens. No shame there. You relax, take a break, put on some Beyoncé or Prince, and try again." Napsugár, hardly subtle, pushed her pastry too hard and caved in the tower on one side. "No worries, Ilona. We can edit that out. Because looky here." I beckoned to the B-camera. Marisol followed me across the kitchen with her handheld to a premade, three-foot triangle of pastry to replace that side of the pyramid. "Through the magic of television, behold the most delicious Lego piece ever."

Nova tapped her watch. I called, "And cut. Moving on." I congratulated my guest baker, then chugged a bottle of Evian while the crew reset to the main event on the veranda.

"WE'RE FIVE AWAY. YOU GOOD?" I flashed Nova my best no-sweat smile. She saw through it and whispered, "Remember. I'm relying on you for the hotfoot. I'll do what I do."

"Are you still here?" Ilona Tábori's voice cut across our crew chatter out on the veranda. She was confronting the Connexion Côte service guy as he passed the open doors from the dining room.

The man turned away, shy or rude, I couldn't see enough of his face to tell. A loop of coaxial cable attached to his tool belt wagged against his coveralls. In heavily accented English, he said, "I need to check all your boxes before I go."

"Certainly there are none out here. Try the kitchen and the maid's quarters. And you're tracking dirt."

He went on his way. After checking to make sure one of his agents remained to cover this venue, Unibrow went off to tail him.

Cammie noticed me staring at the service tech as he strode off in his soiled booties. "What?"

Something about that guy… "Wondering who wears booties outside, is all." Latrell broke my ponder with a question.

"Are you wanting handheld or sticks?"

The enclosed patio was smaller than I'd envisioned. "We're going to have more folks crammed in here than the oligarch and me. He's going to squeeze a security entourage, off cam, plus a visitor from Moscow. Plus Mrs. T."

Latrell gave a conspiratorial grin. "You mean Lap Sugar?"

"She wishes." I gave the area another assessment. "Four at the table, two more crowding around… Not that I don't love your company, but you and Marisol lock off your cams on tripods and clear the set so we can breathe."

"Done, Chef. Lap Sugar. Like that?"

"Later, I will. Maybe."

Chuck Ludik came onto the veranda with four Niçoise salads balanced on his stubby forearm like he was serving chow at the Waffle House. He plunked them down and left. I pulled a paper towel from the utility cart and dabbed the slops of olive oil he'd left on the rim of the fine china. Food effing Sarge, indeed.

Coming from the hallway, heavy footfalls. I heard the same voices that had filtered through the study door. My gut hollowed when I heard the Russian's baritone.

The look I got from Specialized Skills Officer Nova said, "It's on."

thirty-four

Bangs and Beard arrived first. The hospitality twins. I watched their roving eyes sonar-pinging the veranda, no doubt suspicious about the swapping of the dining room for the less secure outdoor space. Or probably suspicious of everything. After all, they were FSO bodyguards. Bangs, the thug who helped me meet Mr. Carpet, must have signed off because he leaned around the door, said something in Russian, and Hungary's richest man stepped in.

On his own turf, Ignaz Tábori was more relaxed than when I ambushed him outside *le WC* at Colombe d'Or. The oligarch called, "Welcome, Chef," and threaded his thin runner's frame between LED light stands to come shake. "Thank you for being flexible and driving up here. This evolved unexpectedly into a business day, and I needed to attend."

"No worries. I'm too happy for the opportunity to talk with you one-on-one. Or whatever." I drew an air circle around Tábori's Russian security entourage. "But who's counting?"

The Hungarian chuckled. "I had to match you. What did you bring, a small army?" Oh, man, I thought, if you only knew. Tábori beckoned to a short, pudgy man lurking near the doorway. "Kasha, come say hello."

As Putin's accountant made exaggerated steps over cables and cords, my first thought was, This schlub is what all the fuss is about? In contrast to Tábori's marathoner body and ease of movement, this specimen looked every bit the deskbound nonathlete showing off a history of gourmandism and indolence his custom tailoring couldn't hide. The presence of the über-apparatchik meant I had done my part. Instead of finding comfort in that, the sight of Arkady Glinka made me feel like a rabid bat was beating wings against my rib cage. The fuse had been lit for the mole's exfiltration, with all its jeopardy.

Tábori made the introductions. Thank God I caught myself before I screwed up. I nearly addressed the Russian by name before I had heard it from my host. A gaffe like that would blow up the whole deal. "Sebastian Pike, meet my interpreter, Arkady Glinka." There. Now I could know the name.

Shaking with the Russian reminded me of the raw choux I'd squeezed out of the piping bag. "*Gospodin* Glinka, I'm surprised our host needs an interpreter. *Úr* Tábori speaks English better than I."

"Oh, but that's not why I came all the way here from Moscow." Do bats have claws? "I came for your food." He patted his gut. Everyone laughed. Who doesn't laugh when Putin's accountant makes a joke? "Look at all these cameras and lights and people. All this to film one lunch?"

I seized the opening to connect the dots for Glinka. "All thanks to my producer. See her over there? That's Cammie Nova. Nova keeps everything running like clockwork." She was busy at the far end of the table removing a floral centerpiece that blocked camera angles. "Cammie Nova, this is all you." What was happening? I had lobbed a softball, pointing her out to the mole by full name, and she barely looked up. Maybe the Russian already knew her. When they moved to take their seats, though, Glinka did steal a second glance at her. Or was that merely horndogging? I began to worry that nothing was in motion after all. Then I remembered Nova's single direction: cover my own base, leave her to hers. "I'll go check on the main." I excused myself to the kitchen.

"Chuck?" The place was empty. I called again. "Ludik?" I walked around the counter to check the floor, imagining the portly Food Sarge slumped on the terra-cotta clutching his infarcted ticker. I even circled the croquembouche in case the pastry tower blocked him from view. No sign of him in the pantry, either. Maybe Ludikrous was outside on one of his relentless smoke breaks. If so, I fantasized one of the security detail putting a bullet in him for the good of all Foodkind.

I feared what would greet me when I opened the oven door, but the pissaladière looked fine. The dumbass had followed instructions for once and set the temp low enough to warm, not bake. Using kitchen towels as mitts, I transferred the sheet pan to the range top. Chuck Ludik strolled in from the hall connecting to the garage. I started misting the surface of the flatbread with EVOO and said, "No worries, Chuck, I can host the show and do your job, too." When he didn't reply, I looked up and found him checking his reflection in the oven door. While he was gone, Chuck had changed out of his Phish tee into a white collared shirt and a gray sport coat.

"What."

"What happened to you? You almost look presentable."

"You're always on my ass. I clean up, and you're still on my ass."

"My apologies. You look swell. Natty, even." I picked up the stainless pan and slid the pissaladière onto a Souleo platter. "But if you got dolled up for the camera, I have news for you. I'm serving." After I garnished the dish with local herbs, I added color with purple thyme and rosemary blossoms. At the door I paused and inclined my head toward the counter. "I notice you left my personal paring knife out when you used it without my permission. Uncool."

As the door swung closed behind me, I heard Chuck mutter, "It's a knife, who gives a—"

Nova had directed Hoss to set up Video Village at the end of the dining room closest to the veranda. I found Latrell sitting inside the

French doors where he had commandeered one of the utility carts to hold his split-screen monitor. He and Marisol planted themselves there with their iPads and would operate zooms and pullbacks on their pre-positioned cameras remotely over Wi-Fi. Declan clipped a wireless mic to my shirt and held the platter for me while I slipped the RF pack into my jeans pocket. "Latrell, you sure the broadband isn't going to bone us?"

The DP tapped his settings. "Full strength. Whatever cable problems they had, we're up now."

"Then roll and speed. I'm going in." I got confirmation and stepped to the threshold.

"Hold the roll." Nova squeezed by me and scurried out to the table where the Táboris and Glinka were already seated. "Excuse me, *Gospodin* Glinka, I need to ask you to adjust your chair so you are out of the camera frame. May I?" He seemed irritated but allowed her to drag his seat a few degrees. During the rocking and scraping of the chair I saw Nova press a slip of paper into the Russian's palm.

thirty-five

Nobody else seemed to register the handoff. Not even the Russian minder's minders, Bangs and Beard. "Do you have everything you need, sir?" asked Nova.

Glinka had made a fist around the note and smoothed the whiskers on his chin with it. "If you are prepared, I am prepared."

"We are." She strode back to Video Village. "Break a leg, Chef."

The Táboris watched with keen interest while Marisol slated each camera to mark the take. But Arkady Glinka's interest was elsewhere. He was pretending to examine the cleanliness of his spoon while he read the note in his lap that Nova had slipped him.

Time for me to play celebrity chef Sebastian Pike. A quick breath, and I swept onto the veranda brandishing the octagonal platter and set the star lunch course in the center of the table. My guest lunchers, Ignaz Tábori and his wife, leaned in to examine it and inhale its aroma. "Oh, Chef..." cooed Ilona Tábori. Arkady Glinka, a man who looked like he loved to eat, appeared interested but kept back out of the picture.

"You like that? Wait until you taste it, Napsugár." I took my seat to the oligarch's right. Latrell had set the cameras to hold a nice two-shot of us with Marisol's C300. On his Gemini he had established a master angle of the entire table. "Before we dive in, let me describe our *déjeuner Provençale.*"

Tábori flicked a concerned glance to Glinka, who sat on his left, then to me. "You are recording already? I ask because I expected we would have a rehearsal."

"Come on, you've seen this show. You think we rehearse this crap?" When the laughter subsided, I added, "Besides, rehearsals tend to lead to questions, and questions lead to setting limits on conversation. Not that you ever would consider such a thing, *Úr* Tábori. Let's be spontaneous. Surprise me."

"Should I be nervous?"

"I guess that's up to your interpreter." I smiled at the Russian. "Will you promise to let us know if the language becomes an issue, *Gospodin* Glinka?"

"Right now, I am more interested in this fine meal."

"I'll jump on that segue. Since we are in Provence, I have decided to go local. And since it's a luncheon, casual." I tipped the pottery serving plate toward the camera briefly. "For our main, I have prepared a regional specialty—a lot like pizza—but in these parts, called pissaladière. The flatbread crust is topped with six onions that were thinly sliced, then slowly reduced and caramelized in the oven for two hours with some olive oil, salt, pepper, and herbs. Then it's layered with anchovies and olives. That gets a second bake, and here you have it." While we ate, Napsugár, the self-styled foodie, asked some questions about preparation, which I answered without listening to myself. The tension of the exfiltration put me on host-autopilot, at least until the interview. Nova had green-lit me to be me, and I had some devilishly forthright conversation planned.

I scrutinized Glinka. The Russian gave no sign of nervousness or care as I described the side dish, a traditional salade Niçoise. "Traditional in the sense of adhering to the strict recipe of a legendary local food purist. Tomatoes, drizzled with olive oil and salted, hard-boiled eggs, anchovies, raw cucumber, purple artichokes, and what else? Nothing else. No potato, no vinegar, no tuna, no kidding." I dabbed my forehead with my napkin while the others dug in.

Glinka finally reacted. "Is good." The others agreed enthusiastically.

"Well, save room. Ilona and I prepared a special dessert." The oligarch's wife beamed.

Her husband used his fork to point at his remaining tomato. "Every salade Niçoise I ever had contained boiled potatoes and green beans. I now must concur with this purist that you credit."

Ignaz Tábori was trying to skate and keep this a food talk segment. No dice. My secret was that I had weaponized my menu, even designed my choice of salad to fire a volley. Which I did. "By the way, that purist? His name was Jacques Médecin. Not only an old-guard gourmet, he was the mayor of Nice for a quarter century. Until he got convicted in 1993. For corruption."

Tábori's eyes drifted to his Moscow handler again. Glinka set his utensils down to monitor the exchange. "I would conclude his real legacy is the salad," said the Hungarian.

"As Hungary's minister of agriculture, what do you think your legacy will be, Úr Tábori?"

Glinka jumped in. "Is this what you do on your little TV program? Come to a man's home and try to embarrass him?"

"Is there something about the agriculture minister's legacy that should embarrass him?" The exfiltration was the mission, but I had researched this sleazebag enough to make it a hot episode, too. Armed with Nova's agreement, I locked horns. "I'm sorry, I should be asking our host. I mean you are only here to interpret, is that right?" Some sweat glistened through the fringe of hair rimming Glinka's baldpate. "What do you say, Minister Tábori?"

The exchange with Glinka had bought time for the billionaire to collect himself and flip the subject. "It makes me want to ask you a question,

Chef. I emphasize chef because that is your expertise. What qualifies you in matters that are not about cuisine?"

Far from getting backed onto the ropes, I charged center ring. "With all respect, food is inexorably linked not only to politics, but also to human rights, and to the land. My best example is right here. Local fishermen, farmers, florists, even the *sauniers* who raked our salt from Aigues-Mortes brought everything to this table. I'll give you a for instance closer to home. Your home. I read about a farmer, less than an hour out of Budapest, whose family has been working the soil for generations, and now is losing his farm and his family's livelihood because of government corruption in the distribution of agricultural land."

"Corruption, you say?"

"Funny. There's that word again."

Glinka leaned in and whispered something in Russian to Tábori. I don't speak the language, but I had a fair idea of the gist. Instead of waiting for a time-out to get whistled, I kept pushing. "If it's not corruption, what would you call it when the EU coughs up a big hairball of five hundred billion euros for ag subsidies, and most of it goes to a handful of the agriculture minister's cronies who bought up all the farmland in a rigged auction?"

"That's a baseless accusation."

"Is this enough base?" I pulled out an index card with notes. "Your predecessor, the former agriculture minister, calls it, quote: 'A crony economy, where friends and political allies get special treatment.'"

"Who said that, Rasko? Bah! Sour grapes."

"Ignaz..." Glinka rested a cautionary hand on Tábori's forearm.

"So, you're denying super-farms like the ones your pals own are killing the family farmer?"

"Name one."

I was ready. "Kishantos. It's been reported that an organic farm there was not only land-grabbed by your political BFFs, but one of his first moves was to begin use of chemical sprays. I would love to give you a chance to respond to that."

The oligarch's simmer was coming up to a boil. "I do not understand your fuss over a few shitty *hektárs* in Hantos. You call them family farmers. I call them dimwitted bunglers who—"

Glinka cautioned him. "Ignaz, *molchi*."

"—who should learn how to make a profit instead of whining like peasant crybabies."

"Was the *New York Times* a crybaby when it reported that selling off twelve state-owned farm parcels to your land-grabbing cronies became known as the Dirty Dozen? Now let's talk quid pro quos."

"Enough," said Glinka. I ignored him.

"I'll bet the friends you made ultrarich are darned generous in return. How do they reward you? I noticed the Panama Papers listed some shell corporations alleged to have ties to you." I flipped my index card. "Raise a hand if the names of any of these LLCs ring a bell." Tábori tried to snatch away my list and called me something rude in Hungarian.

"Ignaz. *My. Sdelali*." That much Russian I knew. "Shut. Up." The oligarch flopped back in his chair and fumed, chastened by his handler from the Kremlin. I put my list away. Tábori regarded me like the dental patient, relieved, but eyeing the drill. I didn't need notes anymore.

"*Ur* Tábori. Ignaz." I inched closer to him, into the money of the B-cam's two-shot. "Something I've always wondered about people of your...situation." He slid his eyes off me and buttoned them on Glinka. I kept it offhand and casual. "I see this opulent villa. Then there's the private jet, the super-yacht, and all. It's quite a life, isn't it? I truly am curious. Is there any part of you, say, when you slip into the spa out there, floating on the bubbles, looking out on the Mediterranean, that you feel even the smallest twinge of conscience that this luxe life was bought and paid for on the backs of the crybaby families you ruined?"

The Russian minder shot to his feet, fluttering his napkin toward the cameras. "Stop. You will stop this slander now."

I struck a pose of innocence. "It's just getting good."

Glinka's face splotched red with rage. "Turn off the cameras and cease this immediately, you silly cook." His shouting startled the FSO bodyguards. Declan, back in audio, had to yank off his headphones. "You…TV clown. I will not permit you to berate a friend and ally by making the…the trapping lies and innuendoes."

"How about facts and figures, would they be OK?"

"Enough. Enough of you and your, your…" In his outburst he sputtered, at a loss for words. "And your fish pizza is shit." Whipping a chunky arm, he Frisbeed the remaining pissaladière over the balcony into a hedge. "Mikhail, Andrei." He snapped his fingers at Bangs and Beard and snarled instructions in Russian. The FSO men balked. The apparatchik growled a command, still in Russian, but loaded with threat. That jolted the pair, and they double-timed out through the dining room. As their clomps up the hallway faded, Glinka addressed the oligarch. "Ignaz, I sent my men to the guesthouse to pack my bags." He took out his cell phone. "I will need to alert…well, you know who…about this so he is not blindsided. I require privacy. You will please wait here while I call him with the unfortunate news." The remaining FSO agent started to go with him. Glinka put up a hand to stop him. As he passed me, he said over his shoulder, "Bastard."

The mole, the object of our mission, suddenly free of his Kremlin minders, stalked off alone to the kitchen. Far from being bothered by the high opera, I relaxed for the first time in days. Because the grin I saw on SSO Nova felt to me like Mission: Accomplished.

NOT ONLY CAMMIE, BUT EVERYONE in Video Village beamed when I slipped into the dining room. With uninitiated ears listening, I crafted my question to carry double meaning. "Madame producer, please tell me that worked."

"Couldn't be better." Clearly satisfied, both as producer and specialized skills officer.

"Should we start, you know, packing up?"

"Mm, let's let things marinate a few minutes." I didn't argue. Whatever was going on was her purview. "Meanwhile, you did great. Pike being Pike."

"As you said."

Latrell, Marisol, Declan, and Hoss, anything but sycophants, chimed in, declaring it hot, one of the best segments ever, etc. As I handed back my RF mic to Declan, I said, "Please tell me you were recording." They all cracked up, then stifled it. I turned. Ilona Tábori flip-flopped in from the veranda. People are fated to be true to who they are. I tangled over injustice, speaking without fear. The oligarch blew his cool trying to justify his corruption. His wife revealed herself, too. She leaned against me, slipping a hand into a back pocket of my jeans. "I would like to serve the dessert I made with you. On camera." Napsugár wanted her moment of glory on *Hangry Globe*.

"I should ask my producer."

But Ilona was already on her way to the kitchen. "Napsugár wait." Nova bolted between her and the door.

"This is my home."

Cammie's wheels were turning but gaining no traction. Before things flew off the rails and she went into that kitchen, I jumped in. "Napsugár, we will absolutely serve your dessert. But I have a plan. I want you to take your place as hostess of honor at the table and allow me to serve you." God damn, the woman's eyes widened. "And for me, personally, making the presentation to you would be the crowning glory of this episode."

Cammie added, "It's probably our promo clip."

Picturing that image, Ilona Tábori's face broke into a wide grin. "Ah, there it is. Now I see why your nickname is Sunbeam. Cameron, why don't you and Latrell go set a mark back at the table with our hostess of honor while I work my magic in the kitchen. Is that a good plan?"

With some hesitation, Nova escorted Ilona back to the veranda.

I didn't know what I expected to see, but I didn't think I'd find the kitchen empty again. I found a stack of dessert plates and quickly set three of them out on a tray, then added a fourth, better to maintain the illusion that Glinka hadn't done a disappearing act. I was fast learning that the trick to living fiction was to act like it was true.

The croquembouche. The damned tower was too big for me to man-handle myself. Nova wanted to keep people out of the kitchen, so I didn't want to call Hoss in to help. Screw it.

Using my bare hands, I plucked choux balls off the side of the pastry tower Napsugár had messed up in the demo and arranged them on the plates. I garnished the pastry with mint, a flower blossom, and the straw-berries Ludik had prepped. I didn't want to take too much time, but if these babies were going on camera, pride made me want to hit them with a dusting of powdered sugar. There was none in the canisters on the counter. Only granulated.

Maybe in the pantry.

I opened the pantry door and froze.

The cable TV guy was standing in there with his back to me. And he was strangling Arkady Glinka from behind.

thirty-six

The attacker pulled hard on the coax cable looped around Glinka's throat. Pulled so hard it lifted the stubby man up off his heels, leaving him to claw desperately at the fleshy folds of his neck. I couldn't see the Russian's face from behind, but his head was crimson on its way to plum.

I lunged. That shocked the cable guy. The garrote slipped. Glinka inhaled a beastly wheeze. But this brute was immovable as a piling. Without letting go of the cord, he twisted and booted me across the pantry. I smashed into a shelf of canned goods and landed on the deck.

The assassin yanked the black cable again. Harder this time, twisting it with his massive hands to cut deeper into his victim's throat. Glinka's rasps cut off. His gurgles stopped.

I threw a can of tomatoes. It bonked the side of the strangler's head. He cursed in French and shook it off. I rushed him, this time shoulder down for a tackle. He saw it coming, scissored up a knee to deflect, and sent me sprawling.

The cable man worked to finish the job on Glinka. The Russian threw desperate flails of his feet, bucking for his life. One of his shoes flew off and landed on a shelf.

Outmatched hand to hand, I scanned high and low for a weapon. A real one, not a can. I bolted out to the kitchen. The knife block was way across the room, but right there on the cutting board where Ludik had left it lay my own Murray Carter Apprentice. I snatched it. Creeping up behind the thug, I wondered—slash his throat or stab his back? The paring knife's blade wasn't long enough for a stab to work, but I remembered what Harrison told me on training day about the carotid. I crept forward, ready to make the cut.

A hand gripped my elbow. Cammie Nova put a forefinger to her lips, then used it to point where to stand, in view, but out of the man's reach. Her face bore a waxen cast. A benumbed look, some icy version of herself. I did as she ordered.

My move drew the attention of the assailant.

SSO Nova slipped close on his blind side. One hand pushed down on his head while the other seized his chin and torqued up hard. Once, in Oslo, I stepped on broken glass in the snow. That's the wet crackle I heard when the vertebra separated from the attacker's spinal cord. His legs gave. His arms fell. He collapsed on the floor, a puppet with its strings cut.

Nova didn't bother to check him. She rushed to Glinka, now face down. I stared at the cable guy's vacant eyes and wet pants. Pissaladière singed my throat, but I held it down. "Is he…?"

"If not, soon." Without turning, she said, "Want to close that?"

By the time I shut the pantry door, she'd unwound the cable. "Slow deep breaths. Deep breaths, that's it." The Russian made nasty sounds. Tubercular coughs, whistling gasps, ragged hawks. The stocked shelves absorbed the racket, sure as the inside of a tomb. "Help me sit him up."

When I stepped around her to help, I stopped, stunned. "Holy shit…"

Glinka wasn't Glinka. The red-faced wheezer on the floor was Chuck Ludik.

IT WASN'T A PENNY THAT DROPPED. The bean machine in my head released a cascade of ball bearings. By the dozens they fell, bouncing over pegs on their way down, sorting out all my whys. Why Nova hired such an incompetent culinary producer. Why she refused to fire him. Why the Food Sarge had changed clothes. Why Chuck had a goatee.

Why? Because Chuck Ludik looked enough like Arkady Glinka to pass as a decoy. Enough to fool his entourage. Also, enough to fool the cable guy into trying to kill him.

"You called him your plan B."

"Yeah, but this wasn't part of it. Hurry. Let's get him on his feet."

Chuck was shaky but breathing. I snagged him a bottle of Evian off the shelf. While Ludik drank, I dared to look at the dead man and figured out what nagged me about him. "I've seen this guy. If I'm right, he was at Ringstad's crib in Marseille while I was getting zapped. Which means Ringstad knows Glinka is here."

Instead of responding, Nova closed her eyes and chewed her lip. I imagined hearing her internal GPS: "Recalculating…" Her eyes sprung open. That quick, she'd arrived at something. "Change of plan."

Chuck tossed the empty. "No shit."

"Instead of driving off in Glinka's car, you're leaving in the cable repair van." She squared her face to his. "Chuck, are you getting this?"

"Uh, yuh. The cable van." He plucked his loafer off the shelf near the Nutella and held it up. "Ha. Check it out."

She moved to the dead man. "We need to get him in his van. He's going with you."

"Why?"

"Because that's the new plan. Are you OK enough to grab hold?" He slid his shoe on and went to the body. I joined them, but she waved me off.

"You need to go back and keep everyone out of the kitchen—this whole area—until I give the all clear."

"How do I do that?"

"Figure it out."

I had my hand on the knob when Chuck's curse stopped me. "Fuck a duck." Ludik pointed to a cabinet door that was ajar in the back corner. Slumped on the bottom shelf was the body of Unibrow. The FSO agent had been folded, knees to nose, and shoved inside. Two ends of coax dangled from his neck.

Nova crouched to test for vitals, then stood. "Leave him. This may help us."

I studied her. "How?"

"Are you still here?"

I hurried to the door and stopped. "By the way, where's Glinka?"

"Pike."

"Going."

thirty-seven

I needed to use my back to open the swinging door from the kitchen because both hands were trying to keep the tray of dessert plates from rattling from my anxiety. All eyes in Video Village found me. Latrell said, "What's it going to be, Chef?"

"A little thing I like to call 'roll-speed.' Marisol, you go handheld to carry me in. Leading shot until I pass you, then break off to hose cutaways of the dessert and reax shots of Ilona. Declan, would you do the honors?" The audio tech mic'd me up. Marisol popped her C300 off the sticks and signaled ready. I paused at the entry to the veranda to await confirmation they were recording. But actually to get my shit together. My nervous shakes had toppled a chou ball off one of the mini-pyramids I'd built on each plate.

To wipe the blackboard clean of the two dead men in the pantry and the minefield ahead, I rolled a mental slo-mo of Astrid in Hemingway's booth mugging at Les Deux Magots on the wall above her. Paris. Our made-to-order moveable feast, a forever banquet table stretching out to the lives ahead of us. For Astrid, I flatlined my jitters. For Astrid, I numbed myself. Same as I'd seen Nova do it, I opened the tap and ran the ice water. For Astrid. For closure.

Leading with my celebrity chef grin again, I breezed out, presenting the tray. There I was, the host-provocateur who beat the drum of authenticity, hiding like a coward behind the skirts of TV host artifice, a masquerade to see me through. *"Qu'est-ce que c'est pour dessert? Is it pâte à choux? Non, mes amis.* It is more special than that." I waited for Marisol to settle her shot on Ilona, who had her hands clenched to her chest in unabashed glee. "It's none other than...*pâte par* Napsugár."

"Oh, Chef Pike, you honor me so."

"What better way to celebrate today's collaboration? I'm delighted that you're pleased."

"And yet."

"...Yet?"

"I was hoping we could present the tower. I had envisioned the entire croquembouche." She windmilled both arms to indicate grandness.

A flare of panic hit me. Deflect, deflect. I took it to her husband. *"Ur* Tábori, may I make a peace offering to you, sir?" I set a dessert before him. The oligarch brushed the dish aside and concentrated on his texting. Not even a glance up to acknowledge.

"I really want my choux tower. Wouldn't that be stunning? Chef Pike, are you listening?"

Ignaz Tábori finally looked up. "Why are you such an asshole? Give her what she wants."

"I'm guessing from your question that my whole peace offering thing didn't wash."

Ilona clanged her fork down. "Why can't you bring it out?"

"I don't think it would be good optics. Visually. Which is what optics are, aren't they? Ha. What I'm saying is it's not so celebratory when your husband looks like I just ran over his dog." I checked Video Village, hoping for Nova and the all clear. No Nova. Not yet.

Stretch. Stall. Improvise.

I drew my chair close to Tábori. "I regret this landed on a sour note. Can we talk it through?"

He quit texting and lobbed his phone onto the tablecloth. "You want to talk? Allow me to share a quaint aphorism we have in my country. Ready? 'Bolond lyukból bolond szél fúj.' You like that? It means 'foolish wind blows out of a foolish hole.' In case you are not smart enough to figure this out, you are the hole."

"I kinda got that."

"Che-efff…" Napsugár, calling me and craning toward the kitchen, amping my nerves. Where the hell was Nova? How long does it take to carry out one body?

"A moment, Ilona." I smiled at the seething oligarch. "Don't you think it would be good PR to repair things and have a moment of coming together on camera?" I heard Ilona slide her chair back. "Napsugár, we need to hold places. For the editing, you see." She stood.

"I will say nothing. Not without my translator here." But Tábori couldn't restrain himself. He spoke low, jabbing me with a finger on one of my Taser burns. "Sebastian Pike, I thought I would like you. Your contrarian manner on television seemed charming. But only on the television, I now see. You offer fake hospitality—erudite conversation, playful ways, gourmet lunch, sweet dessert—and you ambush, pow, asking the rude things."

"It's what I do. And how are any of my questions new to you? It's all over the internet."

"Fuck the internet. And fuck your show. And fuck me for agreeing to be on it."

Ilona started to wander. "Don't worry, Chef. I'll go get it myself. I can handle it."

"No, Ilona, stay here, please. We need you here for the show."

Lordy, she was headed for the kitchen. "I'll be back with the real dessert," she said. My stall was falling apart. What could I do? I turned back to Tábori, speaking loudly to make sure his wife would hear. "You're sorry you did this show? Fine. Tell you what, *Ur* Tábori. Say the word, and it never goes on the air."

Ilona Tábori hit the brakes. "What is this talk?"

The oligarch snorted. "This is more foolish wind from your hole."

I raised a hand and took an oath. "Swear to Emeril."

"You are serious about this."

"Say the word and the whole episode goes straight to the vault."

My ploy had not only arrested Ilona from going to the kitchen, it reeled her back. "Ignaz, you will not dare." Sandals clicked up behind my chair. Ilona bulled between us to assail her husband. "You cannot agree to this. Cannot."

"Ily, please. This is not your affair."

I juggled my hands like scales. "Mm, yes and no." I didn't know where I got the inspiration to pit her ego against the oligarch's fears, but after seeing what I'd started, I fanned the flames. "Napsugár and I did do an exceptional kitchen segment."

"Which is my moment on *Hangry Globe*. It will be the promo."

"There are greater concerns than your silly dessert moment."

"My moment, baking with the great Chef Pike, that is not silly to me. What will I tell my friends? My mother."

"You will tell your friends and, and *kedves anyád*, that there are other factors to consider. Greater concerns."

Still no sign of Nova. I applied more heat. "So that is your decision, then? We kill it?"

"Wait. Is not his decision."

"Oh, no? You enjoy this good life I give you, with the shopping and the face treatments and the frivolous indulgences—"

"*Te szar.*"

"Yes, I am that. I am a son of a bitch because why? Because you are too selfish to be aware of the grave pressures on me." And because he couldn't leave it there, he tagged it with, "*Te kurva*."

"You dare call me bitch?" She picked up the dessert plate to throw at him. But set it down and punched him in the nose. Blood streamed onto Tábori's slim-tailored shirt. He wadded his napkin against his face. She balled a fist to strike again, but the Russian security agent Glinka had signaled to stay put enveloped her in a hold from behind.

While he wrestled Napsugár away, Cammie Nova appeared in Video Village, paused to let them by, then continued onto the veranda. "Chef, if you want to call cut, I think that's a wrap."

I studied her. "Are we good?"

Offhand, with a hint of a smile, she said, "We are good."

"Then cut." I handed my napkin to Tábori to replace his bloody one, then turned to the crew. "Attention, ladies and gentlemen, that is a—" An engine roared. Then tires squealed like a jailbreak from Hell.

thirty-eight

Heads whipped toward the low garden wall overlooking the driveway. A distant voice shouted, "*Arrêtez!* Stop!" Then more of the same in Russian. The FSO agent discarded Mrs. T. and scrambled over the tabletop, sending plates, glassware, and silver flying. He skidded off feetfirst and yanked Ignaz Tábori out of his chair, shoving him to the ground, squatting over him with his gun hand inside his coat. But all the action was outside.

The approaching vehicle growled. The veranda sat atop a knoll, so only the stepladder lashed to the roof of the Connexion Côte van was visible over the hedge as it vroomed by at highway speed. Hard soles in foot pursuit stopped below the veranda. Another warning shout to stop. "*Ostanavlivat'sya!*" A pistol shot. A tinkling of glass.

The man covering Tábori drew his piece.

The feet outside resumed the chase.

The motor noise dimmed as the Opel veered down the slope toward the main gate.

The bang of metal colliding with metal echoed up the rock cove.

The screech of radials said the van broke through the gate.

The racing engine grew faint until it got bleached out by the silence of privileged real estate.

The breathing resumed on the veranda.

We all tasted scorched rubber and gun smoke.

My instinct, aside from wanting to get my folks out of there, was to study Nova. Was that sequence the execution of an exfiltration plan or the sound of one falling apart? Her face gave nothing away.

Bangs and Beard, Glinka's lead FSO posse, raced in from the guesthouse. No pistols for these two. Each gripped compact Vityaz submachine guns in don't-fuck-with-me black. Bangs called out in Russian, then in English. "Where is he? Where is Glinka?" His demand came wrapped in panic. This was a major screwup. The dread of lost careers and hard labor flashed in their eyes.

Ignaz Tábori got back on his feet. Answering in Russian, he held his bloody napkin to his ear, miming a cell phone, and pointed to where Putin's accountant had gone. The FSO pair started in that direction but were met at the edge of Video Village by a breathless member of their FSO team racing in from outside. "That cable repairman. He took off. Noskov is dead."

"Where?" said Bangs.

"His body, it is outside. Behind where the cable van was parked."

Bangs charged off toward the guesthouse, snapping an order to Beard on his way. Beard motioned the two remaining FSO agents to come along. Those three disappeared to search the mansion, calling Glinka's name. More tire squeals, this time from the direction of the guesthouse. Bangs, blasting off in pursuit of the getaway van.

Cammie approached me. "I say we strike this location."

NOVA AND I PACKED UP the kitchen ourselves. Cammie told the crew she had fired Chuck Ludik and sent him away in an Uber for neglecting to bring the main course backups. Nobody seemed surprised or bothered.

While Hoss, Latrell, Marisol, and Declan toted their remaining gear out toward the vans in the driveway, she and I moved quickly, more about speed than fussiness. After two killings in there, what's an abandoned hotel pan or a ramekin left soaking in the sink? The idea was break camp and get out.

One of the Russians came in from the dining room, made a wordless circuit of the island, then disappeared into the pantry calling out, "*Gospodin* Glinka?" He emerged from his recon seconds later holding my knife out to me. "Is yours?"

"There it is! My favorite knife, you found it." I beamed relief and took it from him. "Bless you. I truly appreciate it." The FSO man ignored me and continued his search down the back hall and into the garage.

Nova said, "Good thing I stopped you from using that. He would have found more than a knife."

"Yes, blood. A bastard to explain. Maybe a sauce to go with *Úr* Tábori's rabbit." Nova picked my blade cover off the counter and handed it over. That Carter Apprentice was my pal. Not only because of how beautifully it cut, but deep sentimental value. I sheathed the knife, slid it in my jeans pocket, and kept loading. "Won't these security types wonder where Chuck is?"

"I'll tell them the same thing I told our crew. But I wouldn't sweat it. Security's usually more focused on who's coming in than going out."

"Speaking of." I made a privacy check. "Where's Waldo?"

"Where indeed?"

Beard, the ranking FSO thug, marched through the swinging door with Ignaz Tábori close behind. "You." The Russian addressed Nova. "I am told you are in charge of this…program, yes?"

The Hungarian stepped forward. His shirtfront still bore the indignity of the nosebleed his wife gave him. "I already told you, she is the producer. The boss of this."

"Come." It wasn't a polite request. Beard made that clear by adjusting his grip on the machine gun. "Now." Cammie started for the door. I followed, but the bodyguard blocked me. "Not you. Her."

"Wrap the kitchen, Chef," she said, then was gone.

I had to steady myself on the countertop against a new wave of anxiety. What if she's burned? What if she never came back? What will they do to her? What happens with me and the crew? I told myself stop. Just stop. There lies the black hole. Don't forget Nova handled two attackers at Aigues-Mortes. Hop off the hamster wheel. Do what she said. Wrap the kitchen.

I clawed up a pile of utensils and dropped them in the milk crate on the floor. Then the next handful. Done. I popped the catches of the roadie trunk and opened the lid. And got a jump scare.

Squeezed inside, curled in the fetal position, Arkady Glinka stared up at me in alarm.

I slammed the lid and snapped the latches.

Damn, I wished Nova was there.

"Wrap the kitchen," she'd said. Meaning the roadie case with the prize inside. Simple enough. I gave it a shove. The heavy-duty casters turned and aligned. The cargo trunk wasn't easy to steer, but I humped it around the kitchen counter and aimed it down the hall. On the roll I wondered what to do with it. Ask Hoss for a hand? Fine, as long as the big man didn't open it up. But then, which vehicle? Nova probably wouldn't want Glinka stowed in a crew van; she'd lose control of him. Plus, she surely had a destination in mind. OK, so: help from Hoss; stow it in our SUV; cool.

I pulled open the door leading to the garage. What I saw slammed me to a halt.

The entire crew—Latrell, Marisol, Declan, and Hoss—were clustered behind the two show vans in the driveway. The other two FSO agents were opening the roadie trunks and searching inside.

I eased the door closed so I wouldn't be noticed. In one direction, a Russian with a machine gun, in the other, certain discovery.

Think.

I needed Nova. But this was my call now.

At the Culinary Institute, I learned a French term: *pis aller*. It's a call to take action as a last resort. Do something. I could either piss myself or *pis aller*.

I hustled the ATA case back into the kitchen and tried to remember how much space was left inside it. Maybe I could drape an apron over Glinka and pile on a bunch of utensils and gadgets. Or how about the excess choux balls? Load them in, and it would not only appear full of pastry, maybe I could distract the Russian guards with free samples.

A meteor shower of scary thoughts pummeled me. What if I accidentally suffocated him? Where the hell was Nova? Was she all right? I got to work. And swore I would never again say or think the words "Mission: Accomplished."

thirty-nine

An eternity later I pushed the stern of the roadie trunk down the hall again. This time, Hoss steered the bow. When the big fella muscled the front casters over the threshold to the garage they landed unevenly. The ATA case started to tip over. I called out a "Whoa, whoa," and Hoss managed to bear-hug the side before it crashed.

"My bad."

"Shake it off. We need to get this loaded, not stop for a cleanup." We rolled through the garage toward the driveway. The closer we got to the SUV, the more I worried about what I left behind in the house. I didn't care how resourceful Nova was, I couldn't deal with leaving her. So, I wouldn't. As soon as we loaded the case, I would go back. I had no clue what I could do but, if nothing else, create a distraction she could take advantage of. The plan was desperate, which described how I felt.

"You're only getting to this now?" Cammie strode out behind me into the garage, followed by Beard and the oligarch. "What have you been up to all this time?"

"I encountered a slight complication. Had to make a critical adjustment. Is everything OK? Are you OK?"

She waggled the iffy sign. "Am now, anyway. I got forced into a bit of a negotiation about the segment. Did I say negotiation?" She indicated her escorts. "One of me against two of them and a machine gun. They demanded our digital media—both video and audio—so Tábori could be sure we spiked the segment."

Beard and Tábori strode by us and ordered my DP and audio tech to give up the recordings. Nova hand-signaled her OK to Latrell and Declan, then said, "Let's get this loaded and haul ass." Hoss and I finished rolling the cargo trunk to the rear hatch of the Brabus. The oligarch met us there holding three Red Mini-Mags, a pair of CFexpress cards, and a Seagate Portable.

I looked over our confiscated property. "That's about six thousand worth of media you took from us."

"Invoice my office, you asshole."

"Um, less machismo, more loading?" Nova, keeping this moving. Hoss and I stooped to hoist the case.

"Careful when you slide it in, Hoss. Don't mash my croquembouche."

"*Zhdat'*." Beard strode over. "Wait." He tapped the lid. "Open." When Hoss reached to comply, Nova rushed in and put up a hand to stop him. The FSO agent struck a challenging pose.

Cammie didn't back down. "You said we could go if we turned over the media." She addressed me and Hoss. "Load it in." Beard unslung the Vityaz-SN and rested his finger on the trigger guard.

I stepped toward him. "Hey, hey, be cool, that's not necessary." Beard started yelling something in Russian and shouldered the stock to take aim at me. I tried appealing to Tábori. "Have your pal stand down. We just want to go without any more bullshit delays." No dice. The Hungarian was enjoying this too much. Cammie slid closer to Beard. She stopped when he jammed the muzzle of his machine gun into my chest, spewing more Russian. I relented with a single nod to him. He took a step away but still trained the gun on me.

Making no sudden moves, I undid the catches. Nova's eyes widened. Beard gestured me to back up. I obeyed, and he opened the lid.

A carpet of choux balls topped the inside. Dozens of them, coated in caramel, wall to wall, end to end. A broom leaned inside the garage door. The FSO agent used the handle end to poke the contents. Three inches down, he met resistance. Keeping his weapon in one hand, with the other he used the broomstick to pry up the cookie sheet I had placed underneath the pastry. Nova assumed a combat-ready pose, inching again closer to the machine gun. Beard tossed aside the broom, lifted the cookie sheet, and dipped his head for a peek at what hid underneath.

The milk crate full of utensils and kitchenware.

Nova shot a look at me. I gave up nothing, only said to Tábori, "If you're through farting around, your party sucks, and we're going home."

The crew mounted up and rolled. Nova got behind the wheel of the Brabus. As I shut the passenger door she said, "I'm going back in. No way I am leaving here without Glinka. Where did you stash him?"

"Please, let us now go." Glinka. From the rear. Nova whirled. "*Da*, in here," came the voice from inside the pastry pyramid. I gave Cammie a Cheshire grin.

Nova threw it in gear. Putin's elite team of Federal Protective Service agents stepped aside to let her pass, and she sped to catch up with the crew vans. Her route took her around the villa, crunching getaway glass near the veranda, down the driveway, and through the busted gate, which was gaping and scored by blue paint. When she gained speed on the Moyenne Corniche, she checked her mirrors. Satisfied we didn't have a tail, she swatted my arm. "You dog. In the goddamned pastry tower?"

"I had to do something. They were popping all the roadie crates. It's sort of a Trojan croquembouche. You approve?"

"You're showing me something, Food Boy."

We came to a side road, and she made a sharp last-second veer onto it, breaking off from the *Hangry Globe* motorcade. The pastry tower shifted. A Russian curse came from inside. "Sorry, back there," she said. "We're late for a delivery."

forty

The turn took us off the scenic Moyenne onto a hidden lane. The track ran flush against a cliffside and descended at steep angles over ruts and potholes. The jaggy terrain was no problem for the suspension of the Brabus, but the narrow road wouldn't leave much room if we encountered anyone coming up. As a pro traveler I've learned every trip reveals a theme. That day's motif presented itself inches from my side window: a scrotum-raising drop into the canyon. "Let me remind you of Princess Grace. 'Nuff said?"

"Uh, yuh."

Thankfully, a few meters on, we left the abyss behind. Scrub brush flanked the road. I relaxed enough to complain. "Know what pisses me off? Confiscating our drives. That was one of our best segments, especially Napsugár slugging his nose." Nova wore a sly grin. I said, "Share with the class."

"During the wrap I had Latrell stow the media in his glove compartment. Tábori confiscated blanks." A chuckle came from the croquembouche, followed by a muttered, "*Amerikantsy*."

Even though it was late afternoon, the woods became dense enough to flip the GPS to night mode. As we crawled through the darkling tunnel of figs and Aleppo pines, Cammie took one hand off the wheel to lower the sun visor. She pressed a button. The vanity mirror flopped down to expose a hidden compartment. SSO Nova took out a SIG Sauer P226. She closed up the works and set the 9mm on the center console. I wanted to say that all I got with my Mercedes was a free travel mug, but this was far from smart-ass time, even for me. When we escaped the villa, in my mind, we were done. But her precaution told me we were not in the clear yet.

At last, the road leveled at the foot of the cliffs. It transitioned into a wide alley beneath a pair of beachy motels high enough on the hillside to sell ocean views to tourists, and not much else. Keeping one hand resting on the SIG, Nova monitored all facing windows and archways as she steered the curvature of the shared driveway. Forty meters later, it delivered us to a familiar sight, the Basse Corniche, the main road that hugs the coastline. To the right, it led toward Nice; to the left, Monaco, Menton, and the Italian border. She waited for some cars to clear the westbound lane and turned right.

I made a side mirror check to see if anyone was following. A kilometer back, I spotted the mouth of the Saint-Laurent traffic tunnel, the one that began the no-camera zone where we lost Tábori's caravan two days before. Half a klick onward, Nova carved a hard left into a driveway under a colorful sign illustrated with Jet Skis and windsurfers. Cap Roux Centre de Sports Nautiques. And in English, Rent by Hour or Day!

An incline sloped down to a chain-link gate between a painted cinderblock wall and the water sports rental office. A hand-printed sign was taped in the window: "*Fermé pour Événement Privé.*" The execution of logistics should have put me at ease. Instead, it creeped me out. The innocuous little sign, "Closed for Private Event," spoke volumes about the clandestine world's ease of manipulation, rapid adjustment to circumstances—and reach. For a guy who spent his life taking nothing at face value, this confirmed things I wished existed only in the long nights of me and my twitchy imagination.

Nova braked, idling two car lengths from the gate. She speed-dialed a number, flashed brights, and hung up. The sequence was obviously the safety signal, because a man in a Hawaiian shirt appeared within the gate and rolled it aside. Passing by, I recognized Ortiz, our security agent-slash-sniper from Nice. The PPO toted an M4.

We came into a paved parking area right on the beach. The quarter-acre lot was walled on the landward sides and ringed by nearly every water toy imaginable. Stockpiles of multicolored kayaks and stand-up paddleboards leaned upright against a rail. Arranged in neatly slanted rows sat windsurfers, sailing dinghies, and a giant inflatable unicorn. A gangway spanning the beach led to a small floating dock with a half dozen Jet Skis, two catamarans, and a Bombard rigid inflatable tied to it. Nova turned a tight circle around the lot, bringing into view the rest of the exfiltration team's vehicles that were parked perpendicular to the storage shelter. Following SOP for a rapid exit, all were nose-out: Espy's Volvo, a Renault SUV, and the Connexion Côte van. Its mashed front grille, cracked windscreen, and missing driver-side mirror put visuals to the sound effects we'd heard from Tábori's veranda during its vanishing act. Cammie backed into the wide space between the cable TV van and the seawall, leaving room at one side to haul the Russian out of his pastry cage.

"Everybody good?" Director of Special Activities Gregg Espy emerged from the rental office, tailed by Kurt Harrison, who also cradled a carbine. The PPO's head was on a swivel, checking all flanks: beach, water, hills. The team's paramilitary protection officer had red-lined into high alert.

"Good and sticky," said Glinka when Nova and I unloaded him and half the choux tower out the rear passenger door. Caramel dappled every part of him. His coat, his pants, his face, even his baldpate.

"Clear, and ready for transfer," reported Nova, underscoring the gravity of the exchange with military formality. As with Harrison, she became all eyes, seeing the near and the far simultaneously. While I scanned the reds and yellows of the rental craft on display and, up the sand, the same house where I'd once made breakfast for Bono and the Edge, Nova explored for wall breaches and suspicious boat traffic. I tried to reconcile this Nova with the woman I woke up with that morning, naked and interlaced by legs and arms, who made love with me at sunup. Then, before we left her room, surprised me with a long, silent embrace that felt sacramental. Was this her work mode or who she really was? Or was she all these things because none of us is only one thing?

Espy and Glinka greeted each other more like frat bros than handler and mole. They threw hugs on each other, and their barroom laughter got broken by "Greggorys!" and "Kashas!" and vigorous back claps. More guffaws followed when the CIA man tried in vain to wipe caramel off his hands.

"You must pardon us," said Arkady Glinka. "It has been too long. Encrypted cables and coded emails are a poor substitute."

Harrison leaned in to Espy. "Tick tock, sir."

"Kasha, my security man, hates vulnerability. We'll continue this after we get you out of the red zone. Let me confirm, you did bring everything?"

"Always the rigorous one, Greggory." The Russian tapped his forehead. "Is all in here."

The DSA chuckled. "Oh God, we're in trouble."

"Not to worry." He spread his suit coat and patted a flat bulge like a travelers' pouch under his shirt. "Is also here, in case."

Harrison flicked a hand signal. The outboard on the sixteen-foot Bombard sprung to life. The muscular engine settled to a purr. PPO Ortiz climbed out of the vessel onto the dock to wait. I grinned at Espy. "Please tell me you're going to skyhook *Gospodin* Glinka out of that thing like Bond at the end of *Thunderball.*"

"I'd pay to see that." Espy gestured offshore. "That's the best I could do." Half a kilometer out, a super-luxury yacht waited. The sharp glare of the low afternoon sun put it in silhouette, but through the blinding light I could make out the helicopter on its landing pad. I understood the choice of location. Fast-water exit in a surveillance camera dead zone.

"Now would be good, sir," said Harrison.

"Want me to drive you over?" asked Nova.

Espy scoffed. "All fifty meters? I'll take it from here. Watch the flank, then you and Pike meet me down by the Bombard when we get there."

Nova looked puzzled. "Meet you on the dock?"

"Am I not speaking English?" He motioned for Harrison to take the point and led Glinka across the blacktop toward the ramp. Nova complied and held her place at the front end of our SUV to give cover. I skidded on a chou ball. I kicked another loose one under the Connexion Côte van. It rolled through a small puddle underneath it and changed color. To red.

I slid open the side door of the van. Nova glanced to see what the hell I was up to, then resumed her watch. I startled her by appearing beside her, mouth gaping.

She followed me to the van's cargo bay. Inside rested the body of the cable repair guy where she and the would-be Food Sarge had stashed it. Atop that body lay the corpse of Chuck Ludik. A stream of crimson coursed from a knife protruding from his back. His lifeless hand held an unlit cig wedged between his fingers.

Words choked as I said them. "Who would do this?" She rotated to give uneasy regard to her team. Espy. Harrison. Ortiz.

A shot ripped the air.

Kurt Harrison went down. The security lead dropped his rifle and crumpled on the asphalt. Nova bolted to the front end of the van with her gun braced. On her way she spoke evenly to me. "Keep down and get in the car—now."

Espy tried to pick up Harrison's M4, but another bullet sang off the ground beside it. He retreated, manhandling Glinka to cover behind a trailered skiff. Two shots missed them and punctured the hull of the boat.

The DSA pushed the Russian flat on the pavement and knelt over him, two-handing his pistol.

Down on the dock, Ortiz assumed a crouch behind a piling. The PPO signaled to Espy and Nova, pointing to the scrubby hillside on the other side of the wall. After flashing two fingers to indicate the firing positions, four more shots rang out, each one sending splinters flying from the thick post in front of him. He returned fire to one zone, then braced to draw aim on the second. Before he got off a shot, an explosion of pink mist rose from his skull. Ortiz's body toppled backwards on the dock. His assault rifle made a splash and sank.

I opened the SUV's passenger door but didn't get in. A shot meant for Nova had passed her, hit the windshield, and traveled through the side window right where I would have been sitting if I'd been five seconds faster. I squatted with my back against the rear door, panting.

Then, as suddenly as it all started, the firing stopped. I scanned the beach to see if the gunplay prompted any attention. Hopefully of someone who'd call the gendarmes. But that section of Cap Roux didn't have public sand, and this late in the afternoon, I saw no trespassers. I was about to reach in the Brabus for my cell phone when I heard a short whistle.

Espy. Waving to Nova. "Wall," he said. I gophered up. The windshield was cracked. I was looking through a kaleidoscope, but I saw movement across the lot. A man with a rifle was rolling over the top of the cinder block, coming in.

Nova fired a shot. A puff of concrete dust came off the wall beside the intruder as he made his drop. Accuracy with a sidearm at distance is tough, but she held her brace against the grille of the van. She squeezed off one more. A patient beat, then another. That one scored. Red spatter decorated the paint. The man reeled but stayed up and stumbled out of sight toward the gate. A covering rifle shot from the bluff tore through the front of the cable TV van. I ducked. When I came up, a sharp pang froze me.

Nova was gone.

But she wasn't hit. She was disappearing around the rear of the van, scrambling low along the storage barn toward the gate. Off to stop the attacker from opening it, I guessed. But the squeak-squeak of metal rollers and the rattle of chain link told another story. Engines revved, tires wailed, then two Volvo SUVs raced in, zooming past either end of the skiff where Espy and Glinka were hiding. Espy fired a shot at the first vehicle, but it was going fast, and he missed, hitting the rear window.

Both XC90s skidded to a stop beside Espy and Glinka, boxing them in with no cover. The driver of the bronze Volvo trained a shotgun out the window on them. The driver of the gray one rolled out the far side and aimed his rifle across the hood. Checkmated, Espy flipped his pistol to hold it by the barrel, set it on the ground, and showed hands. Glinka used the boat trailer to pull himself up with a grunt.

"You. Step away from the car." Without hesitation I did as I was told. I knew better than to argue with Sigurd Ringstad.

forty-one

"Let's talk, brother." Espy, easy and cool. A career intel man's de-escalation opener.

Ringstad's reply came instantly. The bullet whizzed past the DSA's head. A close one that made Espy duck from the knees and flinch his shoulders to his ears. The on-purpose miss was a message. Yeah, there was talk to be done. But Ringstad held the conch. An AK assault conch. "Where's your mongrel? Where did she go?"

Espy adjusted his collar. "I thought you took her out with my other two."

When Ringstad glared at me, I returned "search me" hands and tried not to look in the direction Nova had gone. The leader spoke to his other man. "Thorvald." He drew a circle in the air, a signal that sent his partner off on a search. Thorvald. The motorcycle assassin from Paris. Emil Dard's ex. And once upon a time, Cammie Nova's joe. As I watched him disappear with his shotgun, I couldn't still my pulse.

"Planning a trip, were you, *Gospodin* Glinka?"

The Russian tensed at the sound of his own name. He a-hemmed. He fidgeted. He spoke. But his baritone had lost its authority. "Please. I am not a combatant. I do office work."

Sigurd Ringstad laughed. "I know what office work you do. It's why you are here, correct?" The captor's wolf eyes sized up his prey. "Before, I only wanted you dead. But now that I have you here, if you are a good boy, I will let you live to go on a trip."

"...A good boy?"

"One who is smart enough to provide Første Stamme all this money you have stolen from your boss." The Russian blanched. A chalky tongue passed over his lips. "Arkady, don't insult me. I know all about your embezzlement from Putin *khuylo*. And if you deny or play games, I'll shoot you right now." He trained the assault rifle on him. "A quick yes or no. Time's wasting."

With Thorvald gone hunting and Ringstad engaged, Espy maneuvered a half step closer to his pistol on the ground. Ringstad swiveled the muzzle to him. "What the fuck are you doing?"

"There's no need to hurt him."

"Why so protective, DSA Espy? Are you performing your duty? Loyalty to your *nomenklatura* mole? The traitor who shared his many secrets with you? Huh? Or is it because you are afraid you will lose the millions you helped him embezzle from Putin?"

That question exposed a puzzle piece that nagged me since Espy pimp-slapped me for asking what the big deal was about an audit of Glinka. Now came a bold accusation from Ringstad. Could it be? If Espy were dirty, an audit would expose him, too. The DSA didn't answer. The Norwegian pushed some more. "I see you are surprised that I knew about your partnership. That *Gospodin* Glinka embezzled the money, and that you used your Agency position to launder it. Don't look away. This is true, yes?"

I made a hard study of the CIA officer. If this were true it explained a lot. Espy: obsessed with exfiltrating Glinka before he got burned. Espy: quizzing me about Nova's meetups and contacts. Was Espy paranoid about Nova being onto him?

Just when I started to wonder if I was connecting red strings from thumbtacks like a conspiracy nut in his log cabin hideout, Espy said, "I think we could cut a deal here."

So. Some conspiracy theories aren't nutty.

"You're in no position to negotiate. Not with Glinka's money."

Espy gestured a line from himself to Putin's accountant. It might as well have been with red string. "That money is ours."

The man with the AK disagreed. "Not anymore."

Espy said, "There's plenty for a three-way divvy." There it was, the DSA, eliminating any doubt he conspired with the Russian to line his pockets.

But Arkady Glinka said, "I like two ways better," lobbing the first volley of making his own deal, cutting his CIA partner out. I was witnessing a case study of the dark side of human nature. To save his own skin, Glinka sweetened his pitch to Ringstad. "I have passwords for offshore accounts he doesn't know about. And stashes of gold and currency around the globe."

But Espy, he was a survivor. You don't rise up the intel bureaucracy without being quick to self-preservation moves. "Consider me value-added. I can be your eyes and ears in US intel. You need my capability."

"Capability? Who's holding the gun on you?"

"I'm talking inside capability." Espy was selling now. Or, more accurately, selling out.

Ringstad regarded the CIA man with disdain. "You don't think I have my insiders? I'm surprised...what is the word...a gamer like you would underestimate Første Stamme."

"Let's not BS each other, Sigurd. You got lucky and scored one crumb of intel that Glinka was coming out. Otherwise, you've been chasing us like a dog with firecrackers tied to its tail because you don't know jack."

Espy had played him. Pride sucked the Norwegian into dick measuring. "My American friend. Who do you think devised the scenario that got all this moving? Do you think because I hold an ideology that I'm some amateur, some wide-eyed zealot?" He tipped his rifle toward the Russian. "Long ago I knew all about this one's money laundering with you. I set in motion the blackmail to expose *Gospodin* Glinka. I waited. I predicted you would freak and respond with this exfiltration so I could kill him. But now I have him. And can trade his life for his money. Because you delivered him to me here to this beautiful place."

Ringstad gestured to the multimillion-euro villas, the members-only cabanas up the beach, the flotilla of super-luxe yachts bobbing on the golden chop. Then he squinted at the eastern horizon. "Way out there. Boatloads of filth coming to stain our homeland and pollute our culture. They bring their stinky food, and dirty skin, and secret languages. Their dark stares." He addressed his audience. "How long do you suppose the migration would have lasted if those rafts of brown garbage landed here on the Riviera instead of Turkey or Greece or Bulgaria?"

He grew alert to footsteps. Thorvald hustled back. "No sign of her. Eklund's dead by the gate." He showed a grave face. "I found Karlsson in the van. He's dead, too. He must have killed one of their guys first. There's a poor *drittsekk* in there with a knife in his back."

"Use your head, Thorvy. They killed Karlsson. Why do you think his van is here?" Ringstad gestured with his weapon to Espy. "You?"

"Had to be." Espy, ever casual, admitting that he killed Ludik. And then, bolstering street cred, "Hey, brother, Glinka and I needed to pull our disappearing act without witnesses."

"You asshole." I couldn't hold my tongue. "That's why you wanted Nova and me to meet you on the dock. No witnesses." I wondered if Espy planned to shoot the PPOs, too. Or were Harrison and Ortiz in this with him?

"It's a rough business, Chef. But a business it is, right, *bror*?" He had some stones, calling Ringstad brother in his native tongue. Then grinning. "Do we deal?"

Ringstad whipped the barrel of his assault rifle across Espy's face. Glinka shrieked and frogged back. Espy cursed and pressed a hand against his cheek. The AK's sight post sliced him good. A filet of skin hung in a flap. Blood coursed down the CIA man's sleeve. The Norwegian wiped the muzzle on his pants. "Don't patronize me, you shit."

"I can't stop bleeding."

"You won't have to worry soon enough. Welcome to your payday."

I made a desperate sweep for any sign of Nova. She wouldn't take off, but where was she? And what could she do? What could I? When their attention slid off me, could I work a fade? Was the gate still open? If I made a break between the cars, how far would I get?

"Payday for what? I never did anything to you."

"Bullshit. You were washing money through a friend of our cause, a rock star. He told me you recruited him because the music business makes a perfect laundry. The concerts, the merch, all that. Much is still done in cash, and the books are all cooked anyway. You know who I'm talking about."

With his hand pressed against his cheek, Espy's whole body rocked as he nodded.

"Say it."

"Kogg."

I forced myself to relax my jaw before it fractured. Ever since talking to Chipper and Cedric, I figured it was Ringstad who killed Kogg over money. Now to learn that it was Espy's and Glinka's? Embezzled from Putin? When Espy told me Rule Number One for surviving the spy business was having an exit strategy, I had no idea his involved corruption with a side of treason.

His game swagger gone, the DSA pleaded with Ringstad. "Look, none of that was about you. Our arrangement was with Kogg. I caught Kogg skimming from us. Glinka said we had to take him out as a lesson to others."

A trap door opened, hurtling me down a chute in a mad spiral. Disoriented and queasy, I tried to listen—needed to listen—through the surge of blood whooshing in my ears. Astrid and Kogg were dead because Glinka ordered it. And Espy made it happen!

"You call it skimming. Kogg was setting aside a percentage." Ringstad paused to underscore. "Setting it aside for a righteous cause he believed in. And when you killed Kogg, you set back Første Stamme's funding by years."

Espy became more antsy as implications landed. "I didn't know it was going to you."

"Like hell you didn't. How could you not know when you sent that bitch cook to spy on us?" What the hell? Was he talking about Astrid? Spying for Espy?

The DSA oathed up with a bloody palm. "I swear I never sent anyone to spy on you or Kogg."

"If not you, who else?"

"I...I don't know. But let's be forward focused. Right now, you've got Glinka. And me." The CIA man tried to gain traction by repositioning himself from hostage to advisor. "I think you need to not be emotional, Sigurd. Make a business decision."

Reeling, I struggled to process all this. Was Astrid spying for Espy, or was Ringstad paranoid? Either way, it was Espy, fucking DSA Espy, who set up the hit on the rock star that killed her. And the crooked Russian ordered it. My rage blinded me to the weapons around me. "Murderer. You fucking bastard." I charged at Espy.

Thorvald rammed the butt of his shotgun into my gut. The blow knocked the air out of me and threw me backwards against the side of the Brabus. I doubled up and collapsed. Chips of safety glass pressed into the side of my face where it hit the blacktop.

Ringstad said, "Don't be stupid. You would be dead if we couldn't use a celebrity hostage. Thorvald." The man with the shotgun straightened up. "Get out your phone. Before we go, we make a video of this one's execution." He moved in on Espy.

"No, don't."

"You will be on our social media. How did you just put it? 'As a lesson to others'? And also to show the reach of Første Stamme, which is not a bad thing to tell the world." Ringstad pulled Espy to stand in front of him and coached Thorvald on composing the shot. "Make sure Glinka is not in it. Only me, the AK, and our CIA prize." Espy tried to bust away. Ringstad grabbed his collar and jerked him back in place.

While they worked out the pose for the execution video, I pulled myself up to a sitting position on the pavement. The Brabus 900's front passenger door was still wide open. I leaned against the running board to rest the back of my throbbing head on the edge of the seat. My gaze fell on the door pocket. The bill of my cap protruded from it, right where I'd stuffed it at Tábori's security gate to hide my revolver.

forty-two

Ringstad and Thorvald were quarreling. It began in English but lapsed into terse Norwegian, peppered with cursing. Thorvald complained it was difficult to hold his shotgun and frame the video properly. Espy heckled. "Yeah, put the shotgun down. Or give it to me, I'll hold it." Ringstad drove a fist into his kidneys and shut him right up.

I used the distraction to ease my left hand toward the door pocket. I not only needed to get the gun, I had to sort out what to do once I had it. The snubbie had six .357 rounds. But the short barrel made accuracy funky, as I learned from PPO Harrison. I ran a mental dress rehearsal. Should I brace and fire from there or try to get close and surprise them? And who to shoot first? Because once I started, they weren't going to stand there and take it like paper targets. My fingers touched the bill of my cap when Thorvald snapped, "Let that chef make the video. He's the TV man."

Attention fell on me. I let my mouth go slack, pretending to be on the verge of hurling. Yet not pretending much. Ringstad said something in Norwegian. It sounded derisive, so probably about me. The pair snickered, notion dismissed.

When they turned away, I pulled the hat out of the door pocket and flipped it on the floor mat. I also made one more check for Nova. Nothing.

"Please. Must I be here for this?" Glinka wasn't keen on eyewitnessing a social media execution. Ringstad ordered him to stay put. I shifted an inch and slid my hand in the door pocket, and my pounding heart stopped dead.

The snubbie wasn't there.

"Come on, hurry. Do you have the framing?" Ringstad wanted to rock and roll. Espy took on the look of a dead man standing. The only thing missing was the proof-of-life newspaper to hold up.

Thorvald cradled the cell phone with two hands, his shotgun dangling by the shoulder strap. "Is good." Ringstad posed with the muzzle of his assault rifle to the back of Espy's head. He squared himself to the lens, ready to make his manifesto. His partner counted down in Norwegian. "*Tre... to... en.*"

An engine roared. Tires on the bronze Volvo spun, emitting a banshee scream and plumes of blue smoke. The SUV launched across the blacktop. As it sped by, Nova fired three shots at Ringstad, who spun, toppling into the side of the skiff. She aimed the grille at Thorvald. The XC90 plowed him backwards. His body folded forward over the hood until the bumper slammed into the seawall, pinning him against it at the thighs. The crash inflated the airbag, ejecting Nova's SIG Sauer from her hand. It flew over the seawall and into the drink.

Glinka dove for Espy's pistol. Espy jumped on him, and they wrestled for it on the blacktop. A round fired, muffled by flesh. Espy struggled to his feet over the Russian, who was moaning and clutching some nasty blood flow from his gut.

Dazed from the airbag, Nova staggered out the driver's side, shaking the beehive in her head. I got up from the deck, rushing to help her. I was rounding the rear of the Volvo as Thorvald Grepp, pale as death, blood filling his mouth, slid the banger down by its strap to point the muzzle at Nova.

I ran to pull her away. Before I reached her, two shots spanked the air. One hit Thorvald's chest. The next one split his nose. He dropped the shotgun, dead before his head bounced twice on the hood. Nova heard my footsteps and spun, ready to shoot my snubbie again, but tipped it skyward when she saw it was me.

Harrison called weakly from across the lot. "Nova, behind!" The wounded PPO was down but alive. Twenty yards away Espy had his 9mm up and was taking aim at her back.

The DSA got off one shot, a miss that punctured the Volvo. He started to draw a bead on her for a second try. She whirled around and fired. She missed. I made a snap choice and lunged into his line of fire to shield her and tackle him. Espy pulled the trigger.

When his slug hit me, I lost footing on one side and stumbled forward. My momentum sent me colliding into Espy, knocking him down on his back. I started to pass out. His body was pinned under my dead weight, but he wrestled his pistol free as Nova rushed up with her snub-nose. Espy held the muzzle to my temple. "Drop it." Nova hesitated, assessing the odds of a clean shot with the short barrel. "Drop it, or I swear he's—"

The paring knife had traveled the globe with me. Tokyo, Havana, Buenos Aires, Nairobi, Mumbai. That afternoon, I had almost left it in the Táboris's pantry. This time my Murray Carter traveled from the sheath in my jeans pocket into the soft flesh under Gregg Espy's jaw. It sunk into his neck point first. Only three and a half inches, but this chef had knife skills. A slice and a wiggle were all it took to sever his carotid artery. Like a page ripped from training day.

Nova kicked the gun out of Espy's limp hand and cradled me. I could tell I was putting out a lot of blood. She pressed her fingers hard to my wound. "Help's coming, I texted before." I tried to smile, but I knew it was weak. My eyes fluttered. The idling outboard motor kicked into gear. She turned toward the dock. Someone was booking it out to sea on the exfiltration boat.

"Who?" Damn, my voice was thready...

"Ringstad."

"Get him."

"No." She undid my belt and applied more pressure to my wound. "You hear that? Listen." Sirens approached. "Help's coming. Hold on... Pike?"

The last thing I saw before I blacked out was the flicker of emergency lights in Cammie's tears.

forty-three

Still in blackness, but no longer total. More like I was trapped in smoke from an oil fire. Light wanted in.

I made out distant chirps. Not birds, though. Too much cadence. Machines. Definitely monitoring equipment. Either I was waking up or God's gotcha is that when we die, we don't go to heaven or hell but a hospital.

The beeps sounded comforting after the random echoes that haunted the blur of my past however many hours. Or days. I don't remember a lot of what happened. I remember a chopper ride. Then a twilight landing at Princess Grace Hospital in Monaco. Weirdly, I admired the view as we descended. I was fading in and out then. My eyes had been heavy, but I forced them open, and I watched overhead ceiling lights tick by while medics sprinted my gurney to *urgence*. Doctors' voices mixed with psychedelic nightmares about getting chased, tortured, beaten, and shot. Not nightmares at all, as it turns out, but real. You know that because you, dear reader, stayed with me. You heard it all, and the telling kept me going. You were better than company. Having you here helped me survive, and I love you for that. I hope you'll stick around when I open my eyes. This could get interesting.

"You're back." A chair scraped. Cammie Nova smiled down at me through a mist. Her face was haggard; its skin bruised and chafed where it had met the airbag. She wore a butterfly bandage above one eye. To me, I was looking at a meadow of sunflowers.

"Think I'd leave without you?"

Cammie laughed but covered her mouth to hide the quiver of emotion. She wrapped cool fingers around my hand. "Are you in much pain?"

"Can't tell. I haven't been this high since my Willie Nelson two-parter."

"So, this is you? You nearly take the last freight and come back doing stand-up?"

"Making up for lost time." I looked around for a clock or a calendar. "Speaking of, how long has it been?"

"Yesterday." A man's voice. I worked to angle my head to see him. He moved closer to ease my strain. I'd seen this guy before. Cobwebs cleared. I remembered. He was Farrel, the man who tailed Nova to the wine bar in Arles. The guy Espy told me was an enemy agent. Farrel stood tall. He had a boxer's build. Maybe he knew he was an intimidating presence, especially looming over a hospital bed, because he took a step back and smiled. "Welcome back to the hangry globe, Chef Pike."

"This is my colleague, Reed Coleman." Nova said colleague, but her bearing telegraphed deference.

"Reed's good," he said. Instead of shaking, Coleman chinned a greeting. "By way of introduction, I'm with counterintel. I liaise with the Office of the Inspector General. That's a fancy way of saying I investigate the bad apples in various intelligence agencies for the OIG. I know you've been through the mill, but I need to hear about your interactions with DSA Espy." Then he corrected. "Ex-DSA."

I replayed the knife going in, easy as coring a Jersey tomato. I caught Cammie sending me the go-ahead sign. "Yeah, sure. However I can help."

A doctor knocked on his way in. He wore his white coat over camouflage fatigue pants. A nurse followed. "Mr. Pike, I'm Captain Nguyen.

I took the bullet out of your hip. Mind if I see how you're doing?" Nova and Coleman took the cue and stepped out. The doc and the nurse conferred over my vitals and checked the wound. "Incision looks good, if I do say myself. We had to wait to remove the bullet until the ER team repaired a nick in your femoral artery. That's low survivability, but somebody gave you vital first aid on-scene." Cammie, no doubt. "How is your pain on a ten scale?"

"Far out, man."

"Enjoy it now. You're going to experience a lot of discomfort when we get you up and moving."

"Beats the alternative. Question, Captain. Not to sound narcissistic, but did they fly you into Monaco just for me?"

Nguyen and the nurse traded looks. "You're at Landstuhl Regional Medical Center. In Germany." The memory came back in a fogged funhouse mirror. Rising to semiconsciousness, believing I was dead, soaring heavenward and floating on air. But instead of Saint Peter, I found an angel in a surgical mask sitting beside my stretcher in the belly of a medevac jet. It wasn't a hallucination. After they stopped my bleeding, they had airlifted me to the big US military hospital near Ramstein Air Base.

I dozed some. When I woke up, Cammie was leaning against the closet. Coleman was sitting in the guest chair smelling of residual cigar smoke. "Up for a chat?" I treated myself to an ice chip to wet my whistle and said yes. "Good. I want to know what Espy told you. About Nova, about the operation, anything."

Between sucking ice, resting my eyes, and pressing the morphine button, I spent the next thirty minutes describing how increasingly obsessed Espy got about getting Glinka out in time. Little did I know then about his money laundering motive. "He ground on me about Nova, too. Near paranoid. Always trying to discredit her."

"Like how?"

"Like wanting me to report to him about any contacts she made."

"Like with me?" The counterintel man smirked. "Come on, I clocked you peeking in that bar like a wet poodle. I do this for a living."

"Yes. He specifically asked about you. Pushy about it. I didn't know your name, but he described you and called you Farrel."

"You misheard. My code name is Feral."

"Nice. Vicious, but with hints of prior domestication."

Coleman chuckled. "Condor was already taken." The comic relief let me refresh. My interviewer waited and let his gentle stare speak. He wanted more. He got it.

"Espy told me you were a Russian agent, doing us dirty in Ukraine. So you know, I didn't give you up."

"Why not?"

"Because I trust her."

The OIG operative turned to Cammie, then grew contemplative. "SSO Nova, you may step out for this part, if you find it uncomfortable." She crossed her arms, settling in. Coleman continued with me. "Did Espy mention anything about her former fiancé?"

"Pointedly." I shared everything from the strange walk Espy took me on in Nice the night before the exfiltration when he quizzed me about her ex, the Russian double.

"Did he mention any communication coming out of our DIS? Sorry. Detainee Interrogation Site."

"He said he heard rumors Cammie's ex smuggled her a note from there and wanted to know if she told me anything about it."

"What did you tell him?"

My gaze rolled to Cammie. If I acknowledged what she confided in me, it would mean trouble for her. I turned back to the big man. And lied. "That I didn't know anything about it."

Satisfied, Coleman said, "You both seem to have done the right thing here. Nova told me she honored protocol and held this back from you. And after what you've been through, I'm deeming you conscious enough to hear the whole story. Well…the part I'm authorized to share, anyway. You may want to press that happy button."

Can I say I liked this guy's style? Mainly because it wasn't a style. Unlike Gregg Espy, who felt like an Ivy League poser from day one on the Paris bateau, Reed "Feral" Coleman played it straight. His quiet command made him trustworthy. If there was such a thing in tradecraft.

"Espy was right," he began. "A note did get out of DIS Maryland and got passed to Nova. It wasn't lax security. Her ex's message got out because we wanted it to. Although this guy had no problem being a traitor to his country, he did have qualms about betraying her. His note was his make-good, sharing intel that one of our moles in Putin's orbit was in a corrupt enterprise with one of our own. He didn't name our turncoat, so after Nova alerted the inspector general, we narrowed a list of possibles, with Espy on top. But we needed proof. Since Nova had skin in the game, I tasked her to join Espy's Special Activities team to spy on him for us.

"The ex-DSA must have picked up a whiff of this, which would account for his paranoia. On the one hand trying to pump you for what she was up to and, on the other, planting doubt in your head to undermine her and gain your assistance. Glad you didn't take his bait."

I sipped some melted ice from the cup. It made me queasy. Or maybe it was the conversation. "Well, a bullet hole in me says you got your proof."

"For which your nation will be forever grateful." This time I couldn't tell if he was being droll or serious. "I may need a more formal debrief, but let's let you catch some winks."

"One thing first," I said. "After all our trouble, what about Glinka?"

"What about him?"

"Did he make it?"

The counterintelligence man didn't answer. He let his gaze arrest in the air halfway between us. But I got the message. The man who ordered the killing of Kogg and my fiancée was alive. Coleman got up and shook hands. "Don't talk about this to anybody else. We clear?"

"I'll delete my podcast."

"Podcast, now that's rich. I'll remember that one." Coleman laughed his way out the door.

Cammie slid her chair close to the bed and offered ice chips. I waved off the spoon. Spent as I was, I had questions. "My turn to debrief you."

"…All right."

"Starting with how the hell did you get the idea to hide in Thorvald's Volvo?"

"What's my mantra? Tactics and cover. I figured the last place they'd look would be their own car."

"Plus-ten for you."

"Except I didn't figure on the airbag. Pissed about losing that SIG Sauer. I had it since training at Camp Swampy."

"Lucky you had my snub-nose. How did you have my snub-nose?"

"I noticed you hiding something in the door pocket when we got to the villa. When Ludik and I hauled the bodies outside, I peeked in the Brabus and snagged it. You didn't tell me you brought a gun."

I hesitated, then tried out her own advice never to answer more than you are asked. "Harrison thought it might come in handy."

It worked. She didn't dig. "You'd only get yourself killed with something like that." Cammie set down the cup of ice and kissed me. "Instead, you almost got killed saving me."

"I think that should be worth something, don't you? Payback-wise?"

"Like what? And why the look? Are you tired? Do you need something from the nurse?"

Deep fatigue was dragging me down, but I couldn't delay this conversation anymore. "I want you to tell me about you photobombing that picture of me and Astrid. This time, the truth."

She closed her eyes briefly and rocked herself as if she'd been waiting for this. "I owe you that. It began when the money trail was leading to Kogg. I needed someone inside to confirm where it was coming from and where it was going."

"Hold on. Astrid was spying for you, not Espy?"

"Pike, I recruited her *to* spy on Espy. On behalf of Reed Coleman and the inspector general."

Suddenly there wasn't enough morphine in Germany. "Astrid was your...what?"

"My jane, yes."

I wasn't prepared for the heaviness that descended on me. Everything got so crazy at the shoot-out on the beach, I couldn't stop to break down the idea of Astrid as a spy. But it sure explained her changes in behavior, her erratic schedule, her sudden absences. It also explained why she avoided my attempts to talk things through. And why our relationship started to crater.

I worried Astrid was having an affair with Kogg when she was covering up for spying on him. That was what she meant by her "duty." Cedric's picture from Hamburg delivered a twist: how ironic that while I was bending my production schedule to meet up with Astrid, she was straining to fit me in with her spying. Cammie read my reaction. "I know it caused a lot of stress between you two. Astrid and I became friends, and she confided that in me. There's a lot of complication that comes with being in a relationship with someone in clandestine work."

"I can attest to that. Times two."

She let that pass. Cammie had more to say. "Do you know the reason I understand why you hate getting sympathy for her death? Because I go through it, too. I bear the same burden. Astrid knew the risks, but what happened to her... It gutted me." Cammie's lip quivered. "My friend was gone. And my guilt. Pike, I carry so much guilt for sending her out there."

She lowered her face, then brought it back up to mine. "And you, well...I can't imagine what it's like having it end with things...ending like that."

"Cammie, I told her to go." I raced to get it out before I cried. "She offered to come home, and I told her, no, take that trip."

"Listen to me." She cradled my face between her hands and spoke to me dead-on. "Sebastian Pike, you did not plant that bomb. You hear me? Any more than I did." We held that tender pose, that deep gaze, in silence except for the metronome of my heart monitor.

Clarity comes unbidden. It can arrive even under sedation. My aha was that Cammie and I held more in common than each other. And more than tandem guilt about Astrid. We both knew her and loved her, and that said something to me. We talked about her a good while, and it lifted my spirits to be able to express my feelings and memories as well as to hear Cammie's. She even confessed that she thought she blew it that time she called me Basty. She'd heard my nickname from Astrid and let it slip. "Please don't hate me because I lied to you."

I still cleave to truth, but you can't be a purist and function in the world or a relationship. Didn't I just lie to Coleman to protect her? I touched Cammie's cheek. "You did your job. As for Astrid, she was willing, right?"

"All in."

"I'm glad you were lucky to get close to her. But now that I know that, it makes me sorry for your pain."

"Thank you for that." Her expression went somewhere deep. She resurfaced. "We live with this now, don't we."

"We do." She leaned in and we kissed lightly. Then she sat back with a sigh and wiped a tear. I shut my eyes, but sleep wouldn't come. My body was beyond tired, but my brain kept firing. It absorbed. It processed. It wondered.

There was no way to know what was next or where we were going. But I knew one thing. Because of Cammie everything had changed. At her job interview she promised to help me get my mojo back for my show. Because of her I had it back in my life. Call it purpose or relevance, I felt rejuvenated, like I was reaching for something beyond my aspirational grasp again instead of going along and along.

Or going it alone.

But for how long?

There are dues you pay for your freedom. I need to move, you see, but it doesn't mean I haven't wanted someone to ride with. But not just anybody. Someone who's also independent and fearless. That's a tall order.

Without Cammie I wasn't sure I could be satisfied going back to simply hosting a TV show. Not without a sense of—dare I say—mission. I'll admit I wasn't too crazy about the kidnapping, the beatings, the electroshock… Taking a 9mm slug was no picnic either, but I did that for a reason, and didn't even need to think. I just knew. Kinda defining, I believe.

My last thought before I drifted off was the same one I started with. What's next?

When I woke up the next morning, Cammie was still there.

THE END

acknowledgments

Gretchen Young, my Dream Editor of those original Richard Castle books, is now my Dream Publisher at Regalo Press, proving dreams not only come true, they recur. I'm back in Camelot.

Thanks go to Alton Brown—food phenom, TV host, author, and friend—for advice, smarts, inspiration, and laughter.

I celebrate José Andrés, culinary force and a model citizen of the world. His charitable works have made the globe much less hangry.

John Parry, dear friend and veteran Food Network director, shared priceless expertise and encouragement.

Some great author pals deserve applause. Like Peter Blauner, to whom I first whispered the idea for this book, and whose support never faded. I also got a boost from my Magical Mystery Zoomers: Reed Farrel Coleman, Matt Goldman, Charles Salzberg, and Michael Wiley. Linwood Barclay provided scaffolding and inspo. Then there's Howard A. Rodman, Jr., whose Paris pointers were indispensable in setting scenes with cred and vision. Ken Levine, who mentored me as a wannabe TV writer and gave me my start, reminded me (as always) to begin with a murder.

Thanks to my book agent David Hale Smith and teammate Naomi Eisenbeiss at InkWell. Also, to my longtime TV agent, Nancy Josephson at WME, for her wise guidance and encouragement, and to Sanjana Seelam who joined the effort to usher my novel to TV.

Major thanks to my publicist, SallyAnne McCartin, who made sure the only thing secret about this book were the agents in my story.

To the readers, particularly the supporters of my Richard Castle novels; I surfed your wave. Never to be forgotten.

In that vein, I am forever grateful to Terri Edda Miller and to *Castle* creator and guiding hand in my Heat novels, Andrew W. Marlowe. Once collaborators, now friends.

And bouquets to Jennifer Allen, first reader, first believer, first in my heart, forever.